THE WENDIGO WHOOP-DE-DOO

A CHARLIE RHODES COZY MYSTERY BOOK TEN

AMANDA M. LEE

WINCHESTERSHAW PUBLICATIONS

Copyright © 2021 by Amanda M. Lee

All rights reserved.

No part of this book may be reproduced in any form or by any electronic or mechanical means, including information storage and retrieval systems, without written permission from the author, except for the use of brief quotations in a book review.

❦ Created with Vellum

PROLOGUE
ONE WEEK AGO

Rosalie Partridge hated camping. She didn't just dislike it, she outright hated it. Like, if there was a contest for people who hated camping, she would win top prize.

So how she ended up camping in the middle of nowhere, with friends who were supposed to take her feelings into consideration, was beyond her.

Nighthawk, Washington, was located at the edge of the world. At least that's how her boyfriend Paulie Prescott described it. He'd explained that it was near the Canadian border, which was supposed to be a selling point.

"It's the sort of wilderness that you're always gonna remember, Rosalie," he explained to her when selling her on the trip. "You'll tell your grandchildren about it one day."

They'd been dating for more than a year, and Rosalie wanted to ask him if he thought he would be having the same grandchildren, but she feared his response. As fun as Paulie was, as hot as he was, he'd never fully committed to their relationship. For a girl like Rosalie, who wanted to settle down right after graduation, that wasn't a good sign. She was nothing if not determined. She would make him commit. She had faith.

Now, though, standing in the shadow of the towering trees that she was convinced were stalking her, she had her doubts. How could he think this would be fun for her? What's worse, how could he have brought all his stupid friends along? There was only one other girl on the trip — stupid Sadie Milliken, with her model-like blond hair.

"The tents are all set up." Paulie shot her a grin as he walked toward the bonfire pit. He'd built it himself and seemed inordinately proud of it, another thing Rosalie didn't understand. "I put our tent over there." He pointed to a spot a distance from the other tents.

Rosalie frowned. "Why is our tent so far from the others?"

"Why do you think?" Paulie waggled his eyebrows in a suggestive manner.

"I don't know. That's why I asked."

"So we can have some private time." Paulie said it in such a way that Rosalie's frown deepened. "That's why we're here. We want some private time before I head off to Washington State."

If Rosalie thought she was annoyed, the feeling doubled now. She hated talking about his plans for the winter semester. When he'd deferred after their graduation, she assumed that meant he would get a job with his father at the lumberyard and propose to her in a year. That would give him enough time to save up for a ring and then they could start thinking about houses. She was of the mind they should rent an apartment for three years and save so they could get something good rather than buy a fixer-upper right out of the gate. She hadn't yet broached that topic with him. Then he announced that he would be going to Washington State University after all. He was planning to live on campus.

Her entire world had come crumbling down in that instant. All the plans she'd made — granted, without his input — evaporated. He started talking about business classes ... and rushing a fraternity ... and living in the dorms with friends. There was no room for her in the conversation and she was bitter about it.

She'd tried to hide her feelings from him but there'd been the occasional slip. That was when he suggested a trip. At first, she thought he'd take her to a pretty bed and breakfast, a place where they could do "couple" things and pledge their love to one another. She was willing to wait if it meant he would return to her once he obtained his degree.

Instead, he planned a camping trip in the middle of nowhere — there wasn't a Starbucks in like fifty miles, something he'd failed to tell her until they were already unpacking the trucks — and she was now faced with the prospect of five long days camping with people she hated. He'd brought six friends — five boys and stupid Sadie because she was dating Peter O'Neill — and there was nothing romantic at all about their setting.

"So you're saying you brought me here for sex," Rosalie surmised, her eyes flashing with warning when Paulie broke into a wide grin. "Am I reading the situation correctly?"

Paulie was familiar enough with Rosalie's tone to recognize her mood. "Why is that such a bad thing?" He refused to let her ruin this trip. He'd been looking forward to it for weeks. He didn't want to bring her at all, but he knew she would torture him if he didn't. He was determined to keep things between them on an even keel until Christmas. He'd already bought her a gift, although he knew she wouldn't like it. It was more of a parting gift than anything else. There was no way he was going to a busy campus full of pretty girls who wouldn't give him a hard time at every turn with a girlfriend anchoring him to their hometown. It simply wasn't going to happen. Paulie knew better than to break up with Rosalie now, though. He was still months away from leaving and she would make those months torturous if he broke up with her too early. And if he broke up with her right before Christmas? That would be worse.

So he'd sucked it up, bought her a pretty necklace, and made his plans. Classes started January 4. He wanted his last New Year's Eve bash in town to be spent with his friends, not Rosalie. Therefore, on December 29, he would break up with her. He expected tears and recrimination, horrible names and maybe even a slap. It was better for her, he told himself. They didn't want the same things. She would be upset at first, but eventually she'd find someone to give her what she wanted. It certainly wasn't going to be him.

She didn't need to know that now, though. They were still a couple for a few months. It would be easier that way, even though she was annoying. Paulie liked things easy.

"Can't you unclench a little bit?" he asked in his amiable way as he slung an arm around her shoulders. "I mean ... look at this place." He gestured to the trees. "It's amazing. There's supposed to be an abandoned town around here that we're going to explore. There's a river for fishing. We have plenty of whiskey for cocktails at night. It's going to be the bomb."

Rosalie's forehead crinkled. "The bomb?"

He shrugged. "I heard it in a movie."

"Well, it's a stupid saying." Despite her agitation, she didn't shrug off his arm. If he wanted to be close to her, that was a good sign. All the fears she'd been wallowing in might've been misplaced. Maybe he was just nervous about moving away from home. If she played her cards right, he would hate college and move back after one semester. She could deal with a few months away from him.

"I'm sorry." She held up her hands in a placating manner. "I'm not trying to be difficult. I just ... think this place is creepy." She opted for honesty.

"Creepy? It's Mother Nature. Who doesn't love Mother Nature?"

Me, Rosalie thought. *I hate Mother Nature. I would be much happier at a pretty bed and breakfast with rose wallpaper and homemade scones for breakfast.* She didn't say that, of course. He would only ridicule her.

"What's the plan?" she asked, changing course. It had taken them hours to reach the camping site. They couldn't park near their destination. They had to leave the trucks almost two miles away and trek in on foot. "It will be dark soon."

"That's why we started the fire." Paulie was a world-class camper and knew all the things that had to be done before darkness descended. "We're going to cook dinner and have some drinks around the fire. Then we'll go to sleep early because we're tired." He waggled his eyebrows again, as if that was supposed to entice her. "Then we'll get up early and start our adventure."

"What adventure?" Rosalie demanded.

"This."

She waited for him to expound. When he didn't, she glanced around blankly. "What?"

"This," he repeated, using his hands to point to the trees. "We're going to take all this in and have the trip of a lifetime."

Rosalie wasn't convinced. "But ... what are we going to do to make this the trip of a lifetime?"

Paulie had to force himself not to snap at her. She didn't realize she was being difficult. She was incapable of seeing herself as she really was. He blamed her mother for putting ridiculous ideas about home and family into her head, but there was no way he was bringing *that* up. Not again.

"Just try," Paulie prodded. "It's going to be a great trip."

A scream echoed against the trees, causing Rosalie to snap her head up. Eyes wide, lower lip trembling, she turned to him. "What was that?" Her voice was barely a whisper.

Unbothered, Paulie shrugged. "It wasn't a human, if that's what you're worried about."

"How do you know?"

"It didn't sound like a human."

The scream had sounded human enough to her. "Then what was it?"

"I don't know." Paulie pursed his lips as he stared at the trees. "Probably a bird."

"That didn't sound like any bird I've ever heard."

"Well, different birds live out here." He was matter-of-fact.

"But ... ."

He barreled forward, as if he hadn't heard her. "Of course, it could be Bigfoot. For years people have claimed he lives out here."

"Bigfoot?" That was the most ludicrous thing Rosalie had heard. "Bigfoot isn't real."

"Then why have so many people seen him?"

"They're making it up."

"No way." Paulie was amused despite Rosalie. "Bigfoot is totally real and these are supposedly his stomping grounds. Like ... this exact spot."

Rosalie was suspicious. "Is that why we're here? Are you and your stupid friends going to try to make that Bigfoot documentary you were talking about in high school?"

Paulie was sheepish. "We might've brought a camera and a few batteries," he hedged.

"I knew it." Rosalie viciously swore under her breath, although not with curse words. A lady didn't use curse words. Her mother had taught her that. "This trip isn't about us at all."

Paulie refused to be dissuaded from his excitement. "It'll be great, Rosalie. Just wait. We're going to have the best time ever." And if she didn't, he said to himself, that was on her. He was done coddling her. She needed to grow up and see the world for what it really was, not as she wanted it to be. She was no longer a child. It was time for her to embrace adulthood ... even if he had to drag her kicking and screaming into her new reality.

"We should get ready for dinner," he said. "We need to eat the stuff in the coolers first. The ice will last three days. After that, it's the pre-packaged stuff and whatever fish we catch."

Rosalie was beside herself. "When have you ever caught fish that you needed to sustain yourself?"

"There's a first time for everything." He moved away from her and toward the fire, toward his friends, toward the fun. "You need to make the best of things Rosalie. We're all stuck out here for the next five days — including you. It'll be miserable if you don't at least put in a little effort."

She opened her mouth to argue but the strange shrieking jolted her before she could. "Seriously, what is that?"

Paulie's grin was impish. "It's an adventure, Rosalie. It's something for us all to discover together. You need to embrace the possibilities. If you do, you'll have so much more fun."

Was that what he wanted? Did he think she wasn't fun? Perhaps she should embrace the adventure, even if she was miserable. "Fine," she said, forcing a smile she didn't feel. "But if Bigfoot kills me, I'm never going to forgive you."

"Fair enough." He linked his fingers with hers and briefly wondered if she would ever be able to make the true leap into adulthood. She always wanted someone to take care of her. It wouldn't be him going forward, but there was always a chance she might reach her full potential. Eventually.

"What's for dinner?" she asked.

"Hot dogs, potato salad and whiskey."

"That doesn't sound very healthy."

"Live a little, Rosalie," he prodded. "You'll find life so much more enjoyable."

Resigned, she nodded. "I guess I can manage that."

"Good. Let's start adventuring!" He pumped his fist into the air, causing her to laugh.

"I'm still going to kill you if Bigfoot comes after me. You've been warned."

ONE
PRESENT DAY

"Look, Charlie, it's a gorilla!"

My smile seemed to be permanently affixed to my face today, so I turned it on Mike — er, my father — and let him see that I was having a good time. It felt like the right thing to do.

I, Charlie Rhodes, had parents — and a brother. I found them in a few short months, and now they were determined to make up for lost time. Apparently that included a trip to the zoo, something they swore had been a regular outing when I was a child. That was before they put me up for adoption. That was before they'd messed with my memory to make sure I couldn't recall any of the time I'd purportedly spent with them.

I was still bitter but doing my best to move past it. My boyfriend Jack Hanson continuously reminded me that they'd thought they were doing what was right in that moment. Second guessing them was unfair. Rationally I knew that. Irrationally, I was annoyed. I didn't want to forgive them for everything ... at least not yet.

"I love gorillas," I said, although I had no idea if that was true. I had nothing against gorillas. The ones in the zoo seemed happy enough, but I had to wonder if they wouldn't be happier elsewhere. They were meant to roam free, not be looked upon as entertainment. But these gorillas had been raised in captivity, so they didn't know there was another life out there. There were worse things than being protected and not having to hide from poachers.

"They were one of your favorites when you were a kid," Melina offered, her fingers linked with Mike's as they beamed at me. She was my mother, but I'd yet to feel a familial bond with her. Jack swore up and down that I would if I relaxed. He might've been right, but I wasn't there yet.

"Awesome!" I shot her a corny thumbs-up, my shoulders tense until I felt a familiar arm slide around my back. I found Jack watching me with unreadable eyes. My parents hadn't invited him on this outing. I'd invited him. The truth was, I needed him ... even if he could only offer me smiles and silent moral support.

"Hey, baby." He leaned in and kissed the ridge of my ear, grinning when I shivered. He had enough sex appeal for ten men and seemingly knew it. Today his long hair was pulled back in a short ponytail at the nape of his neck. Fall had officially arrived even if the daily temperatures remained confused — and he looked dressed for rugged weather, sporting a flannel with sleeves rolled to show off his impressive forearms.

"Hey, baby," I mimicked, grinning at him.

"Do you want me to play gorilla tonight?" he whispered.

"I was thinking we could play lusty lumberjacks again," I teased. "That game was fun."

From somewhere in front of me, a throat cleared. Mike watched us. He and Jack were having issues, something I preferred to ignore.

Mike, Melina and my brother Casey had last spent time with me when I was a child. I'd remained frozen in their minds for decades. Jack was my boyfriend, and we were moving into a new condo together. It was huge, close to the water, and the sort of place I never believed I would have the money to live in. So, even though they still thought of me as a child, I was an adult, one of the reasons I was convinced I was having such a hard time with this adjustment.

"Do you need something, Mike?" Jack asked dryly. He knew darned well why my father was so agitated. He wanted to hear him say it. It was a passive-aggressive game they had embraced almost the moment they'd been introduced.

"I need you to not talk to my daughter that way," Mike replied, taking the boyfriend by the horn ... so to speak. Most of the time he denied having a problem with Jack's presence. Occasionally, however, he let his true feelings be known. Apparently today was going to be one of those days.

"What way is that?" Jack's social skills weren't always polished, but he was calm when addressing my father. It was as if he understood that a big blowup would hurt us all. While he wasn't opposed to having it out with my parents — I'd seen him biting his tongue more than once — he was careful to limit the arguments for my sake. I appreciated the effort.

"Because ... it's weird."

"Why is it weird?" Jack used his patented "I'm being patient so you should do the same" voice.

"Because it is." Mike was adamant. "She's my daughter. You shouldn't talk to her that way."

"She's my girlfriend," Jack replied reasonably. "How should I talk to her? I don't think constant comments about gorillas is going to do it for her." The statement was pointed, and I shot him a warning look. The last thing we needed was for this afternoon to go off the rails.

Clearly sensing trouble, Melina interjected. "We just thought a family outing was called for," she said. "I mean ... we haven't had a family outing in decades."

"Oh, I don't know," I countered. "I thought the last family outing where we had to fight for our lives in a haunted asylum while holding off the ancient witch who wants to suck me dry and steal my magic was great fun." It was out of my mouth before I realized how it would sound to them. Rather than take it back, I merely shrugged. "Baby steps?"

Melina sighed and nodded. I could tell she was struggling and yet she kept pushing forward despite all the bad feelings. I felt sorry for her, but I couldn't outright forgive her yet. "Baby steps," she agreed. "It's supposed to be a fun day at the zoo."

"It is," Casey agreed as joined us. He had a big Icee in one hand and looked to be shoving a piece of paper into his pocket with the other. He'd excused himself to talk to two women on the other side of the gorilla viewing area, so I could only imagine what was on the sheet of paper.

"Big date planned?" I asked.

He smirked. "We'll see. I don't know that I'll have time for dating, but I don't want to miss out if there's going to be a break in our schedule."

"There won't be a break," Mike said, shooting his son a dark look. They were close but couldn't stop snarking at one another. I found it refreshing, proof that these people were real and had emotions that didn't revolve around trying to make me love them in the weirdest ways possible. "We have to keep our noses buried in work and nothing else. Sybil is out there."

Sybil. Sybil Granger. Sybil Croft. Whatever name she was going by now, she was indeed out there and looking for me. Heck, she could be watching us right now, waiting for the perfect moment to move in and claim what she considered rightfully hers. I was what she wanted most, the magic I wielded a prize she was desperate to claim.

I shuddered at the thought of her watching us and looked around for anyone paying us an inordinate amount of attention. There was nobody, of course. There never was when I had the feeling I needed to look around and search for her. One day she would be there. I had no doubt about that.

"Are you okay?" Jack anchored me closer to his side. "Are you cold?"

I shook my head. It was a pleasant day and I'd layered with a hoodie and jeans. I wasn't cold. I was ... haunted. Sybil might not have been stalking me at this moment, but she was haunting my every move ... and I didn't like it. "I'm fine," I reassured him. "I just don't want you guys to argue." I shot Mike a pointed look. "That goes for you, too."

He made a protesting sound as he held out his hands. "As your father, it's my right to give your boyfriend a hard time."

I wanted to tell him he'd lost that right when he'd given me up. They'd done it for a very specific reason. They hadn't wanted to do it — I believed them on that — but to save me, they felt they had no choice. They wanted me to have a life, even if it was without them. I had to respect them for that, even if this small part of me couldn't shake the idea that I wasn't good enough to keep.

"You need to get over it," Jack said. "We live together."

"Not yet," Mike growled.

"Actually, yes." Jack refused to back down when he was feeling territorial. That was the true problem between Mike and him. They both wanted to be the alpha. Under normal circumstances Jack would have no choice but to defer to Mike. These were hardly normal circumstances, though.

"We're living together," I reiterated, so there could be no confusion. My parents and brother would have to adjust to Jack. I loved him too much to sacrifice him for them. We were a package deal. "Jack still has a second apartment, but it's packed, just waiting for moving day."

"Which comes in less than a week," Jack added.

"What happens if we get called out on a job?" Casey asked.

The three of us — Casey, Jack and me — worked for the Legacy Foundation. In addition to several financial endeavors, the foundation funded a paranormal research group. The head of the foundation, Myron Biggs, allowed his nephew Chris to run that leg of the operation. We worked with Chris. I had magic at my disposal and had always been fascinated with learning more about the paranormal world. After my adoptive parents died, I pursued course studies in that area and landed a coveted internship with the group. I'd since been promoted and was a full-fledged member of the team. We'd been without a job for two weeks now and I was starting to get antsy.

"Then the movers will take our stuff when we're not in town," Jack replied. "I've already arranged it. They have copies of the keys to all three places."

"Is that safe?" Melina made a face. "You can't just let random strangers into your homes. You could lose everything."

"I'm a security chief," Jack reminded her. "I did a thorough check on the company. They've been in business forty years. On top of that, I know the son. Dale Horvath. He'll be in charge of our move. It's fine."

"Plus, I have nothing to steal," I added. "I think all my worldly belongings are worth about a grand."

Jack slid me a sidelong look. "Well, now we're going to share worldly belongings. You're moving up in the world." He smirked as he tugged me close. "Are we done with the gorillas?"

"Sure." Melina's smile was amiable. Of all of them, she worked hardest to be friendly with Jack. It was as if she understood they wouldn't have access to me if they forced the issue with him. I could imagine the unpleasant conversations she and Mike had in their apartment at night — they were renting until everything was settled.

"Where to next?" Mike asked, pretending he hadn't just been in Jack's face regarding our flirting.

"Penguins," Casey replied, his lips blue from his Icee. "I love penguins."

Mike smiled indulgently at his son. "Penguins it is," he said.

I linked my fingers with Jack's as we left the gorilla habitat. There were moments when things almost seemed normal with my family. As if reading my mind, Jack lowered his voice. Mike, Melina and Casey were far enough in front of us that we didn't have to worry about them overhearing.

"Tell me what you're thinking," he prodded.

My automatic response was a smile. "This is fun."

He rolled his eyes. "You're acting as if this is torture. You're hardly having fun."

"But I am," I insisted. "We're together. I always have fun when we're together."

"I love spending time with you too, but that's not what I'm asking."

I shrugged. "It's hard." There was no sense pretending otherwise. Jack knew better than anyone that I was dealing with constant emotional fluxes. "They're trying so hard. This outing today, though, it's like it was planned for a child. It's almost as if they can't accept the fact that I'm an adult."

"They know you're an adult," Jack countered. "They see you, admire the wonderful person you've grown into. But they also mourn. They'll never get the time back that they lost. It's not the worst thing in the world to indulge them."

I shot him some serious side eye. "Coming from the guy who likes purposely talking sexy in front of my father, that's kind of funny."

Jack's grin widened. "I can't help it. He's so easy. He looks at me as if I'm defiling you."

"I was pretty happy with the defilement last night ... and this morning."

"There's more where that came from, little missy," he teased. His smile lingered. "Give them a chance, Charlie. I know you can't forget all the feelings that have ruled your life, but they really are trying. They want you to be happy."

"What about you? Do you want me to be happy?"

"More than anything." He was earnest. "In fact, because I want you to be happy, I made reservations for all of us at your favorite restaurant."

"Muriel's?" I was beside myself. "They have that awesome clam chowder."

"And the stuffed lobster you love more than anything is on special tonight." He paused. "Oh, and that chocolate cake you go gaga over, with the hot fudge and vanilla ice cream? That's also on the menu."

I groaned. "I'll be so stuffed you won't be able to defile me tonight. We're running out of nights in my apartment to make memories."

"I heard that," Mike barked. Apparently we'd somehow caught up without me realizing it.

"Sorry," I said sheepishly.

Jack didn't miss a beat. "I was just telling Charlie I made reservations at her favorite restaurant for when we're done here. I thought you could see the mountains of seafood she eats."

Despite his earlier grimace, Mike chuckled. "I don't care what sort of food they have. If she's happy, that's all that matters."

"Thanks, Dad," Casey said dryly. "I like to know where I stand in the family pecking order."

THE WENDIGO WHOOP-DE-DOO

"We love you too," Melina reassured him, her eyebrows hopping when Jack's phone alerted.

I turned and watched as he checked his screen.

"Chris," he said grimly, all traces of mirth forgotten.

There would be no stuffed lobster or chocolate cake. No delicious clam chowder.

"Don't freak out yet," Jack advised, holding up a finger as he answered. He wasted little time with pleasantries, nodding as he absorbed whatever Chris was saying. When he was done, he smiled as he pocketed his phone. "We can still have dinner."

"We can?" I had no idea why that was such a relief.

"Yes, my love, you can stuff that pretty face of yours to your heart's content." He gripped my chin and gave me a quick kiss before focusing on my father. "Don't give me grief," he warned as my father glared. "She likes her lobster."

"I'm not giving you grief," Mike replied. "I'm curious about what's happening. That was your boss. Do you have a job?"

Jack nodded. "Nighthawk, Washington. It's in the middle of nowhere. Eight campers who were supposed to return yesterday didn't. They're missing in the wilderness ... and people have been hearing strange screams in the area."

"Screams?" Melina's eyebrows collided.

"Chris is convinced that it's either Bigfoot or some sort of paranormal creature," Jack replied. "Apparently the screams aren't human. At least that's what he says. Either way, we're out of here first thing in the morning."

"Maybe I'll really get to see Bigfoot this time," I mused. "You're convinced I imagined it last time."

Jack shot me a look. "Oh, not this again. Bigfoot isn't real. Neither is the Chupacabra, while we're on the subject."

"I saw it!" I was adamant.

"Here we go," Casey muttered, rolling his eyes. "I hate when you guys have this argument over and over again."

"I like it," Mike offered. "If he thinks you're lying, he's not worth your time, Charlie."

"Don't." Jack warned. "As for whether we're dealing with Bigfoot or not, I can't say. Kids are missing. We've been tasked with finding them."

"So ... wilderness?" I asked.

"Yup." Jack's lips quirked. "This time we might be able to stay in the same tent on purpose."

I perked up. "That might be fun."

"Oh, I can't take this," Mike groused. "Come on." He waved his hand. "The penguins are waiting."

"And then dinner," I said. "If we're camping, the food won't be anywhere near as good as at Muriel's."

"And then dinner," Mike conceded. "I'm here to make both of my children happy."

If only I could take solace in that. But it didn't matter. We had a new assignment, and surprisingly I looked forward to the break from my parents. It might be exactly what I needed.

2

TWO

"Ready?"

Jack was up two hours before the sun rose. He turned off the alarm and let me sleep as long as possible, even packing for me. He was such a Boy Scout sometimes it made me laugh. In truth, he always complained I forgot things and preferred being in charge of packing. I think he just liked being organized.

We didn't have time for breakfast, so he promised to pick up sandwiches on the way. I was still a bit bleary eyed — I'd eaten so much food I was uncomfortable until almost midnight the previous evening — and let him lead me out. I had no idea if he'd packed the right things, but I trusted him to come through.

In truth, I trusted him for everything.

I didn't speak during the ride. We stopped at a McDonald's drive-through to order breakfast. He knew what I liked. He also got enough for the rest of our team. We were the last to arrive on the isolated private runway where the Legacy Foundation jet was kept. Chris looked stern until I waved the huge bags of food.

"I was going to give you grief," he said as Jack carried our bags onto the plane. "Since you brought greasy food for everybody, I guess you're forgiven."

"Good deal." Jack beamed at him as he stowed our bags in the overhead compartments. I made sure to snag my sausage-and-egg McGriddle from the bag — along with two hash browns — before tossing the food onto the small table at the side of the plane and getting comfortable in my normal seat. It was a free-for-all when Millie, Bernard, Chris and Casey started digging in. The only two not excited for the food were Hannah and Laura. I wasn't expecting Hannah to dig in. A healthy eater, she was careful about her food intake. Laura often made disparaging comments about our food choices but almost always dug in. This morning she was listless, her gaze directed out the window.

I hadn't seen her in more than two weeks, not since she'd been held captive inside Heavenstone Asylum. Sybil had riled up ghosts to torment her, and she'd been unconscious when we finally found her. She missed the big show, including the arrival of a crossroads demon with attitude and two mouthy witches. They helped us survive what could've been a deadly adventure. By the time Laura woke, she was in a small cemetery outside the asylum. She'd been confused, in pain, and quiet.

Laura was never quiet. In fact, she was one of the most obnoxious people I'd ever met. She was one of those women who earned power by holding other women down. As long as there was someone beneath her on the totem pole, she believed she could claim top place. Seeing her so quiet and disengaged was jarring.

"Breakfast, Laura?" I asked. Normally I wouldn't engage her in conversation — I hated her with a fiery passion — but she looked altogether wretched.

"No thanks." Her voice was soft. "I'm not hungry."

Millie, who could've been the only person who hated Laura more than me, turned her keen eyes to the blonde. "You should eat something. It's going to be a long flight."

"Seven hours," Chris added. "You should definitely eat. All we have are snacks."

"I'm fine." Laura didn't bother looking at us. "I don't need food."

I cast a worried look to Jack. I didn't need to tell him what I was thinking. Laura's disappearance at the asylum had shaken us both. As the head of security, he believed anything that happened to her was his fault. Because Sybil was after me, and Laura had been hurt at her hands, I couldn't help feeling responsible. Laura's inability to bounce back was a blow to us both.

"We'll put your sandwich and hash browns in the fridge," Jack offered. There wasn't a hint of snark to his tone, unusual when dealing with Laura. "You can heat it up later."

Laura didn't respond.

Just to make sure there was something available for her to eventually eat, Jack collected an Egg McMuffin and hash brown from the bag and moved them to the fridge. That way he wouldn't have to worry about anyone else accidentally eating her share of the haul. Unfortunately, Casey wasn't the only one with the ability to inhale two breakfast sandwiches. Chris, Jack and I could hold our own, too.

"Let's eat," Chris said as he got comfortable next to Hannah. "I'll brief everybody in the air."

Jack cast one more look toward Laura and nodded. "Sounds like a plan."

THIRTY MINUTES LATER WE WERE AT cruising altitude. Chris took center stage, using a pointer remote on a huge television screen.

"Nighthawk, Washington," he intoned, sounding very much like a museum guide. "It's an unincorporated community in northern Washington. Extremely close to the Canadian border. There's an active border crossing to the north, but we're talking about wilderness here, people.

"Nighthawk was a booming mine town at the turn of the 20th century," he continued. "We're talking hotels, burlesque houses and everything else that went with a town like that. It's located on the former Great Northern Railroad and is listed as having a population of five ... but nobody knows who those five people are."

I stirred. "They would've had to fill out census forms," I said. "I mean ... there have to be names on record."

Chris chuckled. "I guess I should rephrase that for the literal member of our team. The individuals who supposedly live in Nighthawk aren't up for socializing. They live in the woods — and willingly so — and don't have much to do with outsiders. If they want items from a store, they have to drive at least an hour."

"I'm guessing they can't just pop over to Canada for a beer," Jack mused.

"Definitely not," Chris agreed. "So, as a general breakdown, Nighthawk was a mining district when Washington was still a territory. It was a boomtown by 1903, named after the neighboring Nighthawk mine.

"The town was so big it had six mills, a saloon, and no shortage of men looking to make a quick buck," he continued. "Like other boom towns, Nighthawk started to have issues when mines began shutting down. This usually happened because of operating costs and a drop in metal values. The last Nighthawk mine closed in 1951, but things had died down a great deal by then.

"The town still features structures dating back to 1903," he continued, clicking through photos I found myself grinning at. There was little I loved better than an abandoned town, but explaining my fascination wasn't easy. "The hotel is still there. The mine workers' houses are still there. What they called the 'Nighthawk house of ill repute' is still there." He used air quotes.

"The area is dangerous," he explained. "There are collapsed mines scattered around the outlying area. The buildings that are standing aren't considered safe. Everybody needs to remain alert."

"That's all well and good," Jack said. "Let's hear about the kids."

Chris clicked off the television screen and sat. "I just want you guys to take it in. We're talking rough terrain. We'll have some off-road vehicles waiting for us — Bernard, Jack, Casey and I will drive — but there's going to be a lot of hiking. I want you to be prepared."

Before I realized what I was doing, I made a face and raised my hand. "Um ... why is it only the men get to drive?"

Chris blinked several times, thrown off by the question. Next to me, Jack lowered his face so nobody could see he was smiling. "Um ... because those are the names I gave the rental company," Chris said.

"Yes, but why did you give those names?" I refused to let it go. "I might want to drive one."

"Have you ever driven an off-road vehicle?"

"No."

"Well, there's your answer."

He might've thought it was an acceptable answer, but I felt differently. "Yes, but at one time, you were driving an off-road vehicle for the first time. You had a chance to become good at it. It's only fair that I have the same chance."

Chris worked his jaw and then flicked his eyes to Jack. "Do you want to handle this?"

The fact that he thought Jack should "handle" me was beyond annoying. Before I could lodge another complaint, however, Jack bobbed his head. "Absolutely." He had a smile on his face when he turned to me. "I'll make sure you get a chance to drive, but I'll handle the really rough terrain until you get a feel for things."

"Yay." I clapped my hands before taking in Chris's eye roll. "You may continue."

"Thank you so much," he drawled. Chris was gregarious guy, and he usually loved my outspoken nature. I'd been coming into my own of late, though, and I wasn't quite as amiable as I used to be. "So, where was I?"

"We're going to a ghost town in the middle of nowhere," Laura replied blandly. She was still looking out the window. "It's dangerous because there are abandoned mines everywhere."

"Thank you, Laura." Chris kept his gaze on her for a moment longer than necessary and then continued. "One week ago, a group of eight kids — and by kids, I mean eighteen-year-olds — went camping in Nighthawk."

"Camping?" Jack furrowed his brow. "Is that allowed?"

"Not technically but the people in that area are comfortable with the great outdoors. Camping in that area is frowned upon, but as long as people don't throw trash everywhere and start forest fires the authorities look the other way."

Jack nodded in understanding. "Okay. Continue."

"The individuals in question are six boys and two girls." Chris looked down at the tablet. "We have Paul Prescott, Rosalie Partridge, Sadie Milliken, Peter O'Neill, Vincent Falls, Chase Hall, Greg Landers and Colby Bennett."

I ran the names through my head. Nothing stood out to me, not that I was expecting some "eureka" moment.

"They were staying in tents. At least that's what they told their parents," Chris continued. "They were going for five days. It was some sort of celebration for the Prescott boy. He'd been accepted at Washington State University."

"He might still be alive," I pointed out, drawing multiple sets of eyes to me. "I mean ... I'm just saying. We shouldn't talk about him in the past tense."

"Actually, we should." Chris flashed a smile that didn't touch his eyes. "In the time since I called you last night and this morning, searchers have found several bodies: Paul Prescott, Peter O'Neill and Chase Hall."

Jack straightened in his chair. "What about the others?"

"They have searchers still out. It's rough terrain, like I said. Initially we were contracted to go in as a search-and-rescue team because the locals are convinced they have a rabid Sasquatch on the loose. They believe we're uniquely qualified to deal with the problem."

"Because of all the other sasquatches we've handled," Jack grumbled.

I patted his knee but kept my gaze on Chris. "May I ask how the boys who were found were killed?"

"They were ... ravaged." Chris looked pained when he delivered the line.

"Ravaged?" Jack asked.

Chris handed his tablet to Jack, who started reading through the report.

"Prescott had his throat ripped out and a broken arm," Jack read aloud from the initial report from the medical examiner's office. "O'Neill was missing an arm." He grimaced. "Hall's eyes were gouged out. They all died badly."

"Awesome," Laura intoned from her spot by the window. "There's nothing better than a murderous sasquatch."

I glanced at her, unsure if I should comment, and then opted to keep my focus on Chris. "What about the others?"

"They have dogs out there. They're looking. The terrain is really rough. They feel lucky to have found three bodies."

I didn't like that. "We don't know the other kids are dead," I insisted. "They could be out there, hiding. Heck, they could be being held somewhere. We don't know it's Bigfoot."

Chris didn't like it when I used the B-word — he preferred sasquatch or cryptid — but I didn't care.

"We don't," he agreed. "For all we know there's a deranged human out there killing people. They could've run into a bear, or some other big creature. It might not be fantastical in explanation at all. Still, we've been tasked with looking into the matter."

"How is that going to work?" Jack asked. He looked intense and I could practically see the gears in his mind working. "Are we camping?" He glanced around. "Nobody can stay in a tent alone under these circumstances. And we're going to have issues with sleeping arrangements when it comes to Casey and Laura. Just for the record, I'm not sharing a tent with Casey. I want that recorded and acknowledged."

"It's recorded and acknowledged, Jack," Chris said dryly. "I won't force you to cuddle with Casey."

"I don't care about that. Er, I do. I'm just saying that Charlie is not sleeping in a separate tent from me."

"As of now, we're not camping," Chris supplied. "We'll be staying in Oroville — I think that's how it's pronounced — and driving in. It's four miles south of the border and is home to less than two thousand people. We'll set up a base camp for the off-road vehicles, a place to keep supplies, but spend our nights in a hotel."

If the area was as remote as he was letting on, I could only imagine what sort of hotel. That didn't matter given what we were facing, though. "There are five kids still missing. Please tell me the locals are going to help."

"They are ... as much as they can." Chris held out his hands. "You have to understand, Charlie, this area is remote. They've called in help from the National Guard but we're still talking about a lot of land and too few bodies. I initially wanted to camp, but Uncle Myron shot me down."

"Why didn't he show signs of thinking things through when we were married?" Millie drawled. "That would've made my life so much easier."

Chris ignored her. "We went a couple rounds on it, but he's insistent. If we have to camp at some point, he's agreed to revisit the conversation. For now, the hotel is our home base."

"I can't believe I'm actually saying it, but I'm thankful for Myron," Jack said as he handed Chris back his tablet. "Are we going to have a local liaison?"

"We are. His name is Chad Pace. I don't have any specifics on him. I don't think it would matter if I wanted to trade up, down, or lateral. They made it sound like there was one person I could talk to ... and only one."

"That's fine." Jack grabbed my hand and flipped it over, idly tracing the lines in my palm as he thought. "You said the kids were camping. Did they find the campground?"

Chris shook his head. "No, and they obviously can't tell us where we should look because nobody knows. They found two vehicles parked along Loomis-Oroville Road that belonged to them. It seems they hiked into the woods from there and never came out."

"What about time of death?" Jack asked. "The kids arrived seven days ago. Were they killed right away?"

"I don't have that information yet," Chris replied. "The report I have says that they don't believe the boys have been dead more than three days."

"Which means they survived four days out there," Jack mused. "You have to wonder if they realized something bad was going to happen."

"That I can't answer."

"Maybe we'll find survivors," I suggested. "Maybe they'll be able to tell us."

Jack's eyes were kind when they slid to me. "Maybe."

"You don't think so," I said.

"It's unlikely, but we have to go in assuming the kids are still alive," he said. "It's what's right for them."

"Right." I slouched lower in my chair. I liked the idea of Bigfoot ... except when someone was ripping off arms and gouging out eyes. "Could it be a bear?"

Jack arched an eyebrow as he glanced down at me. "Maybe." He made an attempt at a smile ... and failed. "Don't get worked up about it. We have a long flight. Take a nap. We'll know more when we land."

He sounded sure of himself. I wished I could feel the same. My stomach was a tight knot, and it had nothing to do with the greasy breakfast I'd inhaled.

THREE

We landed at an airport with one runway. I was confused when we exited the plane — this time I was carrying my own bag — and found that the "terminal" was the size of a standard ranch house.

Jack smirked as he took in my reaction. "You're in the wilderness now, Charlie Rhodes."

"We've been in the wilderness before," I reminded him. "We were in the middle of nowhere in Michigan ... and Texas. We still landed at normal airports, even if they were small."

He shrugged. "This is different. Chris got clearance to land here. Otherwise, we would've been driving for hours to get to the town."

"But ... it's a real airport?" I was dubious.

"Obviously. We just landed here."

If he said it was a regular airport, I had to believe him.

We didn't even walk through the building, instead traversing it to where two Chevy Tahoes waited. Clearly these vehicles had seen some rough rides. When I turned to Jack he was already nodding.

"We're going to be driving some rough roads."

I followed him to the back of one of the Tahoes and watched as he tossed in our bags. Millie and Bernard joined us in our vehicle, which left Casey, Laura, Hannah and Chris in the other. I spent a few minutes studying Laura as she climbed in the backseat. Normally she would already be complaining about the location. She was silent and withdrawn.

"It's obvious you're worried about her," Jack noted as he climbed behind the wheel. I was in the passenger seat fastening my seatbelt. "You can say what you're feeling."

That was the problem. I didn't know what I was feeling. "She seems ... lost." I rummaged in my purse for my sunglasses. Jack had made sure they were packed because he was Jack and never forgot the small details.

"I've heard some things," Millie said from the backseat. She didn't look bothered by our remote location in the slightest. "Do you want to know what I've heard?"

"First I want to know where you heard it," Jack challenged as he plugged the location for the hotel into the dashboard GPS. "If it's random gossip, not interested."

"It comes from the front office, smart guy," Millie fired back. "I still have a pipeline to the front office, in case you've forgotten."

"Which means Myron still gossips with you," I said. I had trouble imagining the tempestuous exes sharing information over coffee, but stranger things had happened.

"Myron and I have a monthly meeting," Millie corrected. "We may be divorced, but it's not as if we hate each other. The marriage was simply not salvageable. I don't want anything bad to happen to him."

"Of course not," Jack said. "What do you and Myron talk about in these meetings?"

"Finances. Ours are still linked because I have shares in the Legacy Foundation. He told me about a conversation he had with Ben and it kind of freaked me out."

Ben Chapman was Laura's father. I'd met him once, at least officially, and he hadn't struck me as the warmest of guys. In the wake of Laura's disappearance at the asylum, however, he'd been a man on a mission to reclaim his daughter. It reminded me that people showed love in different ways.

"Apparently Laura was in shock or something after what happened," Millie volunteered. "She wasn't physically injured, at least nothing that would linger for more than a few days. But she was traumatized and afraid to be alone. She moved back in with her parents."

That was indeed shocking. "For good?" I couldn't picture that. Laura enjoyed going out and partying with friends. She didn't like parental involvement.

"She still has six months on her lease, so Ben is paying it, but she's hunkered down with her parents. Myron and I talked a week ago, so this information might be a little dated, but there was talk that Laura was so freaked out that she might not come back at all."

"Oh, if only," Jack drawled.

I shot him a quelling look. "Let's not go there," I warned. "There's no reason to speak poorly about her given what happened."

Jack made a face. "Being kidnapped by a crazy witch and terrorized by tortured ghosts doesn't give her a pass on all the things she's done."

"But there's no reason to pile it on in the aftermath."

"I'll never forget you being thrown in the water in Florida," Jack insisted. "There were sharks, and she knew it. I don't care that she feigned innocence afterward. I know what happened."

I'd been the one stroking through shark-infested waters — and freaking out — and I understood his stance. That didn't mean I was going to have a good time being nasty to Laura. "You don't have to be nice to her. Just ... don't be mean to her."

He muttered something that sounded like "whatever" and kept his eyes on the road.

"Tell him, Millie," I instructed. "It's no fun to be mean to someone when they're not mean back."

"Oh, I'm fine being mean to anyone and everyone," Millie countered. "He's right about Laura deserving it."

"Ha." Jack's eyes flashed. "See, I'm right."

"You're also wrong and Charlie is right," Millie added.

"Ha," I mimicked him.

Jack's lips curved, but he didn't respond.

"Laura makes me nervous," Millie said. She either didn't care about the mild spat brewing between Jack and me or was beyond it. "I don't think she can be trusted as backup right now. Her nerves appear shot. She jumped so hard on the plane when you guys started up the stairs that I thought she was going to come out of her skin."

"I don't think that means she's untrustworthy," I hedged.

"I can't believe you're taking up for her," Jack groused. "She's been horrible to you."

"Which is why I don't want to be horrible to her." I'd been thinking about this since I saw her reaction on the plane. "Maybe her ordeal changed her way of thinking. It's possible she'll come out the other side a better person."

"Oh, I love that you're so sweet," Jack said. "Don't be naive. She's not going to suddenly turn into a good person."

"She could."

"She won't." Jack insisted. "She might be introspective, maybe even convince herself that she wants to be better, but we all know that you can't just change a personality by wishing for it to happen. She is who she is and she'll be back to being nasty in two weeks, three tops."

"I hate to take Jack's side," Millie started.

"But you will," I huffed, crossing my arms over my chest.

"I've been around a lot longer than you," Millie said pointedly. "I've also known Laura longer. She won't keep this up forever."

"Fine. Let's all be mean to the woman who was kidnapped and tortured."

"Even your sarcasm is sweet," Jack teased, poking my side before sobering. "I don't think anybody is saying that we should be mean to her. We're just saying that trusting her is never advisable. Nobody is going to go out of their way to hurt her."

"Fine." I blew out a sigh and focused on the road. We were surrounded by trees. "What sort of town do you think we're going to? I mean ... are we going to have choices for restaurants?" I had no idea when I'd turned into such a foodie. Before joining the Legacy Foundation team I'd considered myself someone who could exist on Campbell's Soup and SpaghettiOs. Now I liked trying new and yummy things. One of my favorite places to visit was New Orleans. The food was amazing. I didn't think we were going to have the same luck here.

"I'm guessing it'll be diner food, pizza, and whatever the hotel restaurant offers," Jack said. "It's probably good you ate your weight in stuffed lobster last night to tide you over."

I nodded. The trees were so thick on either side of us I felt claustrophobic. "You were right about this being real wilderness. Somebody could get lost out here pretty fast."

"They could," he agreed. "That means you're sticking close to me, right? I don't want you getting lost when we're exploring."

He didn't have to tell me twice. "I promise not to go wandering."

"Thank you."

"Unless I actually see Bigfoot and decide to follow." I felt the need to add the caveat. "I mean ... I can't not chase Bigfoot."

"Bigfoot isn't real."

"I bet you thought that about really old witches who want to take young girls to absorb their power."

His hands gripped the wheel tighter, a muscle working in his jaw. "Fair point, but that's still different."

"Yeah, yeah, yeah." I let loose an absent hand wave. "Bigfoot is fake. Blah, blah, blah. Sometimes you're like a broken record, Jack. I wish you would open yourself up to possibilities occasionally."

"I've opened myself to you, fully and completely. That's enough opening for me."

It was a sweet sentiment. That didn't change the fact that we were heading into unchartered territory. "The woods are really thick."

"Which is why they haven't found more bodies. I'm serious about you sticking close, Charlie. No unnecessary chances this time."

Understanding his fear, I nodded. "No unnecessary chances. I promise."

IT TOOK US FORTY MINUTES TO get to the hotel. When we arrived, my greatest fears were realized.

"Moose Lodge Lodge." I tilted my head and studied the faded sign of the two-story hotel and tried to keep my distaste from becoming evident. "Why do you think they used Lodge twice?"

"I think it had a different name at one point." Millie pointed to the sign. "I think it was Bear Creek Lodge, but then they painted over the sign and were too lazy to drop the second lodge."

Well, that explained that. "It says they have a restaurant." I tried to look on the bright side.

"I promise you won't starve," Jack reassured me. He smiled, but his eyes told me he felt the same way about the hotel. "We won't be hanging out here often. We'll be here to sleep and eat. That's it."

"Right."

I loitered at the back of the lobby as Jack and Chris sorted out the rooms. I thought it would go smoothly until Laura received her room assignment and started shaking her head. It was the first signs of life I'd seen from her.

"May I have a different room?" She tossed the keycard envelope back at Chris before he could answer.

Confusion lined Chris's forehead. "I guess, but can you tell me why?"

"I want something on the second floor away from the elevator." Laura was firm. "Rooms with first-floor entrances are more likely to be targeted by criminals."

Bob Sutton, the owner of the hotel, made a face from behind the counter. "We don't have criminals here, Miss." He had an odd drawl that wasn't exactly an accent but was nothing I'd ever heard. "Everybody is armed, including me. Nobody would ever try breaking into one of my rooms. It doesn't happen."

"I still want a different room." Laura insisted.

Jack seemed as if he was about to argue with her, but I sent him a look that slid from stern to pleading in an instant. "Can she please have a room on the second floor, away from the elevator? We're sorry for being difficult."

Bob didn't argue again. He took back the card and started typing on his computer. "I swear this place is safe."

"Of course it is," Jack said amiably. "We're just picky when it comes to rooms."

I waited until we were in our room, which happened to be on the first floor with a separate entrance, to tackle Jack on the bed and smother him with kisses. "Thank you for doing that for her."

Jack laughed as he hugged me. "It wasn't that big a deal. In hindsight, I get why she doesn't want a separate entrance. I should've taken that into consideration. You're much sweeter than me, so you thought of it first."

I lightly sank my teeth into his neck and gave him a little nip, which made him groan.

"Okay, maybe you're not that sweet." He wrapped his arms around my waist and rolled me under him, his eyes earnest as he scanned my face. "You don't have to be nice to her. She probably doesn't like it because she thinks you pity her."

"I'm not going to be mean." I couldn't, even though she'd been mean to me more than once. "Just ... let her do her own thing."

"Fine." He gave me a quick kiss and then his eyes moved to the nightstand. "Holy ... ."

I turned to look. The hotel room was clean, which was the most I could say about it, but given where we were located, I thought there might be some sort of critter invading. Instead, I found an antique device that accepted quarters. "What is that?" I asked.

He belted out a laugh. "That, my little Charlie, is Magic Fingers. You put quarters in and the bed vibrates."

"Seriously?" I looked around for my purse. "Do you have any quarters?"

He laughed as I started pawing at his pockets. "Hold on." He shook his head. "You can't put your hands on me like that or we'll never leave this room. I guarantee Chris will want to head out within the hour."

I frowned. "We were on the plane for seven hours. It's late in the afternoon."

"Not here." He shook his head. "We're three hours behind. This is Pacific, not Eastern."

"So, what time is it?"

"A little after noon. I'm guessing we're going to get lunch in the restaurant and then head out."

I thought that wouldn't happen until the following day, but I nodded all the same. "Can we still try the Magic Fingers? I think I've seen them in old movies."

He moved my head to the pillow. "Prepare to be amazed." He dug quarters out of his pocket and dropped them in the slot. The bed started vibrating so intensely that my teeth rattled.

"Ah, soothing vibrations to sleep to," Jack teased as he flopped down next to me, his hand finding mine. His voice shook with the vibrations and I laughed.

"Can we ... do things ... with this bed doing this?" I asked. It was the first thing that came to mind.

"Of course we can. I'm very athletic."

I laughed again. "This is ... wow. I'm kind of more excited about the bed than looking for Bigfoot."

"It does have a certain charm."

The door to our room opened without anyone knocking, telling me we hadn't latched it properly. That might be cause for concern at night, so I made a mental note to check the door next time. Thankfully, it was only Millie paying us a visit.

"Um, we have a problem," she said when she saw what we were doing. "Bernard and I are right next to you guys."

"So?" Jack was blasé.

"We can hear everything you guys are saying and doing."

"We're not doing anything. We're just ... getting acquainted with our new bed."

"Oh, don't even." Millie wagged her finger. "I know darned well you guys are going to be playing with this bed later. It doesn't matter how exhausted you'll be when you get back thanks to the time change. You won't be able to stop yourselves."

"It's not often you find Magic Fingers," Jack argued as he squeezed my hand. "Maybe you should get a different room."

"We don't want a different room."

"Well, there's no way Charlie isn't going to wear out this machine." Jack said. "She's already in love with it."

"I am," I admitted, rolling my chin onto Jack's chest so I could better see Millie. "This might be the coolest thing I've ever seen."

"You need to get out more," Millie snapped. "I'm serious. We do not want to hear this bed vibrating all hours of the night."

Jack's smirk turned devilish. "You might want to brace yourself for disappointment."

"I'll make you pay," Millie warned.

Jack didn't look worried. She was inordinately fond of both of us. "Bring it on."

FOUR

Four of us went with the first group. Jack drove, Chris in the passenger seat, and I sat with Casey in back. I understood why they were cutting our group in half, at least in theory, but the feeling of unease rolling through me refused to be abated.

There was something out here.

How I knew it, I couldn't say, but it was something I felt deeply.

Jack pulled to the side of the road and parked next to two SUVs. A sign had been erected warning people away from the vehicles. I was the last one out of the Tahoe. Jack and Chris already had their heads bent together when I joined them.

"There's nothing wrong with the vehicles, at least externally," Jack noted, briefly running his hand down the back of my head before continuing to circle the darker SUV. "If they'd been able to run in this direction, I don't see any reason they couldn't have escaped."

"I'm guessing they didn't have the option to run, at least not very far." Chris moved to the back of the Tahoe and removed several packs. "We have time to hike in, look around, and then hike out. I was hoping the four-by-fours would've been delivered by now, but that doesn't seem to be the case."

"Haven't the police already been to Nighthawk?" I asked.

Chris nodded. "Yes, but they didn't spend much time there. Their dogs picked up the scent of the campers, but it seems they fled into the woods. The dogs followed those trails, so nobody has spent much time in the town."

I had to ask the obvious question. "What do you expect to find in the town?"

Chris shrugged. "I don't know. I guess we'll find out."

I flicked my eyes to Jack, who had returned to survey the bags Chris wanted to hike in with. "What's in here?" he asked, knocking his toe against the nearest bag.

"Cameras. Infrared equipment. Some night-vision stuff. I want to set it up around the town."

"Why?"

"What do you mean why? So, we can see what's going on when we're not there ... and maybe even see a little something that might be hidden while we are there. Hannah will make sure the feeds are working from the hotel, although the internet setup is not great there."

"They have Magic Fingers, though," I said. "I think it's the best hotel we've ever stayed in."

Jack sent me a smirk and then straightened when Casey glared at him. "What?"

"Do I even want to know what she's talking about?" He had the air of a big brother protecting his younger sister. Thankfully, Chris was so busy itemizing the equipment in the bags he didn't realize something else was going on.

"The vibrating bed machine," Jack replied. "Charlie had never seen one before today. She's ... enamored."

"Oh." Casey's forehead creased in puzzlement. "You've never seen them?" he asked me.

"I haven't stayed in all that many hotels," I replied. "In fact, before I joined the Legacy Foundation, I'm pretty sure the only hotels I'd ever stayed at involved trips with my parents. They were big fans of Marriott."

"Ah." Casey's lips twitched. Apparently, he was as amused by my reaction to Magic Fingers as Jack. "Well, have fun ... I guess."

"Millie and Bernard are right next to us. They say that we can't have any fun because they can hear."

"Even better." Casey winked at me before grabbing one of the packs. He groaned when he tested the weight. "What do these things weigh?"

"Thirty pounds," Chris replied. "We have five miles to hike. It should be doable. We'll be leaving most of the equipment behind when we get there, so the walk back will be easier."

Jack flicked his eyes to the sky. "I do not want to be caught out here after dark. I wish we didn't have to hike the five miles." The words were barely out of his mouth before the sound of a buzzing engine assailed our ears. When I looked to the left, I found an all-terrain vehicle screeching to a stop. The woman behind the wheel, wearing some over-the-top goggles, grinned. "Hello, sports fans."

I laughed. "Millie, what are you doing here? I thought you were staying at the hotel." I was delighted to see her.

"That's when I thought we were going to have to hike in," she replied. "The rental company called right after you left, said they left these things a mile from where they should've been left. I figured Bernard and I would make sure you got them. There's no reason to make things more difficult."

"Bernard?" My eyebrows clapped together as I searched the road for Bernard. After what felt like a really long time, he appeared. He was driving at a much slower pace than Millie.

"He drives like an old woman," Millie explained, seemingly not caring that she was disparaging her own sex and age group. "Someone will have to take the wheel from him."

"I will!" Casey's hand shot in the air. He looked beyond excited, and I very much doubted it was simply because he wasn't looking forward to the hike.

"Chris can go with you guys," Jack offered. "I'll take Millie and Charlie." He pinned Millie with a serious look. "Which means you need to give me the driver's seat."

Millie was having none of it. "No way. I'm the captain of this starship, buck-o." She was firm. "I'm driving."

"You heard Chris," Jack argued. "He didn't list you as one of the team cleared to drive these things."

"I don't believe I heard that at all." Millie's tone was sweet, to the point of being saccharine. "Not even a little bit. Chris, you didn't say anything like that, did you?"

Chris looked caught. "Um ... ." He'd definitely said that, but Millie was his favorite aunt. In fact, he was closer to her than he was his own parents. He didn't want to disappoint her. "I'm sure she can drive if you serve as a chaperone, Jack," he said finally.

"Such a wuss." Jack shook his head and then darted his eyes to me. "Who do you want to drive?"

There was only one answer to that question. "Her!" I knew beyond a shadow of a doubt that Millie would make the ride fun, even if a bit reckless. "Shotgun!"

Jack's glare moved from Millie to me. "I'm not sitting in the back."

"Then you should've called shotgun," Millie said. "As it stands, you're in the back. Load up our gear and let's get out of here."

Jack worked his jaw, fury bubbling beneath the surface. There was no arguing with Millie when she was in a mood. "Fine. Charlie, fasten your seatbelt." He glanced around the gear attached to the vehicle. "Are there helmets? Charlie needs a helmet."

"Ugh." Millie was disgusted. "You're zero fun. Get in and shut up. I've got this."

RIDING WITH MILLIE WAS INDEED AN adventure. My knees were shaky and my stomach threatening to revolt when we reached Nighthawk.

"I'll bet you're glad you didn't try the chicken salad," Jack noted as he watched me bend at the waist to rest my hands on my knees. He looked amused.

"Yes, mayonnaise would not be my friend right now," I agreed.

"The cold cuts were a much better idea." I made a gagging sound but didn't throw anything up. Then I straightened. "I'm fine."

Jack might've been a killjoy when it came to fun — that's what Millie claimed — but he was sympathetic. He cracked a bottle of water and handed it to me, running his hand over my back as he watched me take a few tentative sips. "Better?" he asked.

"I'm fine," I reassured him. "I just didn't know you could fly through the air like that while still in a vehicle."

"You shouldn't be able to. Millie defies the laws of gravity."

"You're welcome," Millie said saucily, sending him a sunny smile that would've made me laugh under different circumstances. Then she turned her attention to Nighthawk, a forgotten town in the middle of a forest. "And will you look at this place?" She made a tsking sound with her tongue. "This place is definitely haunted."

Jack rubbed my back three more times and then pressed a kiss to the spot behind my ear. I'd pulled my hair back before leaving the hotel, and it had turned out to be a good idea given the thick foliage we'd trekked through. It would be a snarled mess otherwise.

"How do you know it's haunted?" he asked when he pulled away from me, his eyes going to the other off-road vehicle. Casey had clearly been a more conscientious driver than Millie because Bernard and Chris were much less shaken.

"Look at it." Millie gestured toward the buildings. "I mean ... that has haunted written all over it." I was the one with magical leanings, including being able to see ghosts, so she looked to me for confirmation. "Right?"

I shrugged. "I'll get back to you after we look around."

"Speaking of that," Jack took control of the conversation before anybody could take off and start searching. "We need to stay in groups of three or more. That means we either all search together or break into two groups. Either way, Charlie is with me. I don't care how it's sorted for the rest of you."

"Oh, thanks so much for your concern," Casey drawled. "I can't tell you how nice it is to be loved."

"I stand by it." Jack refused to back down. "It's best we stay together for the initial trip through the town. If you want to argue, you can go with a different group." There was an edge to his voice.

I knew what Jack was really saying. He wanted Casey to stick close in case there was some sort of attack. He figured that together they could hold off whatever creature we came into contact with until I could escape. I had no intention of leaving them behind, even though that was likely what he was picturing in his head.

"Let's stick together," Chris said, his gaze keen as he scanned the town. Back when Nighthawk was considered a boom town, they didn't build sprawling metropolises. They simply constructed the necessary buildings and called it a day. "We can do an initial search as a group, get the lay of the land, and then figure out our next move."

Jack checked his watch. "I don't want the initial search to take more than an hour. I know it's going to take two hours to set up the equipment. I wasn't kidding when I said I want us out of here before dark."

"We've got it, Jack." Chris let his annoyance out to play, a rare occurrence. "Sasquatch isn't real, but you're determined to make sure we're not killed by him anyway. You're nothing if not predictable."

Jack's expression didn't change. "My job is to keep us safe. I'm determined to do that ... no matter what. If you don't like my methods, take it up with Myron."

Chris blew out a sigh. His uncle might love him, but Myron always capitulated to Jack's wishes. It was because of that love that Jack was put in charge. Myron wanted to indulge Chris, but it was more important to keep him safe.

"Let's start then," Chris said. "I want to see what we've got here."

JACK TOOK THE LEAD. HE WAS armed — he'd told me that everybody in these parts was armed when he'd holstered his weapon on his hip. We took a methodical approach to walking around town.

"This is the house of ill repute," Casey noted as we stopped in front of one of the buildings. "That's actually what they called it."

"How do you know that?" I was honestly curious.

"I saw the photos online when we were at the hotel."

"It doesn't look safe," I noted, wrinkling my nose. "Also, did they really call it a house of ill repute back in the day? I mean ... I can't see two guys coming back from the mine and saying, 'Who wants to hang out at the house of ill repute.'"

Jack met my gaze over his shoulder and grinned. "They probably called it a brothel, or a bath house. I'm sure the people who surveyed the town after it folded called the building a house of ill repute."

That made sense. Still, I was curious what we would find inside. "Can we go in?"

Chris shook his head. "I had to promise we'd stay out of the buildings to get clearance to come out here. They're not safe."

"They're old, Charlie, and nobody has been taking care of them," Jack added. "I prefer you not have to survive a building falling on you, however old and weathered the wood might be."

"Fair enough." I blew out a sigh and traced my hand over the wood. "It's kind of cool. In fact ... ." I forgot what I was going to say as magic jolted through me. It wasn't the sort of magic that could hurt me. No, it was something else entirely.

Paulie, where are you? It's here!

I whipped my hand away as the memory blasted through me, my heart hammering with fear.

"Charlie?" Jack turned away from Chris and moved toward me. "Are you okay?" He brushed my flyaway bangs from my face.

"Is something wrong?" Chris asked. He was often so lost in his own little world he didn't pick up on weird exchanges. Apparently, that wasn't the case today.

"I just felt suddenly queasy," I lied. "I guess I'm not over Millie's driving yet."

"Which is why I will be driving back," Jack replied, his gaze intense as it searched mine. He knew I was lying. He also recognized he couldn't call me out on it when we had an audience.

"Oh, dream on," Millie drawled.

Jack kept me at his side and slowed our pace as Chris started leading the others to the next building. "What really happened?" he asked in a low voice when the others were far enough ahead of us. "Did you see something?"

"I ... felt ... something," I replied. "When I touched the wood, I had a flash of memory."

"Sybil?"

I shook my head. "It wasn't my memory. It was someone else's."

He slipped his arm around my waist. "The missing kids?"

"I ... don't know. One of them was named Paul?"

He nodded.

"I heard a voice. It was female. She was screaming for Paulie."

"That would likely be Rosalie Partridge." Jack looked as if he was scanning his memory. "She and Paul Prescott were a couple. That's what I read."

"Well, then I guess that would make sense." My palms were sweaty so I dried them on my pants. "She screamed for him, was looking for him. She also said, 'It's here,' but didn't sound excited about whatever 'it' was."

He pressed his lips together, as if debating, and then nodded. "Did you see anything else?"

"Are you asking if I saw Bigfoot?"

"Definitely not."

"I didn't see anything else. It was dark. I couldn't really see anything. It's more that I heard ... and felt."

"What did you feel?"

"Her fear. She was terrified."

"We don't know what happened to her."

"We know what happened to Paul. He's dead."

"He is, and it's sad. But until we have confirmation on the others, we can't assume they're dead. They may be out here somewhere. They may need us."

I understood what he was saying and agreed. "I promise to stick close to you, Jack." I said it for him as much as myself. I was agitated enough that I didn't want to risk being separated from him. If something did attack, I wanted him close to protect with my magic if need be. "You don't have to worry about me wandering off."

He managed a wan smile. "Good. That's one less thing to drive me to distraction."

"You still have to wrestle the off-road vehicle's keys from Millie for the drive home," I reminded him.

"Yes, that's on top of my list of things to deal with. The fact that there might be some sort of monster up here is second on the list, so still important."

I grinned. "It was kind of a fun ride."

"Obviously you've already forgotten how sick you felt."

"I'm sure I'll remember during the ride back."

"Not likely. If I have to wrestle her down and take those keys, I'll be driving."

Something told me he was going to have a bigger fight than he was anticipating. For now, we had other things to worry about ... like a town that time had forgotten, and the teenagers it had seemingly swallowed whole.

FIVE

The further we traversed into the town, the greater the sense of dread surrounding me grew. I didn't like this. At all. Something very bad had happened here.

When we got to the remnants of the general store I purposely moved to the highest standing wall and looked around. I didn't want anyone watching me do this. Once I was convinced that all eyes were directed elsewhere, I tentatively extended my fingers to see if I could get another flash.

I wasn't disappointed.

I can't believe you brought me here for this, Paulie.

Oh, babe, why do you have to be such a pain? You're always such a pain.

Since when is knowing what I want a bad thing?

Since not everybody wants what you want.

Fury burned through me hot enough that I drew back my fingers, and then I almost jolted out of my skin when a pair of arms wrapped around me from behind. For a moment, I was so lost in the flash I thought I'd become the girl at the center of the conversation. Rosalie. That's what Jack said her name was. Then I realized whatever it was wasn't actually happening to me.

"Did you see something else?" Jack asked, his lips close to my ear.

THE WENDIGO WHOOP-DE-DOO

Under different circumstances, I would've shivered because of his proximity and offered up a flirty response.

"The same girl. She was arguing with the Paulie guy. She was angry that he brought her here."

"I can see why this place wouldn't appeal to a teenage girl."

"He was frustrated with her, said not everybody wants the same things. Then I felt ... this incredible sensation of rage. I've never felt anything like it."

He moved my ponytail off my neck and placed his lips there. It was a comforting move. "Was the anger coming from her?"

It was a good question. "That's what it felt like, but I can't be sure."

"I don't know what to say. I'm not all that familiar with your powers."

I jerked my head up to make sure none of the others were nearby. Casey and Millie knew what I could do, at least on a superficial level. That meant Bernard had an inkling, but Chris had no idea. I was exactly the sort of person he was searching for to study. I feared what would happen should he ever learn of my abilities.

"Calm down," Jack chastised in a low voice, turning me to face him. "I would never be reckless enough to out you."

"I know." I licked my lips, feeling a bit like an idiot. "I just ... get nervous sometimes."

"I think you're nervous because of the other thing that's happening. It's amplifying your natural fears regarding your secret. It's okay. Just ... tell me what you think."

"I feel as if I'm connecting with the one girl."

"Rosalie."

"Probably, but I haven't heard her name yet. If she and Paul were together, it makes sense that they would be arguing."

"Why do you think you're connecting with her?"

"I don't know." I knew what I wanted it to be, and I couldn't stop from blurting it out. "Maybe she's alive and I'm supposed to find her."

Jack's expression didn't change, but I swear I could almost hear him internally sigh. "I know I told you we're supposed to approach this with the aim of recovering the other kids alive, but I have to think the odds of that are slim."

"Why?"

"Because ... I saw the photos of the other bodies."

I hadn't. He'd purposely refrained from showing them to me. He believed I didn't need to see the horror meted out to these kids to know something bad was happening in the Washington woods.

"They met hard ends, Charlie." He kept his voice low. "It's possible that when this happened the kids scattered. A few might've initially escaped, but we don't know if they had supplies."

"We don't know that they didn't," I pointed out.

"True, but ... think about it." He used his practical tone, my least favorite. "If you were terrified because some sort of monster, maybe a bear, was rampaging through your camp, would you stop to collect survival supplies?"

He had a point. "Maybe they came back to the campsite after they fled. We still haven't found it. They could still be there, hunkered down or injured."

"The dogs didn't find them."

I refused to let go of all hope. "Some of them might be alive."

"And you think this Rosalie is alive," he surmised.

"I think ... that I'm not willing to give up on them." It was the only thing I could say with absolute certainty. "I just ... can't."

He held my gaze a moment longer and then nodded. "Okay. But I need you to be careful. I know you're now going to walk around to every building in this town and touch it because you're you, but it's important that you're careful."

"I'm always careful."

He snorted. "Yeah, right. Tell that to someone who hasn't had ten years shaved off his life because you're not careful."

"I haven't shaved ten years off your life." I refused to accept that. "We need to live to a hundred, together, and then die the same day. You can't die before me. I'll be wrecked."

That earned a smile. "Then we'll have to work on your survival skills. It will be a gift for both of us."

. . .

AFTER OUR INITIAL SEARCH OF THE town, Chris plotted out where he wanted the equipment erected. I was good with the cameras, compared to the infrared, so Millie and I started mounting them in the downtown area. Jack relented about constantly being at my side and let me walk a whole three-hundred feet away from him. I tried to remind myself that he was only doing it because he loved me, but sometimes his alpha nature was grating.

"Are you deciding how you're going to punish him later?" Millie asked as I dug a hole for the anchor. She'd witnessed our minor spat when Jack balked at the idea of Millie and I going off alone.

"Maybe." I'd talked to her about Jack more than once, so I was comfortable confiding in her now. "He's a butthead sometimes."

"He's afraid," Millie corrected. "He knows something bad happened here. He knows you're sensing something. He can't help himself that he's afraid."

I shot her a sidelong look, surprised. "How did you know I sensed something?"

"I saw you at the whorehouse. There was no covering for whatever it was you were feeling. Thankfully Chris is about the most unobservant person I've ever met."

"I don't think you're supposed to call it a whorehouse."

"I bet that's what they called it back in the day."

She was probably right. "It's still mean. Prostitution isn't always a choice. Sometimes people have to do what they have to do."

"Oh, that's very politically correct." She tapped the end of my nose and grinned. "For the record, I think prostitution should be legalized."

"You do?" That was surprising. I simply assumed she would be against it, which said more about me than her. Assumptions were always bad, and with Millie, they were hardly ever accurate.

"Absolutely." She bobbed her head. "There's a reason prostitution has been around since the dawn of time. Sex is biological. It's necessary. Prostitutes are filling a need."

I didn't disagree, but I had questions. "Do you think it should be regulated?"

"Yup. Make it taxable. Make STD tests and birth control readily available to registered workers. Make them be licensed."

"I think the problem is that those who are poor enough to entertain the thought probably can't afford to jump through hoops to be licensed."

"Probably not, but in my world, nobody is so poor things like that are an issue."

"You should run for president."

"Right?" She beamed at me as I lowered the camera stand into the dirt. "How are things going with your family?"

As far as transitions went, it could've been smoother, but I understood her curiosity. When I'd told her about my family, including the fact that Casey was my brother (something nobody other than Jack knew) she'd been intrigued. Since I'd dropped the initial bomb on her, we'd had very little time to talk.

"Um ... it's going about as well as could be expected."

"Oh, well, that's a diplomatic answer." She rolled her eyes. "I want the dirt. Tell me."

I blew out a sigh and wiped my forearm across my forehead. "They took me to the zoo yesterday."

Millie blinked several times. "Because they wanted to find a place for you to live? Or wait, maybe your father wanted to move Jack in with the gorillas."

She made me laugh. "They did insist I loved the gorillas when I was a kid. That was the problem. They kept expecting me to react as if I was a little kid."

"Ah." She reacted as if she understood. "You know why they're doing that, right?"

"Yeah. They have no context of me as an adult."

"That's it exactly. You were frozen as a child in their minds. Intellectually they knew you were growing up, but they couldn't see it. How did you react?"

"I smiled a lot. Then Mike gave Jack grief for flirting with me."

THE WENDIGO WHOOP-DE-DOO

"Mike is your father?"

"Yeah, but I have trouble referring to him that way."

"I get it. You don't have to feel what you don't feel."

That was the problem. I had no idea what I felt. "It's ... a learning experience. They're nice people, and I can tell they've been through a lot, but I can't create the instant bond they seem to want."

"You can only do what you can do. Don't let them push you."

"That's the plan. Jack and I are moving to the new place in a few days. Or, well, we might be moved in by the time we get back. I'm excited about that. It's beautiful. I've never lived in a place as nice."

"Let your parents help you look at furniture and artwork. That might be a nice bonding exercise, and it will make them feel as if you're including them in your life."

I snorted. "I don't have money for that sort of stuff yet."

"And yet something tells me Jack will spring shopping excursions on you," Millie teased. "If you don't want to listen to him complain, you'll have to deal."

"I don't have to deal right now." I was done with this conversation. It made me feel itchy, and my emotions were all over the place as it was. "Let's talk about something else, like Laura. Do you think ... ?" I didn't finish the sentence because I was drowned out by a bone-rattling scream.

I swung my head so fast I almost gave myself whiplash as I studied the heavy woods to our left.

Then it happened again, another scream.

"Is that ... a person?" Millie asked. She looked more confused than frightened.

"I don't know." The scream was shrill but lacked a human element. "Wait here." I reacted without thinking, Jack's main complaint about me, and bolted into the woods. It was hard going between the thick trees, and I stopped about twenty feet in to listen.

I could hear Millie grousing behind me. When I heard another scream, I readjusted and raced in its direction. I was frightened, but I had more in my arsenal than a normal person. If someone was in trouble — Rosalie or one of the others — I might be able to protect them.

"Charlie!" Jack's voice was a boom of frustration behind me. He'd obviously realized I'd taken off into the woods. He would be angry.

I kept going, keeping a mental picture in my head as I slipped through the trees. I was heading in the right direction. I was almost positive. The terrain was rough, roots sticking out in every direction. It was one of those roots that tripped me up. I wasn't coordinated even when there weren't a million things to trip over.

I gasped when I pitched forward, my hand automatically going out to touch a tree. That's when it happened again. The magical memory flash for something that didn't belong to me.

We're never going to survive this. It's all your fault, Paulie. This isn't what I wanted. Why do you never care what I want?

Shut up! I can't take another second of your whining. We have to get out of here. You need to shut up and hurry up if you expect to get out with us.

Or what? Are you going to leave me behind? Is that what you're saying?

I'm saying we have to run. You can come with us. We're out of time.

I landed on my knees, my breath coming in ragged gasps. Had he left her? Was that why his body had been found and Rosalie's hadn't? Maybe she was still out here. Maybe he'd left her behind and she was hiding.

Or maybe she was screaming.

I heard the sound again and got to my feet. My knees hurt, as did my hip. Despite the pain, I couldn't turn back.

I started forward again, and this time when I reached the row of trees I'd been aiming at I emerged into a small clearing. It was an opening, and it allowed me to breathe ... until I saw what was in the clearing.

There were several tents. They'd been trashed and were sagging. Clothing, some of it shredded and mashed into the ground, littered the area. A cooler was tipped on its side. A body rested in the debris.

I took a wary step toward the body, as if being pulled in that direction against my will. It was a male, facing upward, eyes open and sightless. The features were twisted, as if they'd seen something horrible, and there was a huge gaping wound where his throat used to be.

"Charlie!" Jack emerged into the clearing, his eyes searching for — and finding — mine. He let out a huge breath, his chest heaving, and then extended a finger. "What did we agree on?"

I didn't answer. I couldn't. I gestured to the body.

Jack moved to me first, pulling me in for a hug, and then searched the clearing for signs we weren't alone. "I guess we found their camp," he said finally, grim detachment washing over him as he regarded the body. "And another one of our missing teens."

"It's not Rosalie."

"No," he agreed.

"I heard a flash of her again. Paul was warning her that she had to keep up because they were going to run for it. She was afraid, but he didn't care. He said he would leave her."

"I'm sorry for that." Jack appeared to choose his words carefully. "I'll never leave you."

"I didn't think you would. I ... wasn't fishing." I didn't know what else to say. "I just thought ... ."

"Charlie! Jack!"

Casey's voice drew my attention to the trees again. The rest of the cavalry was obviously coming. "We're here," I called out. I would've liked more time to talk things over with Jack.

"We'll talk about it again," Jack promised. "Just ... look around. Tell me what you see."

"It's a trashed campsite," I replied.

"But that's not all it is."

I was confused.

"Look up," he instructed.

I did, and when I registered what I was seeing — twigs and brush that had been twisted into little people, or maybe symbols — attached to the branches, I swallowed hard. "What in the ... ?"

Millie finally caught up to us. She was breathing so hard I worried she might have a heart attack. She shook her head when I moved to her side. "Don't ever do that again."

"Okay."

She looked up. "Well, that's some Blair Witch-level terror."

It was only then that I realized she was right. The figures did remind me of something out of the *Blair Witch Project* movie. "I ... don't know. We have a body, too."

"I saw that." Millie was grim. "I guess this place really is deadly."

That's exactly what I was afraid of.

SIX

Chris was beside himself with joy when he caught up with us. He attempted to temper his enthusiasm because we had a body to grapple with, but his glee at the tree symbols was hard to contain. I turned from him to focus.

"I'm going to send him back to the vehicles with Bernard," Jack said in a low voice. "We need a body bag."

I stilled. "Are we taking the body back?" That went against everything I'd learned on the job so far.

"No, but we want to protect it from scavengers. When he's gone, you can start touching things. Try to make it quick."

I understood what he was saying. Er, well, more like what he wasn't saying. The four people who were to remain behind were aware of my abilities. He was setting it up purposefully.

"Okay."

He shot me a tentative smile before heading over to Chris. There was a brief argument, but Jack won. He explained to Chris that he thought it best two men return to the vehicles and he stay behind with Millie and me. Chris complained, but then headed out.

Jack craned his neck to watch them go and then nodded to me. "Go for it, baby."

I approached the fallen tents and started touching them. The first three were a loss. The fourth, located away from the rest of the tents, was the only one still standing. When my fingers grazed the tattered material, the memory flashes started.

What are you going to do once you're on campus, Paulie?

How much fun is that going to be?

I can't wait to visit you there, bro.

The first three voices were male. Then I heard the female voice again.

You're going to come home on weekends to visit, right?

It was Rosalie, and I couldn't help but feel sorry for her. She was so desperate for love that she was begging Paul to ease her fears. He didn't.

It's hours to get back home. I don't think I'll be coming back at all the first semester.

But ... how is that going to work?

I couldn't see the shrug, but I could sense it. Paul was not going to give her what she wanted ... ever.

I guess we'll have to figure that out later.

When?

Later.

That was it. Either the statement was enough to shut Rosalie down or the rest was unimportant.

I pressed my lips together as I withdrew my fingers. "I can't decide if Rosalie is needy or if Paul is just a douche," I admitted as I shook my hand. There was a slight tingling at my fingertips and it was mildly uncomfortable.

Jack took my hand and rubbed my fingers. "Maybe it's both," he suggested. "No one person is all bad."

"Right." I took a breath and then dropped to my knees to look inside the tent. The flap was open and the items inside were damp. There was no blood, which was a great relief, but clothes were strewn from one end to the other. "It looks like there was a struggle." I backed my head out so Jack could look inside.

"Not necessarily," he countered. "I mean ... we're talking teenagers.

There are men and women's clothes here. I'm guessing there might've been some romance going on."

"You think there was romance going on despite the way they were arguing?" I was understandably dubious. "How often do we romance it up when we're fighting?"

He arched an eyebrow as he rolled back on his haunches. "How often do we fight?"

"Sometimes we fight about what we're going to watch on television."

He made a face. "We don't have relationship issues. At least I like to think we don't. Paul and Rosalie were clearly having some sort of ... thing. I'm guessing he was excited to escape to college and she was desperate to hold onto him. The more she clung, the more annoyed he got and increased the distance."

It made sense. The whole situation made me queasy. "I don't like this."

"There's nothing to like. We don't know how long they were here before things started to go wrong. It's possible they made it one or two nights. We don't have a time of death from the medical examiner yet."

"When will we have that?" We needed to put together a timeline.

"Hopefully tomorrow." He brushed his hand over my shoulder. "I'm not an expert — and we might have to pull out the big guns and muscle Hannah in on the autopsies — but I'd guess the boy over there has been dead forty-eight hours or so."

I did the math in my head. "It was supposed to be a five-day camping trip, right?"

He nodded. "At this point, they're almost two days overdue."

He didn't grasp what I was getting at. "Shouldn't they have been packing up to leave right about the time he died?"

Realization dawned on his face as he glanced around the campsite again. "You're right."

"So, why weren't they?"

Jack slowly rose and moved over to the cooler, his eyes narrowing as he glanced inside. "There's food in here, not much.

They at least made it through several days before things went south."

"But what were they doing out here?" I dusted my hands off on my jeans as I stood. "I mean ... what's the appeal? Why would teenagers want to camp near an abandoned mining town?"

A small smile played at the corners of Jack's mouth. "Let me ask you something," he started. "Let's say that you and I were fun and frisky eighteen-year-olds who decided to go camping."

I fought a smile ... and failed. "How do you know I was a fun and frisky teenager?"

"I've met you. I'm sure you were fun."

"I *was* fun. People everywhere talked about how fun I was. They wanted to start a fan club."

He choked on a laugh. "If I suggested a camping trip to you, even at that age, would you really have turned down the opportunity to visit a supposedly haunted old town?"

"Probably not," I conceded. "I was fun and frisky, but also weird."

"I guess it's good my favorite combination is fun, frisky and weird."

"Totally." I bobbed my head. "I just feel as if there's more going on here."

The sound of heavy footsteps in the woods to our east signaled Chris and Bernard's return. I would've preferred more time, but Chris was in a hurry to get back.

"Something big happened here," Jack confirmed as Chris emerged from the trees. "It's our job to find out what that is." He pointed to Millie. "You have the good camera. We need photos of how the body was discovered before we move it."

"I've got it." Millie let loose a saucy salute, unbothered by the task she'd been assigned. "There's little I love more than taking photos of dead boys. My childhood dream has been realized."

Jack made a face but didn't comment on her snark. Instead, he flicked his eyes to me. "We need photos of the twig things. Can you handle that?"

The question should've been insulting, but I couldn't muster the energy for outrage, fake or otherwise. "Yeah. When I'm done, can I take one or two back to the hotel to study?"

Jack hesitated and then tilted his head toward Chris, deferring the decision.

"I don't see why not," Chris said. "Just make sure you have photos of the entire setup. We want to cover all our bases. I have small bags to put them in."

We all had jobs to do. Chris, Jack and Bernard had to get the body into the bag. Jack was tagging it with a geotag so the search team would have no trouble returning to claim it the next day. Casey made a big show of taking photos and searching through the remains of the campsite, but I didn't miss the fact that he was close to me as he did so. Somehow Jack had put him in charge of watching me without me realizing it. They'd come up with some sort of shorthand I wasn't familiar with, so I made a mental note to watch them closely and figure it out.

Once I finished taking photos, I turned my attention to the line of trees. I figured there had to be something there to explain this. Or maybe I just hoped. I was halfway around when something caught my eye. At first, I almost glossed over the indentation in the dirt, but then I caught sight of it from a different angle.

"What is it?" Casey asked, appearing at my side. He was getting better at reading my moods and reacted almost as quickly as Jack these days.

I pointed. "Does that look like a footprint?"

"A footprint?" His forehead creased as he studied the indentation. "I don't think ... ." He cocked his head before he finished the statement. "Huh."

"Right? Look. There's another one right there."

"There is," he said.

"Jack?" I glanced over my shoulder, relieved to find that the body had been covered. "Can you come over here?"

"Of course." Jack removed the gloves he'd donned to handle the body and joined us. "What am I looking at?"

"Charlie thinks that's a print." Casey used a stick to point. "There's another one there."

"If those are supposed to be toes, they're longer than any toes I've ever seen," Jack said.

"On a human," I agreed, sliding him a look.

"They don't look like animal tracks," Jack said. "I mean ... a bear print is much wider, the toes more compact. If those are toes, we're talking like three-inch toes too narrow to balance on."

"Too narrow for us," I clarified.

He shot me a "Here we go" look. "What creature has toes like that?"

"I don't know. I'm pretty sure that's what we're here to find out."

Chris picked that moment to join us. "What did you find?"

"Charlie thinks that's a footprint," Jack replied, gesturing.

Chris peered closer, his eyes lighting with excitement. "Good catch, Charlie!" He offered me an enthusiastic high-five, which had Jack making a face. "We need to make a cast of it."

"Of course you think it's a footprint too," Jack grumbled.

"Let's mix the casting plaster," Chris instructed. "We have time to make a cast before we leave."

"Joy." Jack shook his head as I moved away from the spot. "Where are you going?" he asked when he realized I wasn't merely giving Chris room to maneuver.

"Looking for more prints. I'm just going to finish circling the clearing. Maybe we can find some even better than those."

"If they are footprints."

"Oh, don't be a Gloomy Gus." I poked my finger into his cheek, earning a smile. "There's no reason not to take a cast. If I'm wrong, you can lord it over me later when we're enjoying the Magic Fingers."

"I'm never going to get any sleep on this trip, am I?" Jack didn't look altogether upset at the prospect. "You and that bed are going to wear me out."

"Oh, can we not?" Casey groused.

Jack ignored him and remained focused on me. "Call if you find something."

"Don't I always?"

"No."

He wasn't wrong. Still, I was happy to leave the men to argue over the cast. Millie was still taking photos. She showed no interest in getting close to the trees. That allowed me to focus on the ground by the clearing.

I slowly circled, my attention strictly on the ground. When I got to the parallel location from where they were taking the cast, I jolted when my gaze fell on a pair of legs. These legs didn't belong to the dead, though. They were upright ... and moving.

"Oomph." I fell backward as my gaze expanded to include the man standing before me. He wasn't one of the missing boys. In fact, he looked as if he was old enough to be a grandfather – or maybe even a great-grandfather – of the people we were looking for.

"You're all doomed," he announced.

My breath clogged in my throat as I searched for words. Jack was across the clearing before I could respond.

"Who are you?" Jack's eyes were fierce as he arrived at my side.

"Doomed. Doomed. Doomed." The man said in a singsong voice that had my blood running cold. "The Darkness is going to come for you. I told the others. They didn't listen. Now you won't listen, and it will come for you."

"Do you live out here?" I asked, brushing the seat of my jeans off as I regained my faculties. I remained on my knees because I didn't want the newcomer to see me as threatening.

"I'm not the only one who lives out here," he replied, his eyes lighting in such a way that all I could see was madness reflected back at me.

"Who else lives out here?" Jack asked. He kept his gaze on the man, wary, but extended his hand to help me up.

"Oh, so many ... things." When the man smiled, I realized he was missing more teeth. "I told them the Darkness was coming. They didn't listen." His gaze bore into me. "Will you listen?"

"Did you see the kids who were camping here? Did you talk to them?"

"The Darkness got them." The man shuffled toward the trees. "It was always going to get them. You don't mess with the Darkness."

"Wait." Jack moved as if he was going to physically restrain the man to keep him from departing but I grabbed his arm. "Shouldn't I go after him?" Jack asked.

"Let him go." I had no idea why I felt it was important. "I don't think he goes far from this place. If we take him in, he'll shut down ... or maybe worse. I'm guessing we'll be able to find him again." Or he would find us.

"What's worse?"

I shrugged. "He's not all there, Jack."

"I noticed."

"He's like a harbinger," Chris noted as he moved closer to us. I hadn't even realized he'd been monitoring the situation.

"A harbinger?" Jack's confusion was evident. "Like a crow?"

"I think Chris means a harbinger in a horror movie."

Chris beamed at me. "I love that I never have to explain myself to you. You always know exactly what I'm thinking."

"That's not terrifying or anything," Jack muttered.

I lightly elbowed him to keep the sarcasm at bay. "In a lot of horror movies there's a character that essentially warns the stupid teenagers that they face doom and destruction if they don't leave. It's framed as a choice for the kids. If they'd just listened to the crazy man, then Jason Voorhees wouldn't have killed them.

"*Friday the 13th* has a harbinger, as does *Wrong Turn* and *The Hills Have Eyes*," I continued. "It's a staple of the genre."

Jack blinked. "So, what are you saying?" he asked. "Are you suggesting that we take off because that guy told us the Darkness is coming?"

I held out my hands. "I'm not really saying anything. Just commenting."

"Well, guess what?" Jack's smile was a thin line. "We're not going to be the stupid teenagers in the movie. We're going to finish the cast, set the geotag on the body, and get out. I refuse to be here after dark."

"Because of the Darkness?" I was honestly curious.

"Because it's my job to keep us safe. Something in these woods killed a man. I'm guessing it wasn't a bear. I am not going to risk being stuck out here with no help."

"We could set up camp," Chris countered. "It might be the only way to see what did this. I'm sure the local authorities wouldn't give us grief if we just explain."

That sounded like wishful thinking.

"Not happening." Jack's tone was no-nonsense. "We're going back to the hotel in thirty minutes." He tapped his watch for emphasis. "I'm head of security and what I say goes."

The others nodded, resigned. I managed a smile. "You're kind of sexy when you're bossy," I whispered.

"Oh, geez," Casey groaned.

Jack offered his most charming smile. "Just wait until we have dessert in bed with those Magic Fingers. You'll see exactly how charming I am."

"Ah, something to look forward to."

SEVEN

Back at the hotel, I showered to get the grime off me. Jack didn't make a play to join me, instead flopping on the bed. I thought he was going to enjoy the Magic Fingers, but he waited until I was out of the shower, hair still wet, to pat the bed enticingly.

"I have something for you."

I climbed on next to him, convinced he was going to try to romance me to wipe the horrors of the campsite scene from my mind. Instead, he plopped quarters in the box and groaned as it started vibrating.

"That's the stuff."

I laughed so hard I thought I might choke. The bed worked best when lying flat but that meant I couldn't get a look at what he had on his phone screen. "Read it to me like a bedtime story."

He cocked an eyebrow. "What is it you think I'm reading?"

"Autopsy reports."

"Smart girl." He squeezed my hand and then rested his phone on his chest. "You don't need to know."

This was the part of his personality I hated. He wanted to protect

THE WENDIGO WHOOP-DE-DOO

me from things. It wasn't necessary, but he was big, burly bear when he thought something could traumatize me.

"Charlie, I don't want you having nightmares," he said. "Suffice it to say, they died badly."

"Yeah, I'm going to need more than that. Besides, how could I possibly have bad dreams when you're sleeping next to me?"

"Oh, so cute." He poked my side. "You've had plenty of bad dreams when I've been next to you."

"Bad dreams are inevitable when you do what we do." I opted to be practical. "The important thing is that you're there to beat them back when I have them."

His lips curved. "That was the right answer. How did you know?"

"Because I know you as well as you know me."

"Good point." He squeezed my hand one more time and began reading. "Paul Prescott had his throat torn out while still alive. Loss of blood is his cause of death."

"And the others?"

"O'Neill lost his arm when he was still breathing. Loss of blood is listed as cause of death. Hall died from a severe blow to the head. His eyes were removed either at the same time or within seconds of his death."

I stared at the ceiling above the bed. It looked like something out of a 1980s movie. "Did you ever see *Any Which Way You Can*?"

The question threw him. "I ... don't ... know. What is it?"

"It's this Clint Eastwood movie. He has a pet orangutan named Clyde."

He rubbed his chin. "I think I remember seeing something like that. Why are you bringing that up now? Do I remind you of an orangutan?"

I laughed, as I'm sure he'd intended. "No. It's just ... in the movie, they go to a hotel. They steal a female orangutan from the zoo so Clyde can get some loving and get adjacent rooms. Clyde hangs from the ceiling fan to entice his lover. In the other room, Clint Eastwood does the same."

Jack studied the ceiling fan. "I don't want to cast aspersions on

Hollywood magic, but there are very few ceiling fans anchored well enough to hold the weight of a full-grown man — or orangutan."

"That's such a dude thing to say."

"I'm just being practical. If you want me to try to hang from the ceiling fan, it'll have to wait until right before we leave. We both need the white noise of that thing and the air circulation to sleep. Priorities, baby."

I laughed again. He could always do that, no matter what terrible thing was stalking me in my mind. "I'll give it some thought."

I closed my eyes and we lapsed into comfortable silence. After a few minutes, I realized Jack was still working his phone. "What are you doing?"

"Looking for someplace to eat. The rest of the team is eating in the hotel restaurant this evening. I was hoping to find a place we can be alone."

"I'm guessing there aren't many romantic French bistros in town," I said dryly.

"Nope. How do you feel about Subway?"

"I like subs."

He made a face and shook his head. "Subs are fine for a quick lunch, or an impromptu picnic. I like watching you eat. Subway won't do it for me. I appreciate that you didn't put up a fight about it. It proves exactly how low maintenance you really are."

"Yes, I'm a queen." I studied his strong profile. "Do you want to be my dirty knight?"

"You betcha. But it has to wait until after dinner. I'm starving and we're on a time change. We'll be conked out by nine o'clock."

"We're becoming boring."

"We've just had a long day, both emotionally and physically. Between the plane ride, time change, and the stuff in the woods, we need to crash and get a full ten hours. That should acclimate us."

"Awesome. What does that mean for dinner?"

"How do you feel about Jackal Jane's?"

Now that was an interesting name. "Do they have a menu online?"

"Baby, I don't think this is the sort of town where they have to worry about enticing people with strong menus. I'm guessing it's bar food, but none of our team will be there."

Bar food was good enough for me. "I hope they have fried pickles."

He chuckled. "I love how you're gung-ho for anything. It's one of my favorite things about you. You never complain about food, even when you want something special."

"I spent my college years living on ramen and Campbell's Soup. Two meals a day. If I could keep those meals under five bucks, so much the better."

He frowned. "I wish you wouldn't say things like that. It makes me want to drive two-hundred miles to get you a good meal."

"It's not like I starved."

"I still don't like it."

"Well, you can make it up to me later. Now I've got my heart set on bar food. I want mozzarella sticks, fried pickles and cauliflower ... oh, and some buffalo wings would be divine."

"So you're ordering a side of heartburn for me? I see how it is." He rolled so we faced each other, the bed still vibrating. "Hopefully Jane can give us some quarters. I'm going to need to keep my girlfriend and the bed fed this evening."

"It's awesome that you think so far ahead."

"I'm a Boy Scout – always prepared."

"I was just thinking that earlier."

He kissed the tip of my nose. "When these quarters run out, we'll head out."

JACKAL JANE'S WAS BOTH MORE THAN I hoped for and something of a disappointment. It was decked out in kitschy western awesomeness, but the menu was much more thorough than I expected.

"They have seafood linguini," I noted. "Do you think it's okay to eat seafood in a place like this?"

"Of course it is," a raucous female voice answered as a blonde reached the side of our table. She looked to be in her forties, fit and tatted up, and the smile she graced us with was welcoming. "I'm Jane. You guys look like newbies."

"Jackal Jane?" Jack asked.

"Yep. This place used to be called Jackal Jeff's after my father — God rest his soul — but when I took over, I added my own flair."

I glanced around at the items on display. Most had an Old West feel to them, including a mechanical bull at the far end of the restaurant. "What did you add?"

"That." Jane pointed to a sign on the window that I'd missed upon entry. It read: Women drink for free, men can't be gross.

"What sort of gross behavior are you trying to cut down on?" Jack asked. "Just for the record, I'm never gross. You can ask Charlie. I'm a perfect gentleman."

"He is," I readily agreed. "He demanded that I wait to see if he can swing from the ceiling fan until our last night in town because he's such a gentleman. He's good that way."

Jane snorted, grinning as she glanced between us. "I've seen that movie. I believe it was a chandelier. I always wanted my own orangutan after seeing that movie."

She wasn't the only one. "And you thought I was crazy bringing up that movie, Jack," I chided. "Clearly I'm not the only one who loved that flick."

"My daddy loved it," Jane volunteered. "I watched it with him."

"Can I ask why women drink free?" I asked. "I mean ... doesn't that cut into your profit margin?"

"You would think so, but no. Women drink free because they're better than men ... in more ways than one." She sent Jack a friendly wink but her flirty smile was for me. "Women can come in here, not have to worry about a man buying them drinks and have a good time. That's what they do when I'm in charge."

"And that means the men show up just to be close to the women," Jack surmised. "They then buy a lot of drinks to keep themselves entertained."

"Right you are."

"I guess that means your drink is already paid for, Charlie," he teased. "What do you have on tap?"

"I'll get you a pale ale," Jane replied. "You look like a pale ale guy."

"I'm not sure that's a compliment," Jack said.

"You look fine," Jane replied. "She seems smart, which means she wouldn't let an idiot hang around her. I trust her judgement, which means I trust you."

"How do you know she trusts me?"

"Because when she looks at you there's nothing but love. You can't fake that kind of emotion."

Jack's grin widened. "Well, I guess that's good for me. The menu is way more than we were expecting. It's just ... we're here for work. We can't get sick. Is the seafood linguini okay for her to eat? I'm sure the steak and potatoes are fine, but she favors seafood when she can get her paws on it."

"And you don't want her throwing up all over you tonight when you get back to the hotel," Jane deduced. "That'd put a crimp in your romance, even if you have decided to hold off on the ceiling fan swinging."

Jack smirked as he nodded. "Pretty much."

"The seafood is good," Jane promised. "It's trucked in from Canada, so it's fresh."

"I didn't even think of that." Jack rolled his neck. "The proximity to the Canadian border must be interesting."

"It is and it isn't," Jane shrugged. "It's not as if we can just wander over the border whenever we feel like it. There's a crossing, and a lot of wilderness, but if you get caught futzing around at the border the punishment isn't what I would call fun."

"I have no doubt." Jack leaned back in his chair. "How long have you lived here?"

"My whole life."

"You obviously like it."

Now it was Jane's turn to hesitate. "It's a rough area," she said, choosing her words carefully. "There's no Starbucks or mall, not that malls are really a thing any longer. There are no boutiques and the nearest movie theater is an hour away. It wasn't easy growing up in this town when I wasn't considered 'normal.'" She used air quotes. "Lesbians are like unicorns here. But it's home, and I can't imagine living anywhere else. I'm accepted here, so ... it is what it is."

"I'm not judging your town," Jack quickly reassured her. "It's just that we're working on something and I might have a few questions."

Jane eyed him. "Okay, well, order first so I can put it in. Then we'll get to the questions."

"Don't you want to know who we are?" I asked.

"I know who you are." Jane's smile was flat. "You're with the Legacy Foundation and you're investigating those missing kids out at Nighthawk."

Jack went rigid. "Did somebody say something about us?"

"You're the talk of the town." Jane laughed. "We rarely have more than two hotel rooms rented the same night. This isn't a big tourist destination, in case you haven't figured it out."

Jack nodded. "Yes, we are looking into those kids. We were up at Nighthawk today."

Jane's interest was obviously piqued now. "Did you find the others? I know five are still missing."

Jack hesitated and then nodded. "We found one."

"I'm guessing that down look on your face means whoever you found wasn't alive."

"Colby Bennett." Jack rattled off the name. "He was dead at the campsite."

I flicked my eyes to him. "How do you know who it was?"

"I looked at the photos when you were in the shower. It wasn't hard to match them."

"So, that's four bodies," Jane said, her forehead creased in concentration. "All four boys." She smirked when Jack cast her a sidelong look. "We have six police officers in town, and they all eat here at least once a day."

Jack smiled. "I'm guessing it's hard to keep a secret around these parts."

"Try impossible. Word spread like wildfire about the three boys who were found yesterday. Our boys tried to keep the state of the bodies quiet, but you can't stop gossip in this town. Everybody knows they were ripped apart."

"The body we found today was intact," Jack replied. "It looks like he died hard, though. I have to ask about animals in the area. What do you have up here?"

"The standard," Jane replied. If she was bothered by the question, she didn't show it. "Bears. Mountain lions. Moose."

"What about other things?" I asked, making a face when Jack lightly kicked my shin under the table. "What?" I demanded. "I was just asking."

Jane's chuckle was low and full of humor. "I like you two. You're good with each other. That's a bummer for me, because I find your friend here adorable, Jack." She winked at me and smiled at Jack. "You're asking about Bigfoot. We have a lot of legends around here, but I've never seen him."

"Do you believe in him?" I asked.

"Of course." Jane's smile widened. "I believe in a lot of crazy stuff, like soulmates and true love. I believe in Bigfoot, too. But I have trouble believing Bigfoot killed those kids."

"What do you think it was?" Jack asked. "You've been around a long time, as you said. What other legends are there?"

"There are plenty. Some say Nighthawk is haunted. Some say men never emerged from those mines and were transformed into beasts that live underground and come out only at night. Others say there's a witch who lives up there."

A memory of the man we'd seen flew to the forefront of my brain. "What about an old guy who tells people they're doomed?"

Jane snorted. "Ran into Hank Dempsey up there, did you?"

Jack straightened in his chair. "We didn't have time for proper introductions. He basically dropped 'You're doomed' on us and took off."

"Yeah, well, old Hank is something of a weirdo. And that's saying something for these parts. He's harmless. He made a living bootlegging years ago — transporting illegal brew between Canada and here.

The isolation made him a bit of a nut. He doesn't come into town often. In fact, I've never seen him, but others claim they have. They say his social skills are lacking."

"He lives out there?" I asked. "Alone?"

"As far as I know the only friends Hank has are the ones he's made up in his head. He's not dangerous. If you're looking at him as a culprit, you're barking up the wrong tree. There's no way Hank could've taken out eight teenagers."

I'd already come to that conclusion. "He seems to know something. He acted like he'd warned the kids off, but they stayed."

"That's possible. We might not ever know what happened to those kids." She pointedly clicked her pen. "So, let's place your orders and then I'll swing back around for more questions. The boyfriend wants pale ale. What will it be for you, Charlie?"

My eyes moved to the cocktail menu on the wall. "I guess I'll try the Jackal Juice."

"Just one," Jack interjected as he read the ingredients. "We'll be loopy from the time change in an hour."

"Yes, Dad," I drawled, laughing as I rolled my eyes. "Don't worry, there's no way I want to feel sick to my stomach when we have Magic Fingers waiting for us. One drink is my limit tonight."

EIGHT

The food was delicious, and I shoveled it in without taking a breath. Jack, who had ordered a steak, rare, watched me with amusement.

"Breathe, baby," he insisted as Jane returned to the table. "The food isn't going anywhere."

"Leave her alone." Jane gave his arm a playful swat. "I like watching her go. It's a testament to my food."

"Yes, but you don't have to share a bed with her when she complains about her stomach hurting later tonight. We have Magic Fingers. I want her to be able to enjoy them."

Jane's brow furrowed. "The vibrating beds? I told Bob to get rid of those things. They're dated ... and horrible."

"I think they're awesome," I said when I'd managed to swallow. "I've never seen anything like them."

"Were you a circus kid?"

It was an interesting question. I'd met people in a circus. They seemed pretty normal, at least by my standards. Wild and fun, but normal. "No."

"Her parents were Marriott people," Jack teased. "Magic Fingers weren't part of her upbringing."

"Bummer for you."

"Totally," I agreed.

"Jack is right," she said. "Take a breath. You'll get indigestion if you're not careful, and that will make you think harshly on my food. Since I make my living off repeat business, that's a no-no."

"We're definitely coming back," Jack said. "The only other place I know of is the hotel restaurant."

"Breakfast there is fine," Jane offered. "Jordan, the cook, is a cousin. He knows what he's doing. Skip other meals there if you can."

"So we should hit the Subway for lunch and you for dinner," Jack said.

"You know it." Jane winked. She was big on winking. Then she leaned forward and rested her elbows on the table. "You said you have questions. Now would be a good time to ask them."

"Right." Jack used his napkin to wipe his mouth. "The missing kids, were they ever in town?"

"They stocked up at the general store. Merv Butters told me. He's a perv. Merv, I mean. He liked looking at the girls, said they were pretty and definitely didn't belong in this area."

"Merv the perv?" I had trouble containing my laughter.

Jane nodded, amusement lighting her eyes. "We've all had a good laugh about that at the weekly bonfires. Thankfully Merv is a looker and not a toucher. Otherwise, all the fathers in town would've killed him and dumped his body years ago. Given where we live, we know how to hide a body." She acted as if she was imparting some important information.

"We'll steer clear of Merv the perv," I promised solemnly.

"Definitely," Jack agreed. "I'm crazy jealous."

"You might be protective, but you're not the jealous sort," Jane replied. "I've been in this business a long time. I can read people. You're so in love with this girl you might as well have hearts in your eyes. You're not jealous. Not about other people looking at her or how successful she is. You're a giver."

Jack's cheeks colored. "Um ... ." He was rarely rendered speechless.

"So cute." Jane was enjoying teasing him. "You've got a smile that reminds me of the sun. If the thought of playing under-the-covers games with the one-eyed snake didn't make me want to wretch, you'd be the sort of guy I'd want."

I practically choked on the scallop I'd popped into my mouth.

"I guess I should thank you for that," Jack stammered.

"That wasn't a thank you," Jane pointed out when it became apparent he wasn't going to say anything else.

"I'm still debating."

"Sure, honey." She patted his hand and focused on me. "What did you see out there? Obviously, you found a body and saw Hank. Sorry he didn't welcome you proper, but his social skills are limited. What else did you see?"

Fragments of Rosalie's memories burned in my mind but there was no sharing those. "We saw the house of ill repute," I replied. "That was ... interesting."

She laughed. "They can't call it a whorehouse if they want to sell that place as a haunted destination."

I paused, my fork halfway to my mouth. Now we were getting somewhere. "Haunted destination?"

She nodded. "Why do you think those old buildings and mines haven't been touched? They're dangerous and that whole area needs to be razed. A couple of bigwigs have gotten it into their heads that the area can be renovated. Ghost stories have haunted Nighthawk for as long as I can remember. They want to capitalize on that."

"And do what?" Jack asked. "It's in the middle of nowhere."

"Thus its appeal." Jane turned grim. "There's a bunch of land the government is begging people to take off its hands. The developers want to renovate Nighthawk into a tourist destination, refurbish the old buildings and rebuild the ones that have fallen. They want to have stores ... and barns ... and they want to add trails for off-road vehicles."

A picture was beginning to form in my head. "I'll bet they want to get a resort out there."

"They do." Jane bobbed her head in approval. "You catch on quick. They want to put a resort with a spa, and one of those indoor water things with slides and lazy rivers. They want to build a golf course. There's even talk of a casino."

"Out here?" Jack was dumbfounded. "How do they think they're going to sustain that?"

"I'm just a lowly bar owner," Jane drawled. "I don't know much about big developments. If I had to guess, they're counting on border business. We're close enough that it could be a waystation of sorts for the sort of things we can't get on this side, and vice versa."

Now I was lost. "What things can't you get here that you can get in Canada?" The question was pointed at Jack.

"There's Canadian chocolate," Jack said, grinning.

"Is Canadian chocolate different?"

"Totally," Jane replied. "It's better. I stock up when I cross the border, but it doesn't last, no matter how much I buy. There's also Mountain Equipment Co-Op for the sports enthusiasts, Roots clothing, a bunch of food items. There's Molson, too."

"We can get Molson here."

"Yes, but it's better from them." She laughed at my confusion. "It's not so much that we can't get it here, but they plan to make it convenient. It's going to be a novelty thing."

"Will that work?"

"It's an idea," she replied. "I don't know that I'm opposed to it other than ... well ... ."

"Oh, you can't leave it like that," I complained when she didn't finish. "I have to know why you're against it."

"We could use extra money here," she said. "I would never deny that. But there are legends about Nighthawk. A lot of people don't want to mess with that land because they think we'll stir up spirits."

"This is the type of stuff we want to hear," Jack enthused. "What sort of ghost stories?"

"You don't think ghosts killed those kids?" Jane didn't laugh after asking the question. She looked deadly serious.

"Probably not ghosts," Jack conceded. "That doesn't mean there aren't other things out there that can kill."

"Right." Jane looked momentarily thoughtful. "So, the stories vary.

People will tell you there's a lady in white. I've never seen her. Others will tell you that the souls of the men who died in the mines are still there, roaming and screaming."

A shiver went up my spine. "Screaming?"

She nodded. "People hear screams up there all the time. We have a local Bigfoot club that claims the screams come from a whole family of sasquatches that have built some sort of fort up there. They take people on hiking tours."

"To Nighthawk?"

"People hike up there all the time, but they don't stay the night. They're out long before dark."

"Why is that?" Jack queried.

"Those kids aren't the first ones to go missing up there. If you do a search on the internet, you'll find at least ten people have gone missing in the last ten years. All of them were setting out to hike in that area."

Jack cut into his steak. He'd been methodically plowing through the food during the conversation. "Any bodies ever found?" he asked before shoving the forkful of steak into his mouth.

"A few. You've been up there. You know it's not easy to get though those woods. The miracle is finding a body at all. There are too many places for them to be forgotten out there."

"Right." I blew out a sigh. "That's a bummer."

She shot me a half-hearted smile. "That's on top of the mines. A couple of people have gone missing. The locals swear that they were murdered and dumped in those mines."

"I can't imagine carrying a body out there," Jack countered.

"Who said anything about carrying them? Everybody here has a four-by-four. Most people keep them buzzing closer to town. The locals aren't nearly as enamored with Nighthawk as the tourists. And kids from Washington who have heard stories but never been to the area? It's like catnip to them. Most don't even last a night when they get out there. These kids were out there for five nights, unless you're saying they were killed the first night."

Jack hesitated and then shook his head. "We don't believe they were killed on the first night. Or the second. The fourth night seems the point of interest. The kids were supposed to pack up and leave on the fifth day. They didn't."

"You just found the one?" Jane rubbed the back of her neck, considering. "Is it possible the others are still out there?"

Jack slid his eyes to me and sighed. "It's always possible. But not probable."

"I want to believe that at least one of them is still alive," I offered. "I have no proof, but I'm not giving up hope."

Jane reached over and squeezed my hand before standing. "Hope keeps you young, honey. This guy over here might seem like a killjoy, but he's more practical than you." She jerked her thumb toward Jack. "He fell in love with you because of all that hope you carry. He might try to protect you, but he doesn't want to dampen your spirit. That's not who he is."

I'd figured that out about Jack a long time ago. It was still nice to hear.

I WAS STUFFED WHEN WE MADE OUR WAY back to the hotel.

"Why did you let me eat so much?" I complained.

Jack cocked an eyebrow. "Oh, don't even. I told you we could've brought the cake back to eat here. Did you listen? No."

"It was hot fudge cake with ice cream. We can't walk with that."

"They had regular cake."

"It's not the same." I grabbed his hand before he could peel off and head to our room. "Can we pick up sodas? I need a Vernors if they have it."

He swished his lips, as if debating. "I should make you suffer."

"But you won't."

"How do you know?"

"Because when I suffer, you suffer too."

"Sadly, that's true." He grabbed my hand. "Come on. We'll get some Vernors for your tummy. Then I'll rub it while we play with the Magic Fingers."

We were barely through the door when we almost bumped into two people surveying the lobby. My mouth dropped open when they turned and I realized it was Mike and Melina.

"What ... ?" That was the only question I could form.

"Oh, yay." Melina clapped her hands and hugged me as I went rigid. "We didn't think we would see you guys until tomorrow morning. This is a treat."

I slid my eyes to Jack, confused. Were they supposed to be here? Was I supposed to tell them to go?

"This is a surprise," Jack said when he'd recovered. "I ... um ... wasn't expecting you."

"We didn't decide to come until this morning," Mike replied, his gaze landing on our joined hands. "Were you heading upstairs?"

"Charlie ate her weight in seafood pasta and cake, and needs a Vernors," Jack replied. "We were checking the vending machine. Our room has an external door."

"Rooms on the first floor aren't as safe," Mike offered. "You should move to the second floor."

Jack maintained his cool, but I knew it took effort. "Well ... we happen to like our room."

"It has Magic Fingers," I said. "They make the bed vibrate."

Mike stared blankly and then shook his head. "You're probably wondering why we're here."

"Maybe just a little," Jack confirmed. "You guys don't really have a place here. We're on a job."

"Yes, and Sybil is out there." Mike didn't look like he was messing around as he stared Jack down. "You're focusing on missing kids. You should also be watching your backs. That's why we're here."

I remained bewildered. "Is Sybil coming here? Why would she bother?"

"Because you're here," Jack said. "They're worried that she'll make a move when we're busy with something else."

"You're going to be focused on whatever is out there hunting people," Mike clarified. "You're good at your job, Jack. I would never say otherwise. I also know that you would die to protect Charlie."

"I would," Jack agreed. "I would die ten times over if I had to."

"We want to make sure that's not necessary," Melina said. "We can watch for signs of Sybil, and you can focus on your job. If something does happen, we'll all be together to handle it."

I worked my jaw, debating, and then nodded. Really, what was I supposed to say? I couldn't very well send them back to Boston. That would be crushing for them, even if their presence made me uncomfortable. "I guess we have a plan then." I offered up a smile I was certain didn't reach my eyes. "You have to be careful. Nobody knows who you are — and we have to keep it that way."

"This isn't our first time flying under the radar," Melina reassured me. "We know how to be invisible."

"Then I guess we'll see you in the morning."

"We're checking in and going straight to bed. We'll be in contact by phone and can make plans after you treat your stomachache."

I WAITED UNTIL WE WERE BACK IN OUR room to swear.

"This is not good," I said to Jack. "This is the opposite of good."

He was calm as he went to the bathroom for one of the provided plastic cups. We'd put ice in a travel cup he retrieved from the rental Tahoe, and he poured it in the glass before cracking the can of Vernors. "It'll be okay."

"How do you figure that?" I asked. "They're going to get caught."

"You heard them. They know how to be invisible."

"Not with Millie on the hunt. She was just saying today how she wanted to meet them."

Jack shrugged.

"You don't think that's a bad idea?" I demanded.

"Millie knows about you, Charlie." He refused to join me in panicking. "She has resources we might need. She'll never blab your secret."

"I know but ... ."

"Baby, we can't change this." He directed me toward the bed. "Getting worked up won't improve things. You're just going to have to suck it up. They love you and they're determined to get to know you."

"What about what I want?"

He smiled. "I'm right here."

I wanted to be annoyed with him, but he was too cute. "I'll be ready for a bigger fight in the morning." I snatched the Vernors from him. "I'm too stuffed for that now but prepare yourself for full-on angst in ten hours."

"I look forward to it." He stripped out of his clothes and then tilted his head toward the bed. "Get comfortable. I'm going to hit the Magic Fingers as soon as you're ready."

I really wanted those Magic Fingers, and he knew it. "Fine, but I'm doing this under duress. This is a terrible idea with a million ways it could go wrong."

"It could go right."

"What are the odds of that?"

He didn't answer.

"That's what I thought."

NINE

I didn't think I would sleep. My stomach, along with my brain, was too full, but the not-so-gentle vibrations of the bed lulled me within minutes. I drifted into a world of dark clouds and trees. It wasn't surprising that I would dream of the woods surrounding Nighthawk. We'd spent the better part of the day out there. What was surprising was the feel of the trees. They were somehow different from when I'd been there earlier.

They were broadly spaced, enough so that the sun managed to shine through the boughs and offer enough light that I didn't feel claustrophobic. The birds chirped, animals flitted through the trees. It was idyllic.

And then I saw it. When I rounded a group of tightly planted trees, I came upon a small house, flanked by barns on either side. One of the barns anchored a paddock where horses munched grass and lazed about. The other had fences extending from the rear, bordering a field where cows grazed.

In front of the house, chickens rambled. I didn't see anyone, but I heard voices. I followed them.

I tracked them to the horse barn. I didn't bother hiding myself because I figured the people inside wouldn't be able to see me. I'd had similar dreams and it was hit or miss whether I could interact with the people in them. If I could, there was normally a reason for it. If I couldn't, there was also a reason for that.

A man stood in the middle of the barn, a curry brush in his hand. He glared at a teenager. She was small — a little over five feet — and wore dungarees. Her hair was pulled back in a bun.

"I don't know why you would assume something like that, Father," the girl said, her voice strained. "That's not what happened."

The man's voice was deep, gravelly, reminding me of someone who had smoked far too many cigarettes. "No?" He cocked a dark eyebrow. He was tall, probably at least six-foot-five, and his hair was midnight black, shot through with streaks of gray. Given how fair the teenager was, I never would've pegged her as his daughter.

"I just went to town to get a few supplies for Mama. I wasn't there for any other reason."

"People saw you," the father countered. "I heard from two people who said you were with *him*." The way he said "him" made me think there was an untold story to be mined here.

"Nobody saw me with him," the girl insisted. "If they're telling you that, they're making it up."

"Why would they do that?"

"I don't know. I wasn't with him. Why don't you believe me over these people you won't even name?"

"You've lied to me before."

"Once, and I wasn't doing anything then either. I was just talking to him."

"In my barn? You were just talking to him, after midnight, in my barn? Why does that seem unlikely?"

"Because you spend all your time thinking the worst of me."

"I would like to think the best of you, but I can't. I know what happens in barns after midnight. Why do you think I was forced to marry your mother?"

The girl's mouth dropped open. "I ... you ... what are you saying?" She was practically breathless.

"I won't allow you to make the same mistakes. I know what you were doing with that boy. You're lucky I found you when you were still clothed."

"Excuse me?" The girl turned shrill. "We were just talking."

"You have to be pure when I arrange your match. If you're not, I could lose everything. That boy is not allowed on this property. There's no way he will be your match, so you're wasting your time."

"We were just talking!" The girl was near tears. "Besides, I want to pick my own match."

"You know that's not the way it works. We need to plot strategically. I have some ideas. In six months, you'll be of age. That's when the match will be made. Until then, you are to stay away from that boy. From all boys. You may continue to go to school because that's what your mother wishes, but you will not socialize with the others from your school."

"So ... what? Are you saying I'm your property? Are you going to barter me for a better position with the Nighthawk Grange?"

"Why are you surprised by this? I've been telling you for years that I would arrange a worthwhile pairing for you."

"I thought ... I don't know what I thought." The girl looked beaten down. "You can't just claim my life as yours."

"You're of my blood. I say what goes in this family. I can decide your fate. I won't let you ruin it and mate with that boy. I won't let you become ... one of the others."

"What others?" The girl demanded. "I don't know what you're talking about. I haven't done anything to earn your ire."

"And it's going to stay that way." The father extended the brush to the girl. "You are to remain close to this house when not in school. You are to tend to your chores. That is your life until I arrange the match. If you don't follow my instructions, you will not be allowed under my roof. You will cast shame on your family. Is that what you want?"

The girl swallowed hard. "No, but ... I want some say in my own life."

"Unfortunately, you don't get a say. The Good Lord puts the onus of your choices on me. I will do my best to make sure I place you where you're supposed to be. That's all I can offer."

"But ... ."

"It has been decided. If that boy shows up here again, I'm well within my rights to shoot him. You've been warned. His parents have been warned as well. I had a talk with them this morning. They understand my concern and promised the boy will never come here again."

The girl's eyes filled with tears, making my heart constrict. "This can't be my life."

"It is. You must accept that."

I WOKE THE NEXT MORNING FEELING fuzzy. I assumed it was because I'd gotten too much sleep. That rarely happened. I studied Jack. He had his typical morning stubble — which made him even more handsome — and his face was relaxed in sleep.

Then he spoke.

"Are you being a weirdo and watching me sleep?" He didn't open his eyes. Somehow, he just knew I was watching him.

"Yup."

"Why?"

"Because you're far too pretty. In fact, you're so beautiful that I have to wonder if you're real." I poked my finger into his cheek. "Are you sure you're not a robot?"

He cocked an eye and focused on me for the first time. "Would that do it for you? If so, I have a great Terminator impression I've been dying to try out on you."

I laughed as he tugged me to him, snuggling me at his side. "I might be up for the Terminator thing one night. Let's save it for another time."

"You won't be disappointed."

"I can never be disappointed with you."

"That's how I feel about you." He stroked his hand through my hair, untangling the knots, and rested his cheek against my forehead. "What time is it? I feel as if I slept for days."

"I know. I'm a bit slow this morning too." I glanced at the clock on the nightstand. "It's not even seven yet."

"We went to bed at nine," He reminded me. "That's ten hours of sleep."

"Yes, but we played Magic Fingers before falling asleep."

"Oh, please. I got ten bucks' worth of quarters and you were down for the count before the first round of Magic Fingers was done. You were so tired you snored."

"I don't snore."

"Of course you do."

"No way." I shook my head. "I'm a lady. Ladies never snore."

"Too dainty, huh?" He pursed his lips as he regarded me. "Did you sleep okay? You didn't get sick in the middle of the night"

"Why would you assume that?"

"You're a little paler than normal. After all the time we spent in the woods yesterday, I would've expected you to be pink-faced."

"I'm guessing there's an insult buried in there. I slept hard but had a weird dream."

"There's never going to be an insult buried in there. You're the prettiest woman in the world."

"That's laying it on a bit thick."

"It's true."

"How can it be true?" I asked. "Have you seen that Kardashian sister who is a model? She's way prettier than me."

"I thought you hated the Kardashians."

"What's not to hate? The quietest one, the one who isn't always screaming, 'Look at me,' somehow tugs on my heartstrings. I can't explain it."

"I don't want to dwell on it." Jack was firm. "I want to talk about how pretty you are."

"I don't think I'm all that pretty. I mean ... I'm not ugly. I look good in jeans because I have a solid butt. Otherwise, I'm pretty normal."

Jack looked caught between amusement and annoyance. "Your

butt *is* fantastic," he agreed after a beat. "The fact that you can't see your appeal beyond that is frustrating. I noticed you the second you walked into the Legacy Foundation to report for duty. You hadn't even spoken a word. That face of yours kicked me in the hormones. Hard."

It was one of the weirder things he'd ever said and yet I found it unbelievably sweet. "I kicked you in the hormones?"

He nodded.

"I don't exactly remember it that way," I said. "You were mean to me the whole first week we worked together."

Jack was incredulous. "I was mean to you?"

"Yup." I liked reminiscing with him. It was a fun morning game for when we weren't quite ready to give up the warmth of the other. "You talked down to me like I was stupid."

"In my defense, interns are almost always stupid. You weren't, but there have been others. I was simply playing the odds."

"Then there was that incident when we were camped out in the woods to see if we could find Bigfoot. We ended up in the same tent and you acted like it was the worst thing that had ever happened to you."

"Yes," he said dryly. "I remember that morning. I somehow wrapped myself around you in the middle of the night. My hormones took control in my sleep. That's how much I disliked you."

I snickered. "I thought my hormones had me wrapping myself around you. Are you telling me it was the other way around?"

"I think our hormones conspired to make sure we both knew that we belonged together." He brushed my hair back as I propped myself to stare down at him. "I knew the moment I saw you that I was a goner. I fought it, but it was as if my heart recognized you. I can't explain it."

I never would've guessed he'd be so romantic after our interactions that first day. I thought he was kind of a jerk. Sure, he was a ridiculously good-looking jerk, but a jerk all the same. "I really do love you."

"I love you too." He kissed me. "Now, tell me why you're so pale." He settled back on the pillows. "You mentioned a dream. A bad one?"

That's when the reality of our predicament hit me. I rested my head on his chest and told him what I'd witnessed in the dream. He listened without interrupting, his fingers tracing circles on the back of my neck. When I finished, he looked perplexed.

"Do you think it was Rosalie?"

"No." I didn't know much, but I did know that. "The events in the dream took place a long time ago. Even if they held on to antiquated rituals like arranged marriages here longer than the rest of the country, it still would've been more than forty years ago."

"I get what you're saying." He brushed his lips against my forehead. "Why do you think you were shown that?"

It was a good question. "I don't know. There were no landmarks in the dream to tell me where to look for the house. I thought that maybe I was shown the location rather than the people."

"Like maybe Rosalie stumbled across the house and is hiding there?"

"Maybe."

"Baby ... ." He stopped himself and smiled. "Do you think it's possible the father in the dream was the Hank guy we met yesterday?"

"The bootlegger?" My eyebrows drew together. "Unlikely. The guy in my dream was like six-foot-five."

"So, definitely not Hank," Jack mused. "Maybe the guy in the dream was a relative."

"Maybe."

"Do you think you could find the house again if you used your magic?"

"Maybe," I hedged. "We have to be careful with that. Chris will want us all to go back today. If Laura comes along, I'll have to be doubly careful. Using my magic, especially if the locals are collecting the body we left, feels like a stupid way to go."

"And you're never stupid." I felt his lips curve against my forehead.

"Definitely not," I agreed. "I'm the smartest woman you know."

"You're the smartest *person* I know," he corrected. "There's no doubt about that. As for the dream, let me think about it a bit."

"Okay." I glanced at the clock on the nightstand. "Can you do your thinking over breakfast? I'm starving."

"You can't possibly be," he said.

"And yet I am."

"Wow. You and your appetite never cease to amaze me." He took me by surprise when he quickly shifted our positions, rolling us so he could look into my eyes. It was only then that I read his concern. "Don't forget your parents are here. We have to figure out a way to interact with them on top of everything else."

My mood darkened. I went from picturing hearty servings of corned beef hash and eggs to imagining what would happen if the others realized my parents were present. Even worse, what if they realized Casey and I were related?

"It'll be fine," Jack said, as if reading my mind. He kissed the tip of my nose. "I didn't remind you they were here to ruin your day. I just thought we should get ahead and try to deal with this before it gets out of hand."

"How do you suggest we do that?"

"I was hoping you'd know. I mean ... you are the smartest person in the world."

I pinned him with a dark look. "Smooth."

"That is my superpower," he said. "You have to deal with this, Charlie. They're here and they're going to insert themselves into the investigation. We need to be prepared."

"What if I have no idea how to deal with it?"

"Then you need to get inspired."

"How do you suggest I get inspired?"

His grin was lightning quick and he waggled his eyebrows. "It's funny you should ask. I was thinking that maybe we could brainstorm that together. You know, in the shower."

I tried to hold back my laugh ... but failed. "In other words, you want to multi-task," I said.

"We're both good at that."

"Fine. We can brainstorm. I think this is going to blow up in our faces, though. When that happens ... ." I trailed off.

Jack's eyes darkened. "What are you worried about?"

"I love my life. I love you, and the life we're building. I want to get to know my parents. I don't want things to change."

"So?"

"So, what if they do? What if Chris finds out and boots me off the team for lying? What if Sybil finds me and takes me? What if ... I die?" I had trouble swallowing. "I don't want to lose what I have."

Jack's eyes kindled with ferocity. "I won't let any of that happen. We're going to work this out and everything is going to be fine."

I wanted to believe him, but it wasn't easy. The world seemed to be working against us.

TEN

We were the first ones in the restaurant for breakfast, which allowed me to study the menu encased in a wall mount outside the doors. It was standard breakfast fare, and given what Jane said about breakfast being fine, I was looking forward to digging in.

"Don't overdo it this morning," Jack advised as he joined me. He'd collected a newspaper from the stack by the front desk and had it tucked under his arm. "We're going to be hiking through the woods today."

"Oh, I know. I don't want to risk throwing up in case Millie decides she's driving one of those four-by-fours again. That would ... not be good."

Jack made a face. "She's not driving."

"I look forward to you telling her that."

"It will be fine." Jack sounded more certain than I would've in his position. "She's a menace."

"I think she's fun."

"That's because you treat her like a kooky grandmother and not a co-worker."

"Hey, no matter how crazy she is, she's better than my other great-great-however many greats- grandmother who wants to kill me and take my powers."

"Stop." Jack raised a finger and then leaned in to kiss me. "I don't like when you say things like that. It freaks me out."

"I'm just trying to dissolve the tension with humor."

"It's not funny."

"I'll work on it." He gave me another kiss, glancing up when a growl became apparent from behind us. I didn't have to look up — and apparently neither did he — to know who was standing there. "Good morning, Mike," he drawled.

I pasted a smile on my face as I turned, making sure to sweep the lobby for a glimpse of the other members of our team before speaking. "Did you sleep well?"

"We did," Melina confirmed. She looked thrilled to be here. Perhaps she was just glad to have her entire family together, no matter how horrible the reason. "Now we understand all the talk about the Magic Fingers." She sent me a wink so exaggerated I almost choked.

"I didn't think I would be able to fall asleep last night because of the vibrations, but I was out in like five minutes."

Jack's eyes constantly roamed the lobby. "You guys need to be more careful than this if you expect to fly under the radar."

"I told you that we have it under control," Mike countered. "We've been doing this for a long time. Even if your group came in and saw us talking, we'd only have to say that we're strangers and were asking about your business in town."

"Fair enough, but what happens if Laura sees you here and then stumbles across us together back in Boston?" Jack was a worrier of the highest order. "Chris might be oblivious enough to forget, but Hannah and Laura are different."

"Well, we'll just have to take our chances." Mike said. "I can't not greet my daughter when I see her. I went decades living through that. I won't go back."

"Oh, fine." Jack shook his head. "We're meeting with the rest of our group and making plans for the day. After that, I'm not sure how things are going to play out. I'm guessing we'll be heading back to Nighthawk."

"We didn't really get a chance to talk to you last night," Melina said, sliding into a different topic. "Did you find anything?"

"A body and a crazy old bootlegger," I replied. "We did find this." I pulled out the phone and showed her some of the photos of the twig creations. "Do you recognize what these are?"

Melina intently studied the photos. "No, but if you want to forward some of those to me, we can start researching them. It will give us something to do."

"Which is good, because this town doesn't look as if there's much to do here," Mike said.

"There isn't," Jack agreed. "Apparently eating breakfast here is fine. If you want something better for lunch and dinner, go to Jackal Jane's down the road. You wouldn't think the food would be good given the name, but it was surprisingly delicious."

"Very good," I agreed, my eyes lifting when the elevator dinged. Sure enough, Laura was getting off it. "They're arriving."

"We'll go in ahead of you." Melina didn't touch me as she passed, although there was a motherly glow about her as she held my gaze. "Forward me the photos and let us know your plans. We'll see what we can come up with."

"Thank you." I pasted a smile I didn't feel on my face as Laura approached. She looked lethargic and she didn't even offer a snarky comment when she realized Jack had his arm around me. "Did you sleep well?" I asked.

"I'm not exhausted, so I guess so," she replied, her eyes drifting to the menu on the wall. "The food last night was tolerable, like a chain restaurant with mashed potatoes served in a little ball from an ice cream scoop. It wasn't the best meal I've ever had, but it wasn't terrible."

"So you ate?" I knew I shouldn't act so surprised — and pleased — but Laura had easily dropped ten pounds since her ordeal, and she was thin to begin with. Now she looked gaunt.

"Yes, Mom, I ate." Laura rolled her eyes, which made me happy. It showed there was still something of the woman I'd been introduced to in there. "You don't have to worry about me. I won't waste away to nothing."

"We're not worried about you," Jack shot back. "We just want to make sure that we don't have to carry you if you pass out from lack of nutrition."

"I guarantee that won't happen," Laura replied. She studied us for a moment and them made small shooing motions with her hands. "Are we going to stand here forever, or get a table? Sheesh. You'd think you two had never done this before."

WITHIN FIVE MINUTES, THE REST OF our group arrived. We were seated within two minutes of that. Once orders were placed, conversation turned to plans for the day.

"They won't let Hannah in on any autopsies," Chris explained as he leaned back, his arm resting on the back of his girlfriend's chair. "They seem to think she has ulterior motives for wanting to be involved."

"Can't Myron pull some strings?" Jack asked.

"He could," Chris hedged. "But I'm not comfortable asking him just yet. I'm not certain there's more to be divined from the bodies. Right now, they're listing it as an animal attack. They are letting us come in to see the bodies before we head out today."

"Is that good?" I asked, shuddering when I pictured the body we'd discovered. "I mean ... what can we do just seeing the bodies?"

"I might be able to learn something," Hannah replied. "I don't know that I will be able to come up with anything new, but they've given us twenty minutes with the bodies before they're released to the families."

"Are the families here?" Jack asked, leaning forward. "Maybe we should talk to them."

"The families are in shock," Chris replied. "They're barely talking to the locals, and what would they know? The kids went camping.

They weren't in contact for the week because the cell service out there is practically non-existent. Nobody knew anything was wrong until they didn't return on schedule."

Jack scrubbed his cheek. "So, we're heading to the morgue and then going back out to Nighthawk?"

"Yup." Chris bobbed his head. "We've been getting footage from the cameras we erected last night. It's not great footage. I think part of it is the bad wi-fi here at the hotel. I want to move a couple of the cameras and then continue searching."

"What about the body?" I asked. "Colby Bennett. Has he been picked up yet?"

"I haven't gotten confirmation of that, but they said they were going at first light so they're probably on their way now. I don't expect the body to be dropped off at the morgue — which is really the gymnasium at the high school — until after we're done."

My mouth dropped open. "Their morgue is the high school? How can that be?"

"The kids are out this week," Chris replied. "Some sort of local hunting thing. I've picked up orange armbands for everybody so the hunters don't shoot us."

"Is that a possibility?"

Chris shrugged. "I'm just being safe. They're also using the high school because the only other time they've had more than one body to take care of was after a fire. They don't have adequate refrigeration, so they're using the cafeteria walk-in cooler."

That made things somehow worse. "Well, awesome."

Jack patted my knee under the table. "They have a tiny operation here, Charlie. There's no sense spending money on things like a big morgue when it will get almost no use. It's fine. You don't have to look at the bodies if you don't want to."

I balked. "I can look at bodies. I'm not some dainty wilting flower."

"Of course you're not." His tone was soothing. "We'll figure it out when we get there. Charlie and I have some information to add. We went to the only other restaurant in town last night and talked to the owner. Her name is Jane and the food there is solid if you're looking for something else to try. Anyway, she identified the guy who showed up toward the end of our hike."

"Hank," I volunteered. "She said he's a former bootlegger who enjoyed sampling his own concoctions a little too much. Apparently, he used to make money running alcohol over the Canadian line. Pretty much keeps to himself now. She said he's harmless."

"Do you believe he's harmless?" Hannah asked pointedly.

"I think he's a little mentally off. He might not even know what he's saying. I don't think he wants to hurt us. He wasn't aggressive. He just kept warning us to stay away."

"He also acted as if he'd warned the kids to stay away," Jack added. "I tend to lean toward Charlie's way of thinking. He's likely harmless. If his mental illness is bad enough, however, he could've killed the kids and not even realized it. I want everybody to be careful if they see him. Don't engage him. That goes double for the women."

I narrowed my eyes. "Why does it go double for the women?"

Jack realized his mistake too late and the smile he sent me was tight. "Can we just forget I said the last part?"

"No." I shook my head. "I want to know why it goes double for us."

"Because I'm an idiot who doesn't always think before he speaks," Jack replied.

"I don't think the women are any more vulnerable than the men." I looked to Laura for confirmation. "Tell him."

Laura didn't meet my insistent gaze. "I don't really care," she replied, using that listless voice that had become commonplace for her. "I'm not going to Nighthawk, so you guys can hash out your own rules."

I was taken aback. "You're not going?"

Chris cleared his throat. "Laura and I had a talk. She would prefer not going to Nighthawk. She's still recovering and doesn't think she's up for the physical component. I agreed it was best for her to stay behind. She'll research the local lore."

It wasn't like Laura to want to be left behind. "That makes sense." It didn't make sense but there was nothing else for me to say.

"I'll be better off here than you fools will be traipsing around the murder woods," Laura replied dryly. "I'm happy to do the research."

Chris smiled at her but there was something pensive about the expression. Clearly, he was worried. Chris was often so lost in his own head he missed emotional signs in every direction, so his attention on Laura's plight seemed a minor miracle. "So, that's the plan. We'll eat breakfast, hit the morgue, and then head back to Nighthawk."

I tuned out the rest of what he said and started typing on my phone. I'd already sent Melina the photos of the totems, or whatever they were. I was now also tasking her with a different job: *Laura is staying behind to research. She's been off since the asylum. Try to keep an eye on her if you can.*

I sent the message and sipped my juice, waiting. When the reply arrived, it was short and succinct.

No problem. We'll handle it.

Everyone had their assignments, but we still had nothing to go on.

WE GOT TO THE HIGH SCHOOL after our meal. I politely declined going in to view the bodies. Even though I didn't want to be seen as weak, there was nothing for me to gain from looking at them. I wasn't a pathologist. I couldn't read the dead the way Hannah could. I picked a spot in the shade and sat outside.

Jack went inside with the group for a bit before joining me, plucking my hand from my lap and holding it as we waited.

"How was it?" I asked when he hadn't said anything for a full two minutes.

"Pretty much as you'd expect," he replied. "They're putting the time of death at about eighty hours ago."

I did the math in my head. "So ... before they would've been due to leave but sometime in the overnight hours?"

"Very good, my little math major," he teased, though his smile lasted only a few seconds. "They would've been set to leave about eight hours or so after they died. That means they were up there three nights without incident."

"Or maybe they just didn't think the incidents were enough to worry about."

"That's a possibility."

"Will they tell us when they make a determination on Colby?"

"Yeah. They radioed in that they'd found him thanks to the geotag we put on the body."

"So, he was still there."

Jack slowly shifted his eyes to me. "Is there a reason the body wouldn't be there?"

I shrugged. "I don't know. The area is teeming with animals. If a bear stumbled across the body, even in a body bag, it might decide it was looking for a meal."

"Well, that's a pleasant thought." Jack tugged me closer to him. "If a bear didn't find Colby when he was exposed to the elements, it's unlikely that it would go for him now."

"The others are still out there," I said. "Two girls and two guys."

"Yup. Vincent Falls. Rosalie Partridge. Sadie Milliken. Greg Landers."

"And Rosalie is the only one I've managed to make a connection with," I said.

Jack moved his hand to my back and rubbed. "You think it's because she's still alive, don't you?"

"Maybe, but that could be wishful thinking."

"What other reasons might you have made a connection with her?"

"She could have some witch in her blood, even dormant genes. She might've been so frightened she somehow left a mark on the land. I've read stories about that. And it could all be coincidence. Maybe it's just because she's a female."

"Sadie is a female."

"Maybe Sadie died right away without time to be frightened."

Jack worked his jaw. "I can see you've been doing some deep thinking."

THE WENDIGO WHOOP-DE-DOO

"We have no proof of anything," I replied, my eyes going to the door as it swung open to allow the rest of our team to exit. "We're flying blind."

"We're definitely flying blind," Chris agreed. He was grim as he wiped his forearm across his forehead. Apparently he'd been shaken by what he saw, unusual for him. "The locals are calling this an animal attack even though they have no proof."

"They say the marks on the bodies don't match those of a bear or cougar," Hannah offered. "Those seem like the only animals big enough to do what they're suggesting, but they're adamant it was an animal attack."

"That's because the alternative is too much for them," I said. "If they don't come up with a reason, the locals will melt down."

"Even worse, they might arm themselves to the teeth and go on a hunt," Jack said. "Under those conditions, accidents are more likely to happen. They might be trying to make sure that nobody is accidentally shot in the woods."

"It makes sense," Hannah agreed. "There was nothing extra I could get from the bodies. I think we need to head back to the woods. Our answers will have to come from the location."

Chris managed a smile. "We'll drive to the four-by-fours and go in the same way we did yesterday."

"I'm driving," Millie announced, her hand shooting into the air. "I called it."

Jack scowled. "You're not driving. You almost killed us yesterday."

"You obviously survived, whiner," she shot back. "I'm driving."

"It's not going to happen." Jack insisted. "Other people deserve a turn." What he said next caught me by surprise. "Charlie hasn't driven yet. She deserves a chance."

"Oh, look at that," Millie drawled, amusement evident. "You're trying to pretend you're doing it for your girlfriend. I love that."

"That's not why I'm doing it," Jack fired back. "Fair is fair."

"You say so, Mr. Fair." Millie shook her head. "I'll just take over driving duties on the way back."

Jack looked resigned. "This is going to be the longest day ever."

I patted his knee because it was the only solace I could offer. "We'll probably survive. We might puke, but survival seems likely."

"You certainly know how to make me feel better, baby."

"I always try."

11

ELEVEN

Millie got her way and claimed the driver's seat of the four-by-four. Jack insisted Bernard sit next to her, which left Jack and me to buckle ourselves in the rear seat. Jack held my hand for the duration of the white-knuckle ride to Nighthawk. This time I kept my eyes closed, which reduced my urge to regurgitate my breakfast.

"Well, that was exhilarating," Bernard said blankly when she'd parked. He moved to step out of the four-by-four and his knees immediately gave out from under him. Thankfully I was right there to swoop in and catch him.

"Thank you, little lady." His hand shook when he reached up to tip an invisible hat. "Much appreciated."

I sent him a sympathetic look. "I felt exactly the same way yesterday. I get it."

"You're a bunch of whiners," Millie complained as she rolled her sparkling eyes. She looked exhilarated when she took off her helmet. "I can't believe what babies y'all are."

"Y'all?" Jack pinned her with a glare, not bothering to glance up when the four-by-four navigated by Chris parked next to us. "Now you're just trying to irritate me."

"It's not hard, crybaby," Millie fired back. "You have the patience of a two-year-old being told he can't eat the entire bag of M&Ms."

Rather than watch Jack stew, I turned my attention to the others. They looked none the worse for wear. "You guys look like you had a smooth ride," I offered.

"It was pretty cool," Casey agreed. "Chris said I can drive on the way back."

"You can drive this one on the way back," Jack replied, jabbing a finger at our vehicle. "Millie will be riding back with Chris."

"I didn't agree to that," Millie said darkly.

"Well, it's happening. I'm the head of security. What I say goes."

"That's an interesting hill you seem willing to die on." Millie's gaze was speculative when it roamed Jack's face. "I guess I have a fun discussion to look forward to in a few hours."

"It won't be nearly as fun as you think."

"Yeah, yeah, yeah." She waved her hand and then focused on Chris. "Should we check the cameras first?"

"Yes." Chris was all business. "The feeds we checked from the tablet in the hotel room last night showed nothing. I'm interested in the feedback on the infrared."

"What do you expect to see?" I asked. "We don't think we're dealing with ghosts, do we?"

"No, but if any of those kids found their way back here after dark, their body temperatures should register."

"Oh." I hadn't considered that. "Do you think it's possible some of them are alive?" I tried to keep my hope at bay, but it was obvious what I was really asking.

"Anything is possible," Chris replied. He boasted a naive spirit sometimes, something I gravitated toward. He was almost never pessimistic.

"Don't tell her that," Jack muttered. "You're going to give her hope when she shouldn't have any. I love you, man, but come on. Those kids couldn't have survived this long."

"People said Elizabeth Smart couldn't possibly be alive and yet she's a mother and advocate now. The same for Jaycee Dugard and a bunch of other kids who went missing but turned up years later. Miracles happen all the time. We don't know all those kids are dead."

I thought about Rosalie and her broken heart. It was almost as if I could feel her emotions when the flashes came on. Dying on top of realizing her boyfriend wasn't nearly as into her as she was into him felt unfair. Of course, none of the kids deserved to die. I wanted to find her. I couldn't explain why, but it was clear when I focused on the emotions that kept bubbling up.

"Fine. They could be alive." Jack held up his hands. "I refuse to argue about this. Everybody needs to remember that nobody can be alone, even in town. We have an extra person, so Casey, you can pick whichever group you want to go with."

Casey's response was immediate. "I'll go with you guys."

I was expecting the answer. "We can take the cameras by the brothel."

"You just want to get me in a house of ill repute," Jack said on an eyebrow wiggle.

"You caught me." I offered him a grin. "Let's head out. I'm anxious to see if the cameras picked up anything that wasn't on the feeds."

CASEY WAITED UNTIL WE WERE FAR enough away from the others that we wouldn't be overheard.

"I'm assuming you saw Mom and Dad," he started. He almost looked apologetic. "I didn't know they were coming, in case you're wondering. They surprised me last night too."

"I didn't suspect that you had a hand in it," I reassured him. "In fact, it didn't even occur to me that you would. I assumed they showed up because they were antsy being away from us."

"You," Casey countered as Jack got to work on the camera. He'd pulled out the small viewing window and was playing back the footage. Everything looked dark from my vantage point, but he was the expert. "They're not upset about being separated from me, but they can't stand the idea of you being out of their sight."

"Oh, I don't think that's true." It was impossible to ignore the tinge of bitterness in his voice. He might've been the one who got to grow up with our parents but that didn't mean he had a carefree childhood. His life became about the child lost to the family. While I'm sure Melina and Mike did the best they could by him, they could do only so much while mourning me. "They love you, Casey. You have to see that."

He shot me a grateful smile. "I know they love me. It's just ... they're afraid. We didn't know if we would ever find you. We couldn't risk trying to track you through the system when you were a kid. If we had, if we'd known where you were, they wouldn't have been able to stop themselves from seeing you."

"And that would've risked them leading Sybil to me," I said.

"Even if they could've watched from afar and not interfered in your life — something they were not capable of doing — they would never have forgiven themselves if Sybil managed to follow them. They had to let you go, and it changed the course of all of our lives."

I sucked in a breath. I wasn't used to him being so earnest. He was obviously trying to forge a bond with me. Weirdly enough, despite our rocky start, the kinship I felt with him was stronger than the one I shared with our parents. Once everything had been revealed, it was as if he could finally take a breath and be himself. When he wasn't putting on an act, he was a pretty decent guy.

"I'm doing my best," I said. "I know it might not seem like that, but ... well ... I am. It's hard for me because I spent so many years building up a shell around myself. I didn't let anyone in for the longest time."

"Then you met Jack," he said.

I shook my head. "Actually, Millie was the first one who kind of broke down my barriers. Jack wasn't far behind, but he had his own barriers to overcome. Millie had none and she refused to acknowledge mine."

"I didn't have barriers," Jack groused.

I smirked. "You were the king of barriers. I was okay with that because I had barriers too. It seemed like we could somehow coexist with our barriers."

"So what happened?" Casey asked. "How did you find the strength to drop your barriers?"

It wasn't an easy question to answer. "For me, somehow the barriers dropped on their own. I didn't even realize it until one day when I was looking at Jack and wishing he would kiss me."

"What day was that?" Jack asked. "I might want to recreate the moment."

He always made me smile. "It was in Texas when we were talking around the fire after everybody else had gone down for the night. Laura had been mean earlier that day."

"So any day we were in Texas," Jack muttered.

"What did we talk about?" I pinned him with a stern look. "There's no reason to get worked up over what she used to do. She's not doing it now."

"She's not even a shell of her former self," Casey agreed. "I don't even recognize the person she's become. I tried engaging her in some snarky banter yesterday before dinner — you know, just to see if she would rise to the occasion — but she wasn't interested at all. She pretended she didn't hear me. I kind of feel sorry for her."

The kinship I'd been feeling with Casey doubled. "I feel sorry for her too."

"Then you're both saps," Jack said. He shot me a wink despite his words. "She'll bounce back and return to form. That's who she is. You both need to harden yourselves to her. She's not a good person."

"Normally I'd agree," Casey said. "But I can't help feeling a little guilty because of the position she found herself in. Sybil took her. Sybil is after our family. There's a straight line there."

"Sybil is after me," I corrected. "If anyone is to blame, it's me."

This time when Jack snapped up his head there was a fierceness to his eyes. "What did we talk about? It's not your fault that Sybil is a terrible witch who wants to hurt you. You've done nothing to earn her ire. She's the one to blame, not you. Your family isn't to blame.

"Well, maybe those ancestors who made the agreement about female babies are to blame," he continued. "I'd like to have a word with them. You, however, are perfect. I don't want to hear another word about you being to blame."

Silence descended over us, and it wasn't altogether unpleasant. Casey was the first to break it.

"You've got it bad, bro," he said.

"I do," Jack acknowledged. "I'm whipped and proud of it."

Casey barked out a laugh. "Keep it up. Eventually my father will learn to love you even though you do perverted things with my sister."

"That's the plan." Jack snapped the window closed. "There's nothing on this camera. We can run the program that picks up on noises, but there are no visuals."

"Maybe Chris had better luck with the infrared," I suggested.

WE CAUGHT UP WITH CHRIS AT what had once been the general store. He was excited.

"Look." He pointed at the screen. "People were here last night."

My heart jumped as I looked at the screen. Then it sank when I caught what he was looking at: red blobs far enough away — sheltering in the woods — that it was impossible to make out shapes. Thankfully Jack pointed out the obvious because I didn't want to crush Chris' spirit.

"Those could be animals," Jack said.

"They aren't big enough to be bears." Chris insisted.

"I didn't say bears. I said animals. It could be deer, or mountain lions. You're just seeing flashes of warmth. We have no way of proving they're human beings ... or anything else for that matter."

So, in other words, no Bigfoot.

"Apparently I'm seeing something other than what you're seeing," Chris said stiffly.

"Apparently," Jack repeated. He straightened his frame. "There's no reason we can't go over and look where the heat flashes registered. Maybe we'll find more of those footprints."

"Or human footprints," I added.

Jack moved his hand to the back of my neck. "Let's not go crazy."

THE WENDIGO WHOOP-DE-DOO

We spent the next thirty minutes scouring the tree line near the town. After finding nothing, I moved beyond the barrier and started searching the woods. I wouldn't allow myself to wander too far, but I was curious enough to delve deeper.

That was a great annoyance to Jack as he caught up to me.

"So, we're just going to wander into the Bigfoot woods for no apparent reason?" he groused as he took up position at my side.

I raised my eyebrow in mirth. "I thought you said Bigfoot wasn't real."

"It's not."

"Then there's nothing to worry about."

"Except whatever killed those kids." He was quiet for a few seconds and then blew out a sigh. "Seriously, what are we doing in the murder woods? Are we looking for the kids?"

"They're not here. At least not close."

He slowed his pace. "Would you be able to sense them if they were?"

"I think so. I mean ... I can't *know* that, but I think I would."

"Well, that's something." He shot me a hopeful smile. "That'll come in handy when we have kids one day. We can let them ramble around a big yard and then use your magic to find them."

My heart stuttered. "You want to have kids?"

"I believe I've mentioned that."

"Not quite that way."

"No," he agreed, "but I want a kid or two. One day."

"Right."

"With you." His gaze was pointed when it landed on me. "There will be no kids without you."

It should've made me go warm all over. Instead, it had me freezing up. "And what if there's still a murderous witch hunting me when it comes time to have kids?"

"There won't be."

"How can you be sure?"

"I just know."

"You can't know that. Staying with me could ultimately ruin your life. I mean ... what if we have to run? If Sybil is out there, I can't risk ever having a child. You have to know that."

He studied my face, his eyes stormy. When he finally spoke, it was with a calmness I didn't know he possessed. "We're going to fix this. Even if we can't do it alone, we have friends. *You* have friends. Between Harley ... and the Winchesters ... and that mage you bonded with in Michigan, something tells me we'll be able to take Sybil down when it's time."

I swallowed hard. "That's what I want."

"Good, because it's going to happen. When it does, we can start making decisions about our future."

"What sort of decisions?"

"I don't know. Do you want to stay with the Legacy Foundation for the long haul? Do you want to do something else? My job can translate to almost every area. That means we can chase your dreams."

"But what about your dreams?"

"Charlie." He let loose a low chuckle and shook his head. "How can you not realize that you are my dream?"

I thought my chest might burst. "Don't make me cry," I admonished, wagging a finger. "I don't want to cry. We're on the job."

"Okay." He pulled me in for a hug. "No crying on the job. It's like no crying in baseball."

"Yeah." I wiped my nose on his shirt as he hugged me.

"I'm going to pretend I don't know what you just did so we can keep the romance alive." He pulled back and stared into my eyes. "You're okay?"

"I am."

"Good. Maybe now you can tell me what that is?" He pointed to a spot about fifty paces in front of him. I almost fell over when I looked through the tree branches and made out what he'd caught sight of.

I took three long strides and then pulled up short, dumbfounded.

"It looks like an old cabin," Jack noted as I stared. "I think it had two barns, one on each side. The fence fell a long time ago. I doubt the house is worth anything on the market, but somebody lived here at one time."

My eyes felt like they were bulging out of my head when I turned to him.

"What?" he asked defensively, wiping his hand over his face. "A bird didn't crap on me, did it?"

My voice was raspy when I finally spoke. "Jack, that's the house from my dream last night."

His forehead creased. "The dream with the father and daughter fighting?"

"Yeah."

His gaze was speculative as he took in the scene. "Are you sure?"

"It doesn't look the same — it couldn't possibly — but I'm certain."

"You don't dream about things for no good reason," he said. "I guess that means we have to check it out." He extended his hand for me to take. "Don't wander off. I'm freaked out enough. I want you close."

That made two of us. "I'm with you, buddy. Now and forever."

TWELVE

I stood rooted to my spot for what felt like a long time. It was only after my lungs started hurting that I realized I'd been holding my breath. I let out a long exhale and then flexed my fingers.

"What was that?" Jack asked.

I shrugged. "It's real." That's all I could say.

He shot me an amused grin. "I hate to break it to you, Charlie, but you're magical. Almost everything you do, whether in dreams or the real world, is magical."

"Such a smooth talker."

He laughed. "Let's take it slowly, okay?"

"What?" I was confused.

"Looking around."

"Oh, right." Of course we would look around. Jack might've had a stick up his butt about Bigfoot and the Chupacabra, but he never shirked his duties. We had to search the property.

"Do you think one of the kids could be hiding here? It's not too far from town."

"I know what you want me to say, but I still believe they're all dead. It's the only thing that makes sense. If we find one alive, I promise to let you lord it over me forever."

"Oh, now I really want to find one."

He chuckled. "Let's hit that barn first." He inclined his head to the right.

"In my dream, that was the cow barn," I offered as we moved in that direction. "They didn't have many cows. There was a big field that was fenced in on the other side."

"I'm sure the fence posts are still out there. This place is old."

"How old?"

"I'm not an archeologist."

"And here you had me thinking you knew everything."

"Don't give me grief, woman."

When we got to the barn, he held up a finger. The building was still standing, but the roof had caved in years ago.

"Let me." He poked his head through the opening, his lips curving down. When he pulled back, he didn't look happy. "There's some old equipment in there."

"Wouldn't they have packed up the equipment when they moved?"

"Maybe they didn't move. Maybe the man you saw in your dream lived here his entire life."

I chewed my bottom lip. I was just about to suggest we head inside to look around when the sound of footsteps directly behind us had me almost jolting out of my skin. "Call out next time," I ordered Casey when he joined us, slapping his arm. "You scared me."

Casey's gaze was speculative rather than apologetic when it locked with mine. "How did you know it was me? I didn't call out and you didn't turn around. By the way, you guys should probably announce the next time you're heading into the woods. I saw you go in, so I decided to follow. I had horrible images of you doing the dirty out here, but I was brave enough to follow anyway."

Jack gave him a foul look. "Doing the dirty? Do you really think I dragged Charlie in here for that?"

Casey's shrug was noncommittal. "You're a dude."

The answer seemed enough for Jack. "Yes, well, I'm not a sixteen-year-old dude." Still, he smiled. "We were looking around. I'm surprised we didn't find this place yesterday." He took a step back and looked in the direction of Nighthawk. "This house is barely on the outskirts of the town."

Casey walked into the barn without asking if we thought it was a good idea. "Hey, there's a bunch of equipment."

"We noticed," Jack said dryly as he followed. "I bet a museum would like to have some of this stuff."

"There are people who would pay top-dollar for this," Casey said, kneeling next to a rotted wooden frame with a rusty blade. "This is a plow."

Looking at it, I wondered how people ever managed to feed themselves before motorized vehicles. "How would they even use that?"

"Horses," Jack replied, his gaze going back to the door. "You said the other barn was for horses."

I nodded. "This was the cow barn."

Casey's forehead creased. "How do you know that?"

"I had a dream last night." I filled him in quickly. "The house is more rundown, but it's definitely the house from my dream."

"Well, that can't be a coincidence." Casey straightened and looked around. "You've been having visions when you touch things. Maybe you should do that while it's still just the three of us."

I looked to Jack to see if he agreed. "Do you want me touching things willy-nilly?"

He sent me such a hot look I had to swallow. "I meant ... ."

"He knows what you meant," Casey said gruffly. "Good grief. You guys make me want to punch someone."

"I'd aim for Jack," I said as I moved around my brother, smirking as I leaned closer and touched the handle of the plow. "He can likely take a punch better than me."

"There's no way I'm punching Jack," Casey countered. "I've seen the guy in action. He can take me."

Jack folded his arms across his chest and watched me. "Go ahead, Charlie. Casey is right. Now is the time to seek out the flashes if you

THE WENDIGO WHOOP-DE-DOO

can. Once Chris sees this place, he'll be all over it. Now's your chance."

I licked my lips and rested my hand on the plow. Nothing happened, so I tried again. "Nothing."

"Move on to something else," Casey suggested. "Just be careful of the walls, or what's left of them." He was dubious as he regarded the remains of the structure. "I don't think this place will be standing in six months."

"Without the roof there's less of a chance of it falling," Jack noted. "Just be careful, Charlie. The walls are probably full of rusty nails and you're accident prone."

I was offended. "I have raw athleticism buried under here," I argued. "People want a fraction of my grace and agility."

Jack smirked and moved to the other side of the barn. "I've seen you trip over your own feet so I'm not going to comment."

"That happened one time ... or maybe ten times. I always catch myself."

Jack examined the items that had been left behind. "I'm not an expert but I have to think, even outdated, this stuff would've been worth something when the house was vacated. I don't understand why they would leave it behind ... unless there was nobody left to sell the remnants."

"The dream suggested the daughter wanted out," I said as I touched an old rake. It was rusted and the handle was mushy in places, causing me to jerk my fingers back. "Gross."

"Given what you described, I'm guessing the daughter didn't have a choice in the matter," Jack said. "There was a time when daughters were considered property of their fathers and then their husbands. They didn't really get a say in the matter."

"I'm glad those times are gone," I muttered as I reached the far opening and looked out on the overgrown field. "I have opinions and I expect to be able to express them."

Jack snickered. "You're good at expressing them." His hand landed on my back. "I don't think there's anything out there. Let's check the other barn."

"And then the house?" I prodded.

He hesitated but nodded. "The roof doesn't look stable. We need to give it a long look before we commit to going inside."

"You're such a worrywart," I said.

Casey scuffed his feet as we crossed in front of the house again, his gaze keen as he looked around. "There's no road here," he said. "Like ... nothing."

"So?" I asked, confused. "They lived here in olden times."

Jack chuckled. "I love how you think fifty years ago was olden times."

"This house was built way more than fifty years ago," I argued. "I'm thinking it was built when Nighthawk was a boomtown. That was 1903."

Jack didn't look convinced. "They built to last back then but ... come on."

"Some of the structures in the main town are still standing," I pointed out.

"She has a point," Casey said. "I'm trying to remember some of the history Chris told us. Wasn't the last mine still operational in the 1950s?"

I bobbed my head. "Yup, and this house makes sense if you believe it was built after Nighthawk lost its boom but before the end. I'm betting there are other houses around here in the woods."

"Nothing about this location makes sense," Jack countered. "If somebody was living here in the 1950s, why is there no driveway?"

"We don't know that there wasn't a driveway," I said. "It's not as if they would've poured a cement driveway. They simply would've driven on the ground until it became a two-track thing. Once it fell into disuse, it would have grown over."

"Since when are you an expert on two-tracks filling in?" Jack asked.

"I know things ... or at least I can puzzle them out. I'm smart."

"You're a genius," Jack agreed. "I wonder if there's a land deed archive around here. That might give us a name. Did you hear any names in your dream?"

"No. No names."

"There's no mailbox with a family name on it," Casey said as we arrived at the other barn. He held up a hand to slow us and then tested the beams over the door to see if they gave. "Still kind of solid," he said. "A portion of the roof is still intact in that back corner. Let's avoid that area, huh?"

Jack nodded in agreement, making me roll my eyes. They were two strong men making decisions for the lone female because they were worried I wasn't smart enough to avoid being hit in the head by fragments of roof. That was so ... male.

"I think I'll survive." I patted Casey's shoulder and walked into the barn. "There's almost nothing in here." I moved to my right, the tip of my shoe catching on something and causing me to pitch forward.

It was almost as if Jack expected it because he caught me around the waist before I flew into one of the empty stalls. "There's my agile girl on display," he said, grinning.

I couldn't maintain even a hint of fake annoyance. "Thanks for making sure I didn't mess up my face."

"I happen to be fond of it." He released me and knelt to see what I'd tripped over. "Horseshoe," he said after digging at the item a few seconds. "This confirms the horse barn part of your dream."

I took the horseshoe from him and gasped as a memory invaded. *I can't stay here. We have to go. I know it's dark and you hate running in the dark, Solomon, but we can't stay. We have to go right now.*

I dropped the horseshoe and shook my head to dislodge the momentary bout of panic that had overwhelmed me.

"What did you see?" Jack asked, resting his hand on my shoulder. "Was it bad?"

"It was ... strong." That was the best word to describe the lightning-quick feeling of losing myself in someone else's world. "It was like I was feeling her emotions."

"What was it?" Casey asked.

"She was riding a horse. Solomon. She called him Solomon. She said they had to run. It was dark and she was terrified."

"So, she was sneaking away," Jack surmised, his hand rubbing the back of my neck to soothe me. "That kind of goes along with the dream. She didn't want an arranged marriage. Maybe she thought she had to run to escape it."

"Did she get away?" Casey asked.

I held out my hands and shrugged. "I don't know. I just saw her running."

"Try touching something else," Casey suggested. "Maybe if we get more bits and pieces of the story, we'll be able to put it all together."

"To what end?" I asked as I tentatively reached out to touch the stall in front of me. One wall was down but the other remained. "We're supposed to be here looking for a group of missing teenagers. Why am I having flashes of a teenager from forty years ago, maybe even further back?"

"She's not the only one you're having flashes of." Jack was calm as he eyed me. "I thought it was weird that you only picked up on Rosalie's memories when we were in Nighthawk. I figured it was because she was female and you somehow identified with something she was going through, but there was another female with her. Sadie Milliken. You've gotten nothing from her?"

I shook my head. "No, but it's interesting. I really did only zero in on Rosalie. Now I'm seeing this other girl. She entered my dreams before we even found this place. There must be a reason."

"I'm sure there is." Jack drew me away from the stall. "We'll figure it out."

"Maybe there's more to find by the house," Casey suggested.

Jack brushed my hair from my face and stared hard into my eyes, as if looking for something specific. "Yeah, let's check the house," he said.

There was still a front door, but it sagged from its uppermost hinge. Casey reached out to pull the door open, but Jack stopped him with a hand on his arm and flicked his eyes to me.

"You touch it first," he instructed. "Just ... tell us if you see anything."

I was becoming more accustomed to the flashes so I didn't even suck in a breath this time. When I touched the frame, anger coursed through me.

You can't tell me who to love!

I shook my head. "You can't tell me who to love," I repeated. "It was the girl. She was yelling at someone."

"I'm guessing the father," Jack mused. He took a step back and studied the structure. When he met my gaze again, he was rueful. "I know you don't want to hear it, but I don't think we should go inside. This place could topple in on us and ... ."

"Nobody knows where we are to come looking for us," I finished. In truth, I wasn't keen to go into the house. There was a sense of dread washing through me. "Let's look around the house front and back, see if there's a back door and if it looks better there."

Jack kept close to me as we circled toward the left. The foliage was overgrown, and we waded through the weeds and plants. I touched the house a few more times, tracing my fingers over the few remaining windowpanes. I looked through one of the openings, but it was too dark to make out much of anything.

"Some of that used to be furniture," Jack said as he looked in. "Looks like they left a lot of stuff behind."

"I hope that doesn't mean the animals too," I groused.

"I'm guessing the animals were gone long before the last resident. Although ... ." He pursed his lips and glanced around, his gaze on the ground.

"What are you looking for?" I asked after a few seconds of silence.

"Footprints. I was wondering if Hank the bootlegger uses this as a home base."

"What do you think?"

"There are no indentations around the walls or windows. Inside is ... gross. Even a drunk bootlegger couldn't call that space habitable."

I turned to study the trees surrounding the property. "So where does Hank hang out?"

"Not here. Let's finish our circle and see if you sense anything else. After that, we'll head back to Nighthawk and check on the others. I don't want them out of my sight for too long ... just in case."

He didn't say what he was worried about happening in his absence, but I knew. Something was out here, and it was bigger than we initially believed. It might even span decades.

13

THIRTEEN

Jack was frustrated when we left Nighthawk and returned to the four-by-fours.

"Where is the key?" His accusatory gaze landed on Millie, who was making a big show of acting innocent next to the other vehicle.

"Whatever do you mean?" she drawled. "I have no idea what key you're referring to."

"Millie." His voice was a low growl. "You can't take off with Chris and leave us with no way to get back to the regular vehicles. Kids are dying out here, for crying out loud. Do you want us to die?"

"Maybe you." Even as she said it, she reached into her pocket. "I should be the one who drives that one back. I mean ... she's used to me being behind the wheel now. We have an intuitive relationship."

"What a load of crap." Jack looked to me to back him up. "Tell her to give me the key."

"You sound like a toddler," I admonished him and held out my hand. "We're tired, Millie." I used my most practical voice. "We just want to get back to the hotel." That wasn't a lie. I had a lot of thinking I wanted to do.

"I can get you back faster," Millie insisted. "I'm good behind the wheel. Tell her, Chris."

Chris looked caught. She was his favorite aunt for a reason. The stories I'd heard about Millie when she took care of him during his younger years were hilarious. She was big on adventures. "Give Jack the key," he said finally, resigned.

"No." Millie turned pouty.

"It's been a long day," Chris said as he dug in his pocket. "You can drive my four-by-four and Jack will handle the other."

Millie was suddenly mistrustful. "Do you promise?"

"No, I'm lying," he replied dryly. "I so often lie to you, right?"

"Fine." Millie slapped the key into Jack's hand. "I don't think I like you as much as I used to. You should mull that over during your drive."

"You don't mean that." Jack shot her a friendly wink. "I'm your favorite."

"Don't kid yourself." Millie was having none of it. "Chris is my favorite. Charlie is second. The rest of y'all are way far down the list."

Bernard, her boyfriend, made a pointed throat-clearing.

"You're not even on the list," Millie reassured him. "You have a list all your own. Don't worry, my little dove."

I pressed my lips together to keep from laughing at Bernard's horrified expression.

"You swore you would never say that in front of other people," he hissed. "Just ... no."

"This is turning into a conversation I don't want to have," Jack noted. "Let's head back to the vehicles. Millie, don't turn into a speed demon. If one of these things tips over it's going to be a pain to right ... and we're two hours from dusk." He looked to the sky, worry clouding his features. "I don't want to be out here after sunset."

"Because you're worried Bigfoot will eat you?" Millie asked.

Jack glared at her. "Because I don't want my girlfriend to lose an arm," he replied. "This might all be fun and games to you, but it's likely eight kids died, Millie. Not everything is funny."

I was surprised he unleashed his concern. When I shifted my gaze to Millie, I found her working her jaw.

"I didn't say it was a joke," she said, mild contrition filtering through her words. "I just ... ."

"You're you," Jack said, managing a smile. "Normally, even though I don't want to admit it, I like when you're you. This time it feels different."

"You're right." Millie held up her hands. "Sometimes I deflect my feelings of unease with humor. It might not be warranted in this situation."

Chris looked relieved. "Does that mean I can drive back?"

Millie's nose wrinkled. "Absolutely not. Don't be ridiculous. I might, however, be convinced to drive slower on the way back. Just this once."

"Just this once," Chris agreed. He was serious when he turned to us. "Let's get out of here. Hopefully the tweaks we made to the cameras will give us better footage tonight. I really want to know what happens in Nighthawk after dark."

Normally I embraced his enthusiasm, but a cool sense of dread washed over me this time. I just wanted to go back to the hotel and close my eyes for a bit, think things through. There was a lot to unpack and yet nothing concrete to go on.

"Then let's get out of here." Jack pointed Casey to our four-by-four. "We all need a break from this place."

I agreed wholeheartedly.

I WAS A SWEATY MESS AND WANTED A shower when we got back to the room, so I headed straight in and left Jack on the bed to answer emails. When I exited the bathroom, I was in simple cotton shorts and a tank top. I flopped on the bed next to Jack, a towel turbaned around my hair, and closed my eyes.

"I don't know what to make of any of this," I admitted.

The sound of coins clinking told me what Jack was about to do. When the bed started vibrating, I smiled.

"Oh, don't start that already!" Millie's voice yelled from the next room. "You guys are randy perverts. I can't believe you do it so often. What is wrong with you?"

"We're not perverts just because we're using the bed," Jack yelled back. "Mind your business." He opened his mouth to say something to me but a knock on the door cut him off. "I'm going to get in a big fight with her," he growled as he dropped his phone next to me and strode to greet our unwelcome guest. "She is just ... oh, hey." His demeanor changed in an instant when he opened the door.

"Is this a bad time?" a female voice asked, causing me to roll and face the door.

"It's fine." Jack held open the door so Melina could join us. She was alone, which I was thankful for because I didn't want to put up with Mike growling over Jack and I resting on a vibrating bed. "We were just ... um ... ."

"Being perverts?" Melina asked, a sparkle in her eye.

Jack scowled. "I take it you heard that." He glared at the wall that separated our room from the one Millie and Bernard shared. "She's a real pain in the ass when she wants to be."

"And the walls are paper thin," I added as Jack hopped on the bed next to me. Apparently, he wasn't bothered about doing so in front of Melina, who sat in one of the chairs by the tiny table against the wall. "Millie thinks whenever we use the Magic Fingers we're doing something."

"And you're not, obviously." Melina smiled, but she looked uncomfortable. "If I'm interrupting, I can come back."

I was amused at her discomfort. "I took a shower because I was sweaty from our time in the woods. Jack is reading emails."

"I was trying to go through the county website to see if I can find who owns that tract of land where we found the house today," Jack said.

"Any luck?" I was hopeful. Names would help given the flashes I kept getting.

He shook his head. "Sorry. Not so far. I don't think they have anything that far back on the site. It looks like they digitized the process about ten years ago, but there's not many older records."

"You found a house?" Melina leaned back in the chair, stretching her legs out in front of her. "In Nighthawk?"

"Not technically in Nighthawk," Jack replied. "It's hard to figure out exactly where the town's boundaries were. There aren't trees in a certain area, which gives us an idea, but there's only a handful of buildings left."

"And some of them aren't even full buildings," I added. "In some places you can still see the brick foundation poking out, but the structure has long since fallen."

"I would love to see the town," Melina said. "I don't think that's going to be possible with you going out there every afternoon."

"There's not much to see," Jack replied. "Charlie found a house about a quarter-mile from the town today. I think it was built after Nighthawk was a boomtown but before the mines closed. She dreamed about the house last night and then found it today. I was hoping to be able to come up with some information on the owner, but records are spotty in small towns like this."

Melina looked to me. "You dreamed about the house?"

"Yeah," I confirmed. "It was weird." I filled her in on my dream before sliding into the story of the house discovery. "It feels as if I'm receiving these flashes for a reason."

"And you've been getting flashes in the town too?"

I frowned. There was only one person who could've provided that information. "Casey has a big mouth."

"Casey is your brother," she replied. "He's a little worried. I know this is new for you, but families often talk."

"I know but ... ." I broke off. She was right. It wasn't as if Casey had betrayed some big confidence. I hadn't asked him to keep the information to himself, and Melina and Mike were well aware of my abilities. That's how we had ended up in this situation. "It doesn't matter," I said. "I didn't hear anything new in Nighthawk today regarding Rosalie. I did get a few flashes regarding the other girl at the house. I can't figure out how it all fits together."

"Maybe it doesn't," Melina suggested. "Maybe you're picking up on two unrelated traumatic instances."

"But why?" I asked. "I get why I'm hearing things from Rosalie, at least in theory. It's been suggested I'm keyed into what happened to her because we're both female, but that seems sexist. Even if that's the case, there was another girl, Sadie Milliken, with them. Why am I not sensing things about her?"

"I can't answer that." Melina said. "I know you wish you had answers, but that's beyond my ability to give you. I'm sorry."

"I don't expect you to solve my problems," I reassured her. "I'm just ... confused."

"Maybe it's something inside of you that's glomming on to these girls," Melina suggested. "Maybe they were feeling something that you've also felt and that's why the memories are finding their way to you."

Well, now I was intrigued. "What do you mean?"

"Casey said that Rosalie was feeling insecure about her relationship. Maybe you picked up on that."

I balked. "I'm not feeling insecure about my relationship with Jack."

"Definitely not," Jack agreed. "She has nothing to be insecure about. I love her more than anything and she'd better know that by now."

Melina's lips curved. "I think anybody who has seen you together can figure that out. But there's more than one type of relationship to feel insecure about."

Jack flicked his eyes to me, debating. "You think Charlie is feeling insecure about her relationship with you. That might explain why she's picking up on the memories of the other girl too. She was having trouble with her parents."

I hated being put on the spot like this. "I'm not insecure about my relationship with you guys," I insisted. "I'm just ... feeling things out."

Melina's smile never wavered. "Charlie, there's no shame in feeling insecure. We knew you as a little girl. We loved you with our whole hearts. You were adopted by loving people — and we're so grateful for that — but I'm sure you spent a lot of your childhood wondering why we gave you up."

"Even more so after I realized I was magical," I admitted, chewing my bottom lip. "I thought maybe that was why I was abandoned."

"I don't particularly like the word 'abandoned,' but I get what you're saying. You were given up because of the magic, but not for the reasons you think. We can't just all reunite and say 'poof, we have a relationship now,'" she continued. "It's going to take work. That's one of the reasons we're here."

"We have to be careful," Jack insisted. "Some members of our group know about you, at least in a vague sort of way. Millie knows most of it, despite the fact that she's a complete and total pain." Jack shot a dirty look toward the wall. "Chris doesn't know. Hannah is too oblivious to pick up on most things. Laura is ... not a good person. She's distracted right now, but if she were to pick up on any of this it could spell trouble for us."

That reminded me of something. "Speaking of that, you kept an eye on Laura for us today. Did she do anything?"

"As far as I can tell, she did her job all day and nothing more," Melina replied.

Disappointment bubbled up. "I thought maybe this was all an act or something and she really was up to something else."

"Sorry," Melina said. "She went to the local library, worked there for hours, poring through books. She talked to the owner of the hotel and got a history lesson. He directed her to a local historian, a woman in her eighties. Laura spent two hours at her house. I obviously couldn't hear what they said, but I don't think anything hinky went on."

I rubbed my chin and flicked my eyes to Jack. "Maybe she has changed."

"And here we go." Jack rolled his eyes. "I'm not saying we should be mean to Laura. I'm simply suggesting that we don't drop our guard around her. She was a guttersnipe before and it's likely she'll return to form once the shock and trauma of her interaction with Sybil and those ghosts fades."

"Or she might turn over a new leaf."

"Ugh." Jack moved his hand to his forehead and began to rub. "I love that you have an open and giving heart. You want to believe in people, even when they don't deserve it. I'm including myself in that statement. You make excuses for me when I have a bad attitude."

"Like when you took the key from Millie this afternoon?" I asked.

"Don't start." Jack wagged a finger. "I have no intention of going after Laura. I already promised you that and I intend to keep that promise. But I refuse to believe that she's suddenly a good person. I've spent too much time with her to ever believe that."

"Fine." I turned back to Melina. "Thank you for keeping an eye on her."

"It was no problem." She waved off the gratitude. "We weren't doing anything but researching. We did find a restaurant outside of town — about twenty minutes away. We hoped we could all have dinner there tonight." She opened her mouth as if she was going to speak again and then shut it. She was making herself vulnerable and she almost looked as if she expected us to shoot her down.

"Can we go out of town for dinner?" I asked Jack.

He nodded. "I don't see why that should be an issue. We'll just say we're handling our own meal. We'll have to take Casey."

"The food has good reviews online," Melina assured us as she stood. "I'll text you the information and make a reservation. Is two hours enough time to get ready?"

"Two hours is fine," I said. "I don't expect to do anything but enjoy the bed with Jack." I realized what I'd said too late to haul it back. "You probably shouldn't tell Mike I phrased it that way."

Melina chuckled as she moved toward the door. "Your secret is safe with me."

"Hold up." Jack climbed off the bed and intercepted her. "Let me make sure nobody is outside. Chris likely wouldn't even recognize that you were leaving our room if he saw you — and Hannah doesn't notice details like that — but it's better to be safe."

"Absolutely." Melina bobbed her head and then sent me a smile as I started rummaging through the change Jack had scattered on the nightstand. "Have fun doing ... whatever it is you're going to do before dinner."

Jack grinned and gestured to the door, indicating it was safe with a simple wave. "You're looking at what we're going to be doing. Charlie isn't hard to entertain."

"No, I gather she's pretty easygoing for the most part."

"That's only one of the things I love about her," Jack admitted. "I have a list of the other things if you ever want to see it."

Melina chuckled. "I'll keep that in mind. Have a good few hours of downtime."

"We'll see you in two hours," Jack promised. "Charlie will be ravenous by then and looking to stuff her face with red meat and cake."

14

FOURTEEN

The restaurant Melina had found was cute but not extraordinary. The food was decent — I indulged in a steak and baked potato — and the conversation was heavy. We dissected everything that had happened.

"It's not Bigfoot," Mike said. "You can't possibly think it's really Bigfoot."

For some reason, the declaration made me smile. "You and Jack finally have something to bond over. I'm so excited."

Jack poked my side and offered up a smile. "Bigfoot is not going to spend his time making those twig things you found."

"You don't know." I'd come to the conclusion that it was definitely not Bigfoot. I still liked irritating Jack. "Bigfoot might be lonely and trying to come up with a hobby. It has to be boring hanging in the woods all day with nothing to do."

"I guess I do have something in common with Jack," Mike conceded, although he didn't look happy about it. "I don't think we'll be bonding anytime soon, but it's nice to be understood." His smile was almost feral.

"They're disgusting perverts with one another and you're just going to have to get over it," Casey interjected, earning tandem glares from Jack and Mike. "Oh, don't look at me that way." After stuffing himself on lasagna and fresh bread, he looked ready for a nap. "You didn't have to spend the better part of the day listening to them coo at one another."

"I'm a manly man," Jack deadpanned. "I never coo."

"Oh, please." Casey practically choked on his snort. "You guys are gross. I want to punch you at least five times a day."

"Go with that feeling," Mike suggested.

"No way." Casey said. "I've seen that guy at the office gym. He can totally take me. I'm a survivor, not a moron."

"I think you could qualify as both," Jack countered.

Casey's smirk was back. "I love you too, man." He offered up a fist bump, which Jack ignored.

"Just because we're not dealing with Bigfoot doesn't mean we're not dealing with something paranormal," Jack said.

I cast him an appraising sidelong look. "You know, when we first met, you would've always erred on the side of a human explanation," I noted. "Well, in this case, maybe not human. You would've been pushing the bear angle six months ago."

"That's true." Jack was brutally honest most of the time, including with himself. "I know better now. Besides, a bear couldn't have made those twig things."

"Those do add a certain element of ... um ... what in the hell is this. They were made by someone. I just can't figure out what they're supposed to signify. I mean ... are they a warning? Were they meant to mark the scene for some other reason?"

"The photos I saw were very reminiscent of the *Blair Witch Project*," Mike noted. "Maybe humans made them to cover up what they did. Stranger things have happened."

"They have," Jack agreed. "I would be willing to go with that theory if not for one thing."

Mike inclined his head, as if to encourage Jack to continue.

"We're talking about eight kids. They were at the same campsite together, or at least close to one another when it all went down. Even if a group of humans did this, how did they contain all eight kids? They would've scattered."

"Maybe they had weapons," Mike suggested. "Maybe they forced the kids to comply with multiple weapons."

"Maybe." Jack bobbed his head. "How did they rip off an arm? How did they keep the kids compliant as they were digging out an eye? How did they rip out a throat? Once they attacked one of the kids, the others would've fled, which would've forced someone to shoot. None of the bodies have gunshot wounds."

"You haven't found all the bodies," Mike insisted. "Don't you think it's telling the two females are among those missing? Maybe the females were the target."

He didn't come right out and say what he was thinking but I understood. He didn't want to get into the ugly side of human nature over dinner. I couldn't blame him. There were holes in this theory, though.

"How does that work in your mind?" I wasn't trying to be combative — no, really — but what he suggested didn't make sense. "Do you think they took everybody captive and then stopped long enough to make twig creatures to throw off investigators? Why not just clean up the area after the fact and make it look like the kids were never there?"

Mike held out his hands. "That I can't answer."

"There are the things I heard when I touched the buildings," I continued. "In one of them, they said, 'It's coming.' That doesn't sound like they were talking about humans. They would've said, 'They're coming' or even 'He's coming.'"

"That's true." Mike looked resigned. "So, what could we be dealing with? Bigfoot is not an acceptable answer. I don't want to hear anybody say it was Bigfoot."

Casey snickered. "I once tried to tell him that Bigfoot messed up my room when I was a kid. It didn't go over well then either."

"It didn't," Mike agreed, although he shot his son a fond smile. "If there's a creature out there killing people, ripping off arms, we have to know what it is if we expect to come up with a way to fight it. The fact that Melina and I can't go out there and look around is troublesome. I don't like the idea of you two out there when we can't get to you."

"Apparently it's fine if I'm out there, though," Jack noted with a grin.

Mike nodded without hesitation. "Absolutely. If you lose an arm, it's one less appendage to grope my daughter."

"Oh, geez." I couldn't contain my annoyance. "Can we please not argue about this again? Jack and I are living together. We try to grope one another in private as much as possible, but sometimes we slip."

Melina and Jack laughed. Mike and Casey didn't look nearly as amused.

"You think you're funny?" Mike's expression relaxed after a beat.

"I'm hilarious."

"She's the funniest person I've ever met," Jack offered. "That's why, no matter how hard I tried not to fall in love with her, it didn't work. The whole package she presents is ... amazing."

"Aw." I leaned in and rested my head against his shoulder. "I love you too."

Jack pressed a kiss to my forehead and lifted his eyes to Mike. "We're doing pretty well getting to know one another. We should have regular meals like this, even though it feels dangerous doing it out here."

Mike's lips curved. "Agreed. We'll keep at the research. I need you to be careful when you're out at Nighthawk. If something happens ... ." He broke off and his features twisted. It took him a good ten seconds to pull himself back together. "We won't be able to run to the rescue if something happens. Be vigilant."

"I'm always vigilant," Jack promised.

"He is," I agreed. "He's a regular Boy Scout. Besides, I don't need people to swoop in and save me. I'm a self-rescuing princess."

The smile that took over Mike's face was profound. It was as if the sun had suddenly come out. "You always were, Charlie. Even when you were little and we played games, you would demand to save yourself.

"I know you're strong," he continued. "I know you're ... an amazing woman. You might chafe when I say you're still my little girl, but I don't mean it as a slight. We missed out on you growing up and that's always going to hurt. We want to know you as an adult."

I had to swallow the lump in my throat. "I want to know you."

"Good." He leaned back in his chair. "Let's get some dessert and call it a night. I'm guessing you guys will be back in Nighthawk tomorrow. You'll need your rest."

"That's a good idea." Jack snagged the dessert menu. "They have turtle cheesecake, Charlie. One of your favorites."

And just like that, we were a normal family having dinner. Sure, we had more baggage than most people, but it was nice to have a bit of normalcy with our monsters.

I CRASHED HARD WHEN WE GOT back to the room. Jack didn't even bother with the Magic Fingers. He spooned up behind me, whispered he loved me, and then we were out.

Dark dreams chased me where he couldn't serve as a barrier.

I woke in the woods outside Nighthawk. Given the memory flashes I'd been having, it was only natural that my mind would start filling in the gaps. What I found as I walked around the town, I never expected.

"What the ... ?"

The Nighthawk of my dreams bustled with activity. It looked like the standard town you might see in an old western movie, complete with noise spilling out to the street from the saloon. People wandered the streets as if they had important business to conduct.

"Not like today, eh?" a woman asked.

I wasn't surprised to be addressed by one of the dream people, but when I turned, I found the woman in dated clothing watching me had a familiar face.

My heart stuttered.

"Sybil," I gasped.

She laughed at my response, throwing her head back and braying at the sky. If it had been anybody else, I would've found the sound warm and inviting.

"You act as if I'm a monster about to eat small children," she said.

"Aren't you?" I saw no reason to be nice to her. Even if my subconscious had thrown her face on a random person, I knew better than to trust strangers in my dreams. "That's why you want me."

"To eat you?" Sybil cocked her head. "You must be mistaking me for someone else."

"I know better." I made sure to keep several feet between us. It was a dream, so she couldn't hurt me, but I was not inclined to allow her to get closer. "Why are you here?"

She held out her hands and shrugged. "Why did you bring me here?"

"I ... don't think that I did. I think you're standing in for someone else in my dream."

"Such a rational thing to say." She made a tsking sound with her tongue. "I'm disappointed. I thought you would be willing to think outside the box."

"Apparently not." I folded my arms over my chest. It was only then that I realized I was dressed in my cotton sleep shorts and a T-shirt with a Bigfoot silhouette. It read "Don't stop believing." I'd pulled it on before falling asleep next to Jack. "Why are you here?"

"To send a message." Sybil's smile slipped. "It's not the sort of message you're expecting, so don't work yourself into a tizzy. I'm not in the mood."

Was this real? Had our minds somehow connected for a dream? "What's the message?" I asked. I wanted her to say what she had to say and leave. I had no interest in hanging out with her longer than necessary.

"You're looking in the wrong place."

I waited for her to continue. When she didn't, I let a hissing sound escape. "That's it? That's what you wanted to tell me?" I was dumbfounded. "Thanks. I guess."

"Oh, don't be petulant." She wagged her finger in admonishment. "There's no reason to be difficult. I'm here to help."

"You're not being all that helpful. Instead of being cryptic, why don't you tell me where to look? Saying that I'm not looking in the right place doesn't exactly fill me with warmth ... or hope."

"Hope is a wasted emotion."

"Okay, well, it was nice talking to you." I moved to leave but she reached out to stop me. I sidestepped her grip, making sure she couldn't graze my skin with her outstretched fingers. "Let's not go there."

She halted and held up her hands in a placating manner. "You really do have so many things wrong. Now is not the time to discuss most of them. Tonight, we're discussing Nighthawk."

My heart sank. I thought she was here to impart wisdom regarding her motivations. "You know where we are?"

"Of course. Once I found you again, there was no way I would lose you. We'll talk about that later. You're in trouble." Her eyes were turbulent when they locked with mine. "I can't have you dying before I get a chance to state my case, Charlie. You need to get it together and look around at your surroundings. It's not Bigfoot you're after."

"Oh, geez." I was so sick of hearing that. "I never really believed it was Bigfoot."

"Maybe not, but part of you was thrilled with the notion."

"Fine. It's not Bigfoot." I was already sick of this conversation. "Is that all you've got?"

"Do you know what a wendigo is?"

I had to take a moment to settle my skipping heart. "I ... ."

She waited, arching an eyebrow.

"I know what a wendigo is," I said finally, my mind going a million miles a second. Could we possibly be dealing with a wendigo? That wasn't quite as thrilling as Bigfoot, but it was nothing to sneeze at.

"Tell me," Sybil prodded.

"It's a folklore creature," I started. "It originated with the First Nations, although there have been a lot of tweaks over the years. It's supposed to be a Canadian thing ... though there are a few local versions in some parts of the United States."

"That's a bit clinical, but I'm glad you're aware of the term," Sybil said. "Wendigos are described as malevolent spirits, but that's not exactly right. They take physical form, start out as humans, and when that human is corrupted, you get a wendigo. Wendigos are created through multiple methods, usually when one of the seven deadly sins gets a foothold."

Now she had my attention. "The seven deadly sins? Like ... gluttony, sloth, lust ... and the rest?"

She nodded. "When one emotion considered destructive takes over and fuels an individual, becomes the only thing they live for, wendigos are the outcome. They used to be more prevalent. It's harder for a human to be able to go through the process now without being discovered because the transformation isn't instantaneous. It takes time."

"And that's what you think we're dealing with?" Rather than focus on her, I turned my attention to the town. "Does it have ties to Nighthawk's past?"

"Every paranormal creature has ties to the past," she replied. "That's how it works. History can't be ignored."

"What history should I be looking for?"

"I'm not here to do your job for you." She pushed herself away from the bank wall. "There's more than one thing going on here. You've seen hints, but not the reality of it." She waved her hand and I found myself transported away from the town. I was at the cabin from my dream. "You can't forget the past, but you can't overlook the present," she insisted. "Do you know what I'm saying?"

I shook my head. "Not even a little."

"Well, you'll have to figure it out." She was calm. "If you don't, we'll never get a chance to work out our own issues."

That's when reality hit me in the face. "You don't want me to die here because that will ruin your plans."

"Oh, see, you are smart." Sybil broke into a wide grin. "And here I thought your boyfriend was simply throwing around that word to make you feel better. I'm glad to know that he wasn't just pumping your ego."

I glared at her. "I'll never give you what you want."

"We'll worry about that at another time," she said. "For now, focus on what's in front of you. Stop screwing around with Bigfoot. Chase the wendigo. That's how you'll get your answers."

"I don't suppose you have something a little more ... concrete ... than that?" I challenged. "I mean, you're not really telling me where to look."

"Of course I am. The question is, are you smart enough to figure that part out? I suppose we'll both have to wait and see."

I opened my mouth to press her further, but she was already gone. She'd dissolved into nothing, leaving me alone in front of the cabin.

"Thanks for the help," I called out. "You're not creepy and weird at all. I have no idea why everybody is so terrified of you."

There was no answer, of course, but I did have a new direction to explore.

FIFTEEN

I woke before Jack and started working on my phone. I tried to be quiet so he could get as much rest as possible. If he was sleeping late, he needed it. I'd been working only thirty minutes when he stirred.

"What are you looking at?" he asked in a sleepy voice.

"Porn."

"Intriguing. Anything good?" He rolled to look at my screen, frowning when he got a good gander at what I was studying. "Baby, we need to discuss the sorts of porn that are appropriate. I'm not into the whole furry thing."

I laughed and kissed his forehead. "I had a dream last night."

He was still waking, but he forced himself to alertness. "The cabin again?"

"Kind of." I explained the dream. When I finished, he looked more annoyed than intrigued.

"You don't think that was really Sybil?"

Of course he would focus on that. "Likely not, but I guess it's possible. I have to think she'd be more frightening."

"Unless she's trying to get you to drop your shields."

"Like on *Star Trek*?"

"Yes. She's the Borg. She thinks resistance is futile. Never trust her."

"You're such a geek with the *Star Trek* stuff."

"Says the woman who thinks Worf is hot."

"I didn't say he was hot. I said he had sex appeal. There's a difference."

"How so?"

"It's hard to explain. I don't think he's hot, but I would totally like to do a Klingon ritual with him."

"And you think I'm the geek." Jack shifted his arm around my back and looked at my phone screen. He was fully awake now. "What do you have?"

"I studied wendigos in school, but I'm trying to refresh my memory." There was little I loved more than a good monster story, and because this was something new, I was enjoying myself. "Wendigos originated in First Nations lore but, in typical fashion, we've developed our own lore around them. They're described as giant humanoids with hearts of ice, a foul stench, and the ability to chill the area before their arrival."

"That's ... lovely. Who doesn't love facing off with a creature with a foul stench? What's the point of these things?"

"In the dream, Sybil said wendigos were essentially fallen humans, people who had been corrupted by one of the seven deadly sins."

"So ... gluttony, wrath, lust, sloth, pride, greed and envy."

"Very good." I cast him a sidelong look. "Which would be your downfall?"

"Lust," he answered without hesitation. "But only for you."

"Good answer."

"It's the only answer as far as I'm concerned. What about you?"

"I'll go with lust too."

"For me?"

"And Worf."

He laughed, as I'd intended. "You don't have many troublesome facets to your personality, Charlie. The truth is the only annoying things you do stem from an overabundance of eagerness, loyalty and curiosity."

"I've never considered loyalty troublesome."

"It is if you put others before yourself. You're a giver, and I worry people will take advantage of that."

"I guess it's good I have you around to make sure that doesn't happen."

"Totally," he agreed, inclining his head toward the phone. "Give me some more on wendigos. If that is what we're dealing with, I want to be prepared."

"They're considered rare, so I'm not sure how much of this is factual or myth," I warned. "There is one interesting tidbit here. There's something called 'wendigo psychosis.' It's categorized by the intense craving for human flesh. Other symptoms could be insatiable greed and destruction of the environment."

"Does that come from the First Nations lore?"

"How did you know that?"

"It makes sense. We stole their land and were willing to profit off their enslavement."

"That does make sense."

"I'm a veritable genius," he said. "Tell me more."

"You're so demanding in the morning," I teased, although I was more than happy to share my knowledge with him. "They've been associated with winter, northern climates, coldness and famine. They supposedly look gaunt to the point of emaciation and give off the odor of decay, as if they're barely clinging to this world and already have one foot in the one beyond."

"Yeah, I don't want to meet one." He brushed his lips against my cheek. "They sound wretched."

"But it could be what we're dealing with," I pointed out. "They're supposed to be strong, the embodiment of greed and gluttony. They're never satisfied with killing just one person and always want more."

"Do they eat people?"

I hesitated and then nodded. "That's part of the lore."

"None of our victims were eaten."

"That we know of. Several are still missing."

"So, you've gone from thinking that Rosalie is still out there to thinking that she was eaten by a wendigo?"

I had no answer for him. "Don't be rational. Mornings aren't for being rational."

He laughed. "I'm glad you spelled that out for me. Can wendigos communicate?"

"It says they can talk, or at least communicate. It doesn't give specifics."

"So, the foul-smelling beast will taunt us. I love when that happens."

"You're hilarious. Has anybody ever told you that?"

"Yes, we're the funniest couple known to man," he said. "Tell me about the cannibalism. I don't really want to know and yet I feel as if I have to."

"It says humans overpowered by greed turn into wendigos and it's all about consumption. The cannibalism aspect falls into that consumption. Supposedly, wendigos sprang out of groups forced into cannibalism in olden times."

"I love when you say 'olden times' like that's really a thing." He gave me a tickle and then sobered. "So, members of the Donner Party could've turned into wendigos?"

"I guess. I don't remember any stories about wendigos when I learned about that in school."

"They probably would've left that part out," he said, stretching his arms over his head. "It's a lot to consider. I like a little proof with my conjecture." He shot me a smile and then sobered when I didn't return it. "I like the idea of a wendigo over Bigfoot, but this really isn't my area of expertise. You're the smart one."

"I happen to think you're a veritable genius, just like you said."

"And I think you just like feeding my ego." He tugged me to him. "I'm not opposed to the idea." He gave me a kiss. "We need more proof. I don't suppose those articles mention anything about the twig creations?"

"I haven't found mention of those." And it was really starting to annoy me. "Whenever I type 'twig creations' into the search bar I get suggestions for craft projects."

"You can make something for the new condo," he teased, grinning as he covered my mouth with his. I pinched him.

"I'm serious." I adopted my sternest face. "Those things must mean something. It's driving me crazy."

"I hate when you're going crazy." He gave me another kiss, collecting my phone and depositing it on the nightstand. "You know what we should do?"

I had no doubt what he was going to suggest. "Something perverted?"

"Don't taint our love." Another kiss and he had me convinced that whatever he was going to suggest was likely the smartest idea in the world. "We should spend a bit of quality time together before breakfast. That way our brains will be clear when we start planning the day. That's important in this line of work."

"Our brains will be clear, huh?" I'd almost completely forgotten about the wendigo because he was so good at kissing me senseless. "That's a smart move. Then we definitely need to head to breakfast, because I'm starving."

"You eat like a Viking."

"Complaints?"

"Nope. I like it."

"Is there anything you don't like about me?"

"Nothing I can think of right now. I'll have to get back to you later."

"Good idea."

JACK CONVINCED ME NOT TO BROACH the subject of wendigos during breakfast. I was confused until he pointed out we couldn't explain why we would be tracking that information.

"You can't tell Chris you dreamed it," he said as we walked into the lobby. "He'll have questions ... and maybe want to send you to a dream clinic or something. About a year ago he mentioned he thought paranormal truths could be uncovered in dreams. I don't want him experimenting on you."

I wasn't entirely opposed to the idea. "Can you get the name of that clinic from him? You know, for later."

He studied me a bit and then nodded. "Sure. We can go. I want to be with you for whatever they have planned. If they see something freaky in your head, I don't want them pushing things."

"It could be quack science," I reminded him. "They probably won't see anything."

"Probably not, but if they do, ..." He didn't finish. He didn't have to. We both knew what would happen if the truth about me found its way to the wrong person. I kept picturing the movie *Splash*, except they wouldn't lock me in a tube of water. They would choose some dark, underground lab. I might never see the sun again.

I shuddered at the thought.

"I won't ever let anybody take you," he promised, his gaze thorough as it searched my face. Sometimes I believed he could read my mind. He laughed at the notion whenever I mentioned it, but he was intuitive to the point of being psychic sometimes.

"I know." I squeezed his hand as we walked into the dining room and started searching for our team. "I'm not afraid that you'll never race to the rescue." I was afraid that he would be killed in his zeal to protect me from Sybil, but that was a conversation for another time. "They're over there." I inclined my head.

He held my hand for the duration of the walk. The others were engaged in serious conversation, so I took a few moments to catch up.

"I'm not saying it's definitely Bigfoot," Chris, annoyed, insisted to Millie. "I'm just saying we can't rule out Bigfoot."

"And I'm saying Bigfoot isn't big on the Etsy scene and isn't making twig sculptures in the woods," Millie insisted. "It's not Bigfoot."

"What did we miss?" I asked, hoping to defuse some of the tension settling over the table.

"The normal stuff," Laura replied blandly. She seemed disinterested in the conversation. "Chris believes Bigfoot is out there killing kids, and Millie is mean."

"I'll show you mean," Millie fired back, seemingly catching herself when Laura didn't rise to the occasion to engage in the argument. "You haven't even been out there," she pointed. "I'm not sure you should have an opinion on the subject."

"I don't," Laura replied. "I don't have ... anything." Rather than continue the conversation, she got to her feet and walked to the coffee bar. She was not the Laura I'd learned to loathe.

"I'll get us coffee," I said to Jack as I started to follow her.

He reached out to stop me, but I lightly swatted his hand away. "I've got it," I insisted, refusing to allow him to pull me back from what I knew I needed to do. "Somebody needs to talk to her."

"It doesn't have to be you," Jack argued.

"Definitely not," Millie agreed. "You should talk to her, Jack. You're in charge of security. Tell her to shape up or ship out."

"Yeah, I'm not doing that." Jack said. "I'm not going to kick her when she's down. There's no reason for you to go out of your way either, Charlie. She's been nothing but horrible to you."

"I know." I didn't want to be best friends with Laura. That would never be the case. "I don't want to sit around and watch her disappear. I'm just going to talk to her. There's no harm in it."

"I agree," Chris said, his gaze contemplative. "I have no intention of pushing her, but if she's not going to contribute to the team, well ... you know."

Was he talking about firing her? That wasn't like him. It wasn't as if Laura had been falling down on the job for weeks or months. She'd gone through a trauma. It seemed we should be trying to help her ... at least as much as we were capable of.

"Just ... fight about what we're going to do today," I insisted. "I'll be right back."

Jack made a disgruntled sound when I headed for Laura. I took a moment to watch her without her knowing, debating my approach, and finally decided that a frontal assault was warranted.

"You don't want to go to Nighthawk?" I asked when I'd closed the distance.

"Nope." She didn't bother looking at me.

"May I ask why? I mean ... you're usually on the front line for this stuff. You don't like being left out of the action."

"Yes, well, I was in the middle of the action last time, wasn't I?" Her tone was bitter.

"I'm sorry about ... all of that. You're on the other side of it now, though. I ... know it must've been hard for you." It was difficult to get the words out. "If you ever want to talk, you can talk to me."

Her laugh was hollow and humorless. "Are we chat buddies now?"

"No, but ... you know."

"I honestly don't." When she turned to face me, there was a blankness in her eyes that had my heart sinking. "You're not my friend, Charlie. I'm certainly not your friend. When I look at you, all I see is the person who came into my group, stole all the attention, and even seduced my crush. What's funniest is that you did it all under the guise of being this sweet and innocent person who would never hurt a soul. As far as I'm concerned, there's nothing to like about you."

I was taken aback. "I ... didn't seduce Jack," I said. It was all I could say. "Things between us just happened. They were never going to happen between the two of you. You're not his type." I didn't mean for it to sound so mean but there was no hauling it back.

"Fair enough, but ... you need to let it go." She needed tough love, and I was going to be the one to deliver it. "You act as if you don't want to be part of the group any longer."

"I don't." She was matter-of-fact. "I have no interest in hunting ghosts any longer. I have no interest in finding Bigfoot. The only thing I care about is the irrational fear that grabs me by the throat and chokes me whenever I think about going into the field."

My heart went out to her despite the dislike that I felt whenever I looked at her. "You have PTSD over what happened in the asylum."

"My therapist has told me as much."

"You're seeing a therapist?" That was news to me — good news.

"That's probably best. Tell Chris. He'll understand. You can stick close to Boston until you're feeling better."

"You seem to be missing the point," she said. "I won't be feeling better. I don't want to be part of this team any longer. It's not worth it." Her gaze briefly landed on Jack. "None of it."

I was bewildered. "So, what are you going to do?"

"My father is looking into that right now. I'm stuck until he comes up with something."

I licked my lips. "You could wait it out a bit longer, see if you change your mind."

"I won't." She gripped her mug and offered me a tight grimace. "Don't worry about me, Charlie. Your halo won't tarnish if you let me fade into the background. I cede the group to you. I no longer have any fight in me."

With that, she headed to the table. She seemed lost. She'd been a pain far more than she'd been helpful, but I didn't like seeing a human being — *any* human being — in pain.

Laura clearly believed her pain was insurmountable, and it was big enough that I hurt for her. How did that even happen?

16

SIXTEEN

Jack's move to deftly divorce us from the group heading to Nighthawk confused me. I didn't voice my questions in front of the group, opting to wait until we were in the rental vehicle.

"What's the deal?" I asked. "Are you trying to keep me from Nighthawk because you're afraid something will happen to me?"

"I'm always afraid something will happen to you," he replied. "But that's not why. I want to stop at the county registrar's office to see if we can find information on that cabin."

"Oh. Then what?"

"Then we try to learn something about the family. Records here are spotty, but I don't know that there's anything else to discover in Nighthawk."

"Other than bodies."

He hesitated and then shook his head. "We've been all through the town. The surrounding area could contain bodies but it's like looking for a needle in a mountain of needles. They would've been out there for days now, likely torn apart by animals. You need to understand that it's likely we'll never find the rest of them."

"I don't want to think about that."

"I know you don't, but it's reality."

"Not my reality. I can't leave without knowing what happened."

"Ugh. You're so stubborn." He was disgruntled, but Jack was a controlled individual, something I both loved and loathed about him. Just once I wanted him to freak out over something little. Well, other than Millie's driving.

"Trying to track the family is good," I said. "We could've done that and still joined the others at Nighthawk. We didn't have to completely remove ourselves from that group."

"I didn't want to promise we were heading out there when we don't know how things are going to go."

"Okay, but what about the group going out there? It sounds as if it's just going to be Chris, Hannah, Casey, Millie and Bernard. What if something happens to them and we're not there?"

"They know how to take care of themselves."

"Yes, but I'm magical. If something did attack them, I'm the best shot we have to fight it off. You have a gun, but that might not work if we're dealing with a wendigo. They're alone out there with nobody to protect them."

"That's true." Other men might have issues with their girlfriends saying they were more powerful, but Jack always wanted to build me up. "I've been thinking about your dream. If we're dealing with a wendigo, it was most likely a human being at one point, right?"

I had no idea where he was going but I nodded.

"What human turned into a wendigo? I have trouble believing this creature has been hanging around since Nighthawk was a boomtown. People hike that area frequently. Some have gone missing, but not enough to make the local authorities itchy."

That's when what he was getting at dawned on me. "You think the wendigo is more recent?"

"I don't know, although that doesn't feel quite right given how isolated it is out there. None of it makes sense. If it's an older creature, why haven't people reported it? If it's fresher, where did it come from?"

"You think the wendigo called that cabin home at one time."

"You're getting ahead of yourself." He let loose a frustrated chuckle. "I love you, Charlie, but you commit to a story before we have any evidence. It's possible the wendigo lived in that cabin. Maybe the father was too greedy ... or prideful. Maybe he obsessed so much about his daughter it turned him into something he didn't expect."

The suggestion made me distinctly uncomfortable. "Oh, god. You don't think he cannibalized her, do you?"

"I'm really hoping the cannibal stuff is nonsense. I don't want to go that route."

"This area is remote," I said. I was thinking things through. "A hard winter when the family was cut off from everybody else might lead to them eating the horses ... and cows ... and then still running out of food."

"Do you have to do this so close to breakfast?"

"It's your fault for having that big plate of sausage." I shot him a sly wink. "They say everything goes into sausage, right?"

"Don't make me gag you, Charlie."

I continued as if I hadn't heard him. "You're right about me jumping to conclusions. I do have a tendency to do that. I'm kind of a downer."

"You're anything but a downer. You're my little ray of sunshine."

"Oh, that's both cute and corny."

"I'm fine with that." He reached over and squeezed my hand, keeping his attention on the road. "I want to get names for the property out there. Then I want to run the family names. I don't know if that'll lead to anything. I'm pretty sure spending another day at Nighthawk moving cameras and complaining about bad footage won't lead anywhere."

"There's that Boy Scout in you again," I teased. "You're a practical man, Jack."

"See, that's not sexy. Nobody ever says, 'He's so hot. He's got a great brain. He's so practical I want to rip his clothes off.' I prefer being sexy."

"You're totally sexy. I find practicality the sexiest of sexy."

"You're such an odd girl."

THE WENDIGO WHOOP-DE-DOO

"You love me anyway."

"More than anything." He was earnest. "You're right about me not being able to forgive myself if something happens to the others at Nighthawk. We need to see some forward momentum. It feels important given your dream last night."

"Forward momentum is good. I'm game for whatever you have planned."

"I feel flirty when you say things like that."

"I'm game for that too."

He groaned when I sent him a saucy smile. "Work first. Play later."

"There's that Boy Scout again."

JACK TURNED OUT TO BE RIGHT about what a mess the records were. Instead of searching the records for him, they made him pay — five-hundred bucks — to print copies of all the land deeds from the area. It was either that or sit in the musty, windowless room in the back of their office and go through them.

Jack had no intention of doing that. He whipped out his corporate card, paid, and then we waited a full hour for them to print the records. They delivered them to us in a huge box.

"Ugh." I knew I sounded whiny, but I couldn't stop myself. "This is going to take all day, Jack."

"Now you know why I didn't want to commit to going to Nighthawk this afternoon." He was grim as he pulled onto the two-lane highway.

"You couldn't possibly have known that their computer system would spit out this." He was smart. Nobody was that smart, though. "Come on."

He shot me a wink. "Charlie, I've been doing this for a long time. This isn't the first tiny town that I've had to get records from. You're used to tracking things down in bigger cities. They have the money and manpower to computerize. Places like this don't."

"Still ... it's such a waste." I shook my head as I stared at the paper. "What are we going to do with all of this when we're done?"

"Toss it in a dumpster."

"Can't we find a place to donate it?"

He was quiet so long I didn't think he'd heard me, but when I looked at him, I found a smile waiting for me. "What?" I demanded.

"You're just ... so freaking cute I can't stand it. If anybody else had made that request, I would've shot them down. Now, for you, I'm trying to figure out what we can do with the extra paper so it's not wasted."

"You're a good guy, Jack." I beamed at him. "While you're feeling warm and cuddly, can I put in a request for lunch?"

"Jackal Jane's?"

"Yup."

"I was thinking the same. We'll drop this in our room and then go to lunch."

WE'D BARELY MADE IT INTO OUR ROOM when there was a knock at the door. Jack had deposited the box on the small table — which I swear let out a groan at the weight — and he held up a finger to still me near the bed.

"What are you doing?" I asked when I realized he was reaching for his gun. "You can't shoot somebody for knocking."

He shot me a wry look. "I have no intention of shooting a random person," he hissed. "Also, as much as I love your voice, baby, it carries. Take it down a notch."

"Oh, whatever." I watched him, holding my breath as he peered through the peephole. He was still for a second, as if debating, and then holstered the gun and pulled open the door.

"This is kind of dangerous," he said as he ushered Melina and Mike inside. "What if somebody sees you?"

"We saw the rest of the group leave," Melina replied. "We were watching from our room this morning. When we didn't see you with the group, we were concerned. We were heading to lunch when we noticed you in the parking lot."

"Yeah. What gives?" Mike turned his full attention to the box.

"Please tell us you aren't considering moving in here because of the Magic Fingers. Melina told me what you were doing yesterday when she stopped by for a visit."

"It's not as if it was dirty," Melina shot back. "Let it go."

"You said there was groaning."

"Because of the bed." Melina shook her head and then offered up a pretty smile. "Aren't you going to Nighthawk today?"

I cast Jack a questioning look, briefly wondering how much I should tell them. I held out my hands. "I had another dream last night." I told them because there was no sense dragging it out. When I finished, Mike asked the same question that had tripped up Jack.

"You don't think it was really Sybil?"

I shrugged. "I don't know. I don't think that's important right now."

"Of course it is. If Sybil is invading your dreams and knows about Nighthawk, she could be on her way here."

"I hate to break it to you, but Sybil is well aware of who I am and where I spend my time." It was the truth, however brutal. "She left that freaking teddy bear for me outside the asylum, the one from when I was a kid."

"The one we have locked in a safe deposit box because Charlie is afraid it will come to life and kill her in her sleep," Jack added.

"Not kill me," I countered. "I just ... don't want to let it in our new place in case it's cursed or something."

He held up his hands. "Fair enough. You have a new teddy bear to love."

I smiled. He'd bought me one when he found out I'd been separated from my favorite toy as a child. I wasn't nearly as scarred by the story as he was — mostly because I didn't remember the bear — but the new toy had melted my heart. It was perched on my bed ... or maybe my new bed at this point. I hadn't been paying attention to updates on our move.

"There's nothing we can do about Sybil right now," Jack said. "Even if it really was her in Charlie's dreams, she hasn't made a move. We have to focus on the case and deal with Sybil later."

"That's easy for you to say," Mike groused, arms crossed over his chest. "You didn't lose your daughter because of that woman."

"I'm going to make sure I never lose Charlie to that woman," Jack said. "I want a future with Charlie. We're going to figure this out ... just not today."

"He's right," Melina said, gripping Mike's hand and drawing his eyes to her. "We have to follow their lead. If they want to focus on this case, we have to help. That's why we're here."

"I don't like any of this," Mike muttered.

"None of us do," Jack said. "For now, we have property records to go through. I have to think that if there is a wendigo it's tied to that cabin Charlie dreamed about. Unfortunately, the records system here isn't great."

Mike nodded as he took in the box with fresh eyes. "That's what you guys are doing with the big box of paper."

"We don't have an address," Jack explained. "We have to go through the paperwork bit by bit. If we can find the right parcel and get a family name — I'm willing to bet only one family ever lived there — it will give us a place to start looking."

"I get it." Mike rubbed his jaw. "That's a mountain of paper. You should let us help."

Jack seemed surprised by the offer. "You want to help?"

"That's why we're here."

"Okay, well ... ." Jack broke off and licked his lips. "We were going to get lunch at Jackal Jane's before starting. The rest of the team is at Nighthawk, so I don't see why we can't have a meal."

"Sounds great." Mike beamed at him. "I'll walk with Charlie."

Jack didn't bother to hide his eye roll. "Give it a rest. This protective father stuff is giving me an ulcer. I love her. I'm not going anywhere. Get over it."

"Definitely get over it," I echoed as Jack opened the room door.

He reared back when somebody fell inward on him, his instincts kicking in and allowing him to catch Millie before she hit the floor.

"What the ... ?" Melina's eyes were wide with fear.

"Millie!" Jack's annoyance was on full display as he righted the

THE WENDIGO WHOOP-DE-DOO

older woman. "What are you doing?" His eyes drifted to the glass that a second before had been pressed to Millie's ear and our door. "Were you eavesdropping?"

True to her nature, Millie straightened and gave him a haughty look. "Of course not. I was just looking for a glass of water. I'm parched."

"You were looking for a glass of water outside our room?"

"Maybe." Millie shifted her gaze to Mike and Melina, a smile playing at the corners of her lips as she took in the scene. "What's going on here?"

"Nothing," Melina replied. "We're just ... staying in the hotel and were out of glasses. We came to ask if they had some we could borrow." I knew Millie wouldn't buy it.

"Some glasses, eh?" Millie's smile broadened. "You're Charlie's parents. Her biological parents. I didn't realize you'd followed the team here."

Melina looked horrified. "We're not family."

I took pity on her. "It's okay," I reassured her. "Millie is familiar with our situation. She knows ... pretty much everything."

"Pretty much?" Millie turned an arched eyebrow in my direction. "What don't I know, missy? Have you been holding out on me?"

"Only a little, and not on purpose. I can't keep up with what I've told you."

"What are you even doing here?" Jack asked. "Why aren't you with the rest of the team?"

"Because I knew something was up when you guys decided to stay back. I saw you outside the hotel last night." She inclined her head toward Melina. "I thought you were Charlie from behind. Then I saw your face and couldn't shake the feeling that I should know you. Something felt off, so I decided to stay behind and figure out what you guys were up to."

"We're working," Jack insisted. "This other stuff ... is none of your business."

"Thanks, killjoy." She slapped his shoulder. "I want to get to know the folks. You can't keep them from me. I'm an excellent judge of character and it's only fair we all get to know one another since we'll be working together to keep Charlie safe."

Jack worked his jaw, annoyed. He'd already lost and he knew it. "Fine." He blew out a sigh. "We're going to lunch. You can come, but you need to keep this to yourself for now. I'm not sure how it'll play out and I need to think."

Millie was the picture of innocence. "I just want to get to know Charlie's family. I'm not interested in anything else. You have my word."

Jack looked dubious but acquiesced. "Lunch ... and introductions. Then we need to get to work."

"I love work." Millie sidled between Mike and Melina, looping her arms through theirs and smiling. "I know it doesn't seem like it, but you're going to love me by the end of lunch."

"I'm looking forward to seeing if that's true," Mike said as he grinned at her. He was clearly already charmed. "Shall we?"

SEVENTEEN

Millie was a chatterbox as we walked to Jackal Jane's for lunch. She had no interest in talking to Jack and me, who trailed behind, but was solely focused on Mike and Melina.

"So ... evil witch, eh?" Millie made a tsking sound with her tongue as she shook her head. "That's the absolute worst."

Melina managed a smile, but I could tell she was struggling to adapt to Millie suddenly being part of our group. "Yes. Evil witches are the bane of my existence."

"We'll figure it out." Millie liked to tackle a problem head-on, and that was on full display today. "I've got money if we need to hire experts ... or specialized security. We just need to come up with a plan."

"You have money?" Mike was confused. "If you have money, why are you working for the Legacy Foundation?"

"I'll be bored if I don't work," Millie replied simply. "If you have nothing to do, you die. I don't want to die."

I felt the need to explain. "Millie's ex-husband runs the Legacy Foundation," I volunteered. "They were married for years. Chris is her nephew, and she enjoys spending time with him."

"I also like driving four-by-fours and torturing my ex-husband," Millie said. "It keeps me young."

That drew a smile from Melina. "How long have you known about Charlie?"

"Oh, for a long time." Millie cast a look over her shoulder and winked at me. "I knew there was something different about her right from the start. I wanted her to be my sidekick from our very first assignment, but she was always a little shy.

"Then, when we were in Texas, we were attacked by these murderous thugs," she continued. "Chris got knocked out, and to save us, Charlie used her magic."

I glanced around to make sure nobody had heard, but the sidewalks were empty. "Millie, don't throw around the M-word," I chastised.

"Mountain Dew?" She feigned confusion and then rolled her eyes. "I'm not new, Charlie. I've kept your secret for the duration, and that won't change."

"You haven't told your nephew?" Mike asked. "If you're so close and Charlie is the sort of individual who would interest him, why haven't you told him?"

"Because it's not what's best for Charlie." Millie's answer was simple. "What's best for Charlie is to figure things out at her own pace. I love Chris. I would do anything for him. But he doesn't need to know about this."

"Because you think he would try to study Charlie?" Melina queried.

Millie hesitated, tilting her head, and then she shook it. "He wouldn't try to put her in a cage and study her. That's not who he is. His excitement might get the better of him, though. He wouldn't understand the necessity to keep things quiet.

"He's not a bad man," she continued. "In fact, he's one of the best men I've ever met. He just can't contain his excitement sometimes."

"You're including me on that 'best man' list, right?" Jack demanded as he offered me a smile.

"Sometimes you're on there," Millie conceded. "But when you tell me I can't drive, you slide right off that list."

"I tell you that you can't drive because I'm trying to protect the other people in our group."

"You're such a Nervous Nellie," Millie muttered. "Seriously, I've been driving longer than you've been alive."

"That doesn't make you good at it."

Mike's laugh was low and warm as he listened to the banter. "Does that mean you think Jack is a good match for my daughter? I'm asking because I go back and forth on the issue. I think he might be a little overbearing."

"Oh, don't even," Jack warned. "I'm not overbearing in the least."

"You're a little overbearing," Millie countered, "but it's okay. That's necessary in a security chief. That's what's needed to protect Charlie."

"So you do think he's a good choice," Mike surmised.

"For her? He's the best choice. If you sit back and watch them, you'll realize that he's the best possible match for her."

"He seems kind of pervy to me."

Millie snorted. "So, what? You don't want a guy who openly loves to be with your daughter? Let me tell you something: It's hell when your partner doesn't want to show affection. Jack is free with his.

"Not only that, he's always there to listen to Charlie when she has an idea," she continued. "He talks things out with her, never makes her feel like she's the junior member of our team, and praises her constantly. What's not to like about that?"

Mike worked his jaw. "I ... don't know. I just see her as a little girl."

"Well, she's not." Millie was firm. "I understand why you did what you did. It was better for Charlie, even though she still struggles with feelings of abandonment. But she's an adult. You can't force her to your way of thinking. You did what was best for her and she has to come to grips with that. As her parent, it's your job to continuously do your best for her. It's not just a one-time thing."

Mike pursed his lips. "And you think Jack is what's best for her."

"I certainly do. All you have to do is watch them interact for five minutes to feel the love. He's the sort of man most women would kill for, and most fathers should come to appreciate."

"So I'm a jerk," Mike surmised.

"Jerk? No. You're territorial. You've got to get over it. Jack has already won her heart. He loves her. He puts her needs first. He would die for her. What more could you want from him?"

Mike made a face. "If he could stop being so handsy, that would be great."

Millie snorted. "Oh, suck it up. I think they're gross half the time and adorable the other half. They're not hurting anyone. If Charlie's not complaining, why are you?"

"Because ... because ... ." Apparently Mike didn't have an answer, which I found intriguing.

"Because you're her father and you thought you would have time to bond with her when you finally found her," Millie provided. "It didn't work out that way. You're disappointed, but you have to adjust. Charlie has done enough adjusting. Besides, you're the parent. You need to be the bigger person."

Mike offered up a flat-lipped grimace. "I was really starting to like you," he said.

Millie wasn't bothered in the least by his words or tone. "You're going to love me before it's all said and done. More importantly, you're going to love Jack. Give him a chance. He's a pretty good guy ... when he's not trying to wrestle keys from me just because I'm a woman."

"It wasn't because you're a woman," Jack shot back. "It's because I don't want to die. I would appreciate if Charlie didn't die because of your driving as well."

"Yeah, yeah, yeah." Millie waved a dismissive hand. "I've had it with this conversation. Let's talk about something else."

"What did you have in mind?" Mike asked.

"Tell me about Charlie when she was little. I've always pictured her with a filthy face, racing through the woods and building forts."

Mike relaxed into the question, and the change that came over his expression was breathtaking. He looked like a different man. "That's pretty close. She wanted a treehouse something fierce, but because we were in hiding, I could never manage it. I did help her build a fort

THE WENDIGO WHOOP-DE-DOO

inside. I snagged a bunch of boxes from the local grocery store. She declared herself the queen and wouldn't let Casey in unless he bribed her with chocolate."

Next to me, Jack laughed. "She can still be bribed with chocolate. I use it all the time when I want to motivate her."

I narrowed my eyes. "You make me sound lazy."

"Not lazy, baby." Jack squeezed my hand. "You're just set in your ways. You like watching monster movies on the weekend. It takes something fun — and chocolaty — to drag you away from the screen."

"You loved monster movies when you were little." Mike took on a far-off expression. "You loved weird horror stuff. We had to be careful what you watched because you were open to anything, including slasher movies. Finding monster movies for kids back then wasn't as easy.

"I did find this old movie called *The Monster Squad*," he continued. "It was an '80s movie and you loved it. You walked around spouting lines from it all the time, even if you didn't understand them."

Something clicked in the back of my head. It was like a puzzle piece fitting into place. "I think I vaguely remember that movie. There's something in my head about the wolfman having 'nards.'"

Mike beamed at me. "We'll get a digital copy, maybe watch it together when we get back to the city."

"We can have a movie night at the new condo," Jack suggested. "We'll order pizza and a bunch of other food."

For a moment, I thought Mike was going to turn down the suggestion because Jack would be involved. Then he smiled. "A family movie night with all the fixings. Sounds good."

"Great." Jack squeezed my hand even tighter. "We'll plan it as soon as we're unpacked and settled."

WE JUST MISSED THE LUNCH RUSH AT Jackal Jane's — most everybody was leaving as we were going in — and there were only a few diners scattered at tables as we got settled.

"Oh, it's my favorite couple," Jane called out when she saw us, a broad grin on her face. "I knew I'd see you again. My food is just too good to pass up."

"It is," Jack agreed, accepting a menu from her. "I have another question if you have a minute."

"You guys are just full of questions, aren't you?" Jane shook her head. "You're young and pretty — like really, really pretty — and you should be spending your time in bed, not asking questions."

"We have jobs to do," Jack replied.

"Okay, what's the question?"

"You mentioned Hank the bootlegger," Jack started. "We haven't seen him since that first day at Nighthawk, but we did discover an old, deserted cabin. I've been wondering where Hank lives."

"I don't think anybody knows where Hank lives," Jane replied. If she was bothered by talking about Hank again, she didn't show it. "He supposedly has a shack out there somewhere — complete with a still if you believe the stories. But I'm pretty sure that old cabin of his was condemned. He shouldn't be hanging out there."

My heart skipped. "Wait ... are you saying that cabin was his?" That felt somehow off given my dream. There was no way Hank and the unhappy father were the same person. Time could change someone, but not that much.

"It was his brother's place at one time," Jane replied. "You're talking about the cabin with two barns?"

Jack nodded. "We went inside the barns. One of them doesn't have a roof so it didn't seem all that dangerous. The other was a bit iffier. It probably won't last another winter."

"Frankly, I can't believe those structures are still standing. I saw them when I was a teenager. My brother and his friends went camping up there and I demanded to go along. The cabin looked as if it was on its last legs then and that was more than twenty-five years ago."

"Well, it's still there." Jack rubbed his chin. "You're saying Hank's brother lived there?"

"Colin." Jane nodded. "He died in a farming accident a long time ago. Long before I was born. I think my parents were teenagers when it happened."

It was hard for me to do the math, so I didn't tax myself. I knew Jack would do it for me when we were alone later.

"So ... Hank hung out at his brother's place after he died?"

"Hank took over family duties after his brother died," Jane clarified. "Somebody had to run the farm, and supposedly Colin was a real hard ass. He was so difficult to live with he ran off his sons. They wanted nothing to do with the family farm. That left a wife and a younger daughter behind."

The girl from my dream. It had to be her. I sat straighter. "Do you know what happened to the girl?"

Jack shot me a quelling look. I ignored him and kept my focus on Jane.

"The daughter?" Jane shrugged. "There are stories."

"We wouldn't mind hearing the stories," Jack prodded. "Ever since we saw the cabin, Charlie's imagination has been running wild. She can't picture how anybody could live out there."

"I'm country — like strumming banjos and town potluck country — but even I couldn't imagine living out there," Jane said. "As for Emmalynne – that's the daughter – she disappeared."

"Disappeared? I don't understand."

"Nobody does. She and her mother disappeared a couple years after Hank took over the house. There are rumors, but nobody knows which are true."

"We like rumors," Jack said. "We know that you can't verify them as fact, but we'd still like to hear them."

"I guess it couldn't hurt anything." Jane lowered herself into the empty chair at the far end of the table. "So, the story is that Hank took over more than just the farm. He also took over Colin's 'husbandly duties,' if you know what I mean." She used air quotes.

"You mean he started schtupping the wife," Millie said.

"Yes." Jane bobbed her head. "I love that word, by the way. I can tell we're going to be fast friends."

Millie beamed at her but otherwise stayed quiet.

"Hank supposedly ruled the house with an iron fist. Some people say he was cruel. Others say he just liked order. I lean toward cruel because I've seen him and there's nothing orderly about him.

"Anyway, about five years after Colin's death, Emmalynne and her mother Jessica went missing. Most people never saw Emmalynne, except when she was working with the animals. Jessica came to town once a week for supplies. It was like clockwork ... until she suddenly stopped coming."

"What happened?" Melina asked. She seemed fully invested in the story.

"There are two theories," Jane replied. "One is that Jessica got fed up with Hank and his overbearing ways, packed up Emmalynne, and took off to live with one of her sons."

"Did anybody ever confirm that?" Jack asked.

"Not that I know of."

"What's the other theory?" I asked. I was almost afraid to hear the answer, but I had to know.

"The other theory is that Hank killed them in a fit of rage. Even back then, Hank was considered a hard drinker ... and because everybody in these parts is a hard drinker, he had to be really bad for anybody to notice."

"Didn't the cops go out to check on them?" I asked.

"They did, but you've seen those woods. Hank said they up and took off. There was no way to find the bodies if he was lying. Nothing seemed out of place. Emmalynne was an adult at that time. She should've been married off. Instead, she was considered a spinster at like twenty-two, which is utter nonsense. Still, as an adult, she was allowed to take off whenever she wanted."

"She never married?" I ran the dream I'd had through my mind again. "I thought her father was arranging a marriage with a local."

Jane made an odd face. "Now, where did you hear that story?"

I shrugged. "I don't remember. We've been going through a lot of old documents." It was a lie, but one I had to commit to. "I must've read it in one of the documents."

"I vaguely remember that," Jack confirmed.

"Well, that's also part of the story." Jane smiled. "Emmalynne was supposed to be married to the son of the owner of the Nighthawk Mine. Even though it was no longer booming, there was money there. People say she pitched a fit the day of the wedding and tried to run. The wedding was called off because the miner's son was embarrassed. Colin was furious. It was too late to fix the match. To my knowledge, Emmalynne never married."

"She could've been killed," I noted. "I mean ... our only options seem to be that she was killed or ran away."

"Pretty much." Jane pushed herself to a standing position. "So, that's the sad story of the cabin. It's all conjecture." Jane shifted the conversation without taking a breath. "I have brisket on special if that's anybody's cup of tea."

"I love brisket," Jack said, his hand on my back. He seemed to understand that I was having trouble with the story. It wasn't something I wanted to entertain. Even though I knew the flashes I'd seen in my dreams were from long ago, part of me wanted to believe Emmalynne had found a way to escape her overbearing father and forge her own life.

"I like brisket too," Mike said. "I'll have an iced tea and fries as well."

Once everybody placed their orders and Jane left, I looked to Jack. "I kind of wanted her to have gotten away," I admitted in a soft voice.

Sympathy lining his features, Jack brushed my hair from my face. "I know, baby. I kind of wanted her to have gotten away too. We don't know she's dead."

"It's a fair conclusion," Millie countered. "This whole thing is a mess. How are we going to track down this wendigo thing, if that's what we're even dealing with?"

That was another thing plaguing me. I had no idea where to start.

"I don't know." Jack leaned in and pressed a kiss to my cheek. "We'll figure it out. We always do."

I could only hope he was right, for all our sakes ... including a young woman likely long since dead. Somebody had to avenge poor Emmalynne.

18

EIGHTEEN

The hotel room was too small for all five of us to conduct research, so Jack doled out stacks of paper and told everybody to put aside anything that looked interesting. Mike argued about splitting up before Jack waved his arm across the tiny room.

"No offense, but there are only two chairs in the room," he said. "You're going to pitch a fit if Charlie and I are on the bed."

"Besides," Millie added, making a face as she readjusted her stack of papers. "Jack wants to talk to Charlie in private about what Jane had to say at lunch. She's feeling emotional about the girl, and Jack wants to make her feel better."

"Why can't Jack do that with us here?" Mike asked.

Millie shot him a "Well, duh" look that would've made me smile under different circumstances. "Because he might want to make her feel better with his tongue," she replied.

Mike's disgust was obvious, but he was suddenly done arguing about staying in cramped quarters with us. "We'll be in touch by text."

Millie saluted before she left.

Once we were alone, Jack put his full focus on me. "Tell me what you're thinking."

THE WENDIGO WHOOP-DE-DOO

"I think Emmalynne was killed by her uncle, that crazy old dude we saw in the woods, and it's likely he's responsible for all of this."

"There's a problem with that scenario."

"What's that?"

"How did he manage to subdue eight kids, rip off arms and gouge out eyes, and not get overpowered by those boys? You saw the photos. They might not have been muscle-bound jocks, but they were young and fit."

He had a point, loath as I was to admit it. "Well ... ." I broke off and chewed my lip. "I don't know. It feels as if we're missing a few puzzle pieces."

"I agree, but I have an idea."

"Does it involve the Magic Fingers?" I pointed to the coin slot.

Jack's grin was lightning quick. "No, but we might be able to fit in a session while we're waiting for my idea to arrive."

Oh, well, now he definitely had my attention. "Your idea is a person?"

"An old military buddy," Jack confirmed. "Quint Roscoe. We served overseas together for two years. He's ... kind of outrageous. You'll love him. He's set up shop as a private investigator about an hour away."

That was a lot to unpack. "I ... you ... a friend." I realized how that sounded a second later. "I mean, a local friend. I wasn't surprised that you had a friend, just that you had one nearby."

Jack made a face. "I have friends."

"You spend all your time with me."

"You're my best friend."

I went warm all over. "I think of you that way too. But I do have other friends."

"I'm apparently going to have to start hanging out with friends occasionally to prove to you that I have them. I'll worry about that later. I didn't remember that Quint was close until we were having lunch. Like I said, he's a private detective, and he'll be able to help us dig deeper."

"Do you really think he'll help?"

"Yes. He's also going to tell you ridiculous drinking stories about me when I was in the military. Don't believe them. He's a gregarious guy who will grill you mercilessly, but he'll help us get through this information faster."

"Then invite him. The more the merrier, right?"

"You might not say that after the fifth time he asks you to leave me for him. He's competitive when it comes to women, and he's going to love you."

"I like being loved."

He grabbed my chin. "Just remember who loves you most." He gave me a quick kiss. "We can enjoy the Magic Fingers while we wait for him to get here."

"Awesome." I flopped on the bed. "This day is looking up."

MY MOUTH FELL OPEN WHEN QUINT ROSCOE, big as a dump truck, appeared in our doorway.

I'd always considered Jack a big man, but he looked like a little kid standing next to Quint.

"Hey, jackass," Quint said by way of greeting, slapping Jack so hard I couldn't fathom how Jack's knees didn't give way. "Long time, no see."

"Quint." Jack rotated his shoulder and offered up a smile. "It's nice to see you."

"It's nice to be seen." Quint took one look around the room and made a face. "Can't you afford a better hotel, man?"

Jack chuckled as he shut the door. "This is the closest location to Nighthawk. It's a work thing."

"Well, it's a dump." Quint's eyes fell on me. "But it does have some interesting perks. Hello, darlin'." Rather than extend his hand to me for a shake, he plopped down on the bed next to me. "Are you one of the amenities in this fine establishment?"

It was one of the weirdest greetings I'd ever been privy to. "Not last time I checked."

"She's definitely not an amenity," Jack said.

I shot him a look. "I could be a great amenity."

THE WENDIGO WHOOP-DE-DOO

"Fine. She's not an amenity for you, Quint. This is Charlie." His lips curved up when he met my gaze. "In addition to being my co-worker, she's also my girlfriend."

"Oh, well, howdy-do." Quint tipped an imaginary hat. He didn't seem surprised to hear the news and yet he was obviously intrigued. "You're a cute little thing, aren't you?"

"I am," I agreed. "I don't know how little I am, though."

"I could fit you in the palm of my hand." Quint held out a massive paw as if to prove it. "You're dainty."

"She's spoken for," Jack reminded him.

"Oh, don't get your panties in a wad, Jack." Quint's smile never dissipated. "I'm just checking her out. Last time I saw you, I believe you said you were never settling down. This hotel room might be a dump, but you're clearly settled."

"Yes, well ... Charlie has magical powers." Jack winked for my benefit. "She reeled me in the second I saw her."

Quint lifted my foot and studied it. "Girl, you are all sorts of adorable. I'm sorry Jack got to you first, because I would love nothing more than to take you out to dinner — and maybe to a real hotel — and show you a good time."

"We have Magic Fingers." I gestured toward the machine on the nightstand. "They're all I need for a good time."

Quint threw back his head and brayed out a laugh loud enough to jolt me. "Yup, I definitely like her. I approve." He patted my foot as he dropped it. His gaze was speculative when it landed on Jack. "You look pretty good, other than that ridiculous haircut. What's with the male model look?"

"I happen to like the hair." Jack nudged him away from the bed. "Sit in the chair."

"There's no way I'm sitting in the chair. I'll break it and I don't want you to laugh." Instead, Quint moved to the other side of the bed and lay down next to me. "I'm good here."

Jack glared at him. "You can't be on the bed with my girlfriend."

"I don't hear her arguing."

Jack slid his eyes to me, waiting.

"I don't want to get distracted," I whined. "Millie already partially derailed the day. Can't we focus on the important stuff and forget about the nonsense?"

Jack muttered something under his breath and then took his spot in one of the chairs. "Fine. I hope you brought your computer, Quint."

"It's in the bag I dropped when I came inside."

I hadn't noticed the bag, but I looked anyway, as did Jack.

"We have a situation." Jack calmly laid out what we were dealing with, leaving out nothing but the magical aspects that had been gleaned from me. When he finished, he watched Quint for a reaction.

"So, you want me to run searches for people who have been missing for twenty years?" Quint didn't look impressed. "Sounds kind of boring."

"I'm pretty sure they've been gone longer than that," Jack replied. "I've been doing the math. I think that cabin was built in the late '40s or early '50s. That would've been right before the Nighthawk mine shut down."

"So, seventy years ago?" Quint shook his head. "Even worse."

"Not that long. Jane looks to be early forties, maybe late 30s. We'll go forty to make it easy. She said that Emmalynne and her mother went missing when her parents were teenagers. If you assume they were roughly twenty-five when they had her, that makes them sixty-five now. Subtract back. We're talking roughly forty-seven to fifty years ago."

"That's so much better," Quint said dryly. "I still don't understand what a missing girl from fifty years ago has to do with what's happening out there today. How does she fit into what happened to the teenagers?"

Jack hesitated, making sure to keep his eyes from landing on me. "Do you know what the Legacy Foundation does?" he asked.

"Looks for missing kids?"

"We hunt paranormal phenomenon." Jack said. "We were called here because the locals believe what happened to those kids can't be explained."

Quint was silent for a long time, his eyes bouncing between Jack and me. Finally, he shook his head. "Are you messing with me?"

"No."

"You're a ghost hunter?"

"I'm head of security for a group of paranormal investigators," Jack replied.

"I'm a ghost hunter," I told Quint with a grin.

"You're adorable," Quint said as he smiled back. "In fact, you're so adorable I don't care if you're a nut. As for you, how can you work with ghost hunters, Jack? You're the guy who said I was drunk when I saw the mummy in the desert."

"You were definitely drunk," Jack replied.

"You saw a mummy?" I was officially intrigued. "Do tell."

Quint's smile was flirty. "There's nothing I love better than talking about myself." He rolled onto his side and rested his head on his torpedo-shaped bicep. "So, it was a stormy night in the desert, wind whipping sand so hard it blasted my backside smooth."

"Didn't you have clothes on?"

"No. I like being naked. I'm sure you'd like it too."

"Oh, geez." Jack slapped his hand to his forehead. "I knew it was a mistake introducing you."

I laughed at Jack's reaction as much as Quint's mischievous smile. "Tell me more."

"No more." Jack was firm as he shook his head. "If you want to chat about things like that, do it on your own time. We're on the job."

"Looking for a monster that rips arms from teenagers," Quint noted.

"Yes."

"Well ... I can run the names. I'm not sure what you expect to find, Jack."

"I'm not either," Jack conceded. "Any information is good information at this point."

"Fine. I'll look, but your girlfriend has to crank up those Magic Fingers while I do. I could use a good massage and cuddle."

"She's not cuddling with you," Jack argued.

"Since when are you the boss of her?" Quint's eyes landed on me.

"Tell him."

"Sorry." I offered up a rueful smile and a shrug. "I only want to cuddle with Jack."

"You're breaking my heart, cutie pie." Quint clutched at his chest. "You wound me."

"We can share the Magic Fingers," I offered. "Jack can climb on, and we'll all enjoy the ride as you search."

"A threesome, huh?" Quint cocked his head and pretended to consider. "I guess I can deal with that."

"There will be no threesome," Jack growled. "There will be a twosome and a onesome."

"Which will you be partaking in?" Quint asked.

"Now I remember why you were such a pain to hang around with," Jack muttered as he slid onto the bed next to me. "Not every woman finds you irresistible."

"Whatever helps you sleep at night. Now, fire up this bed. I haven't seen an actual Magic Fingers coin slot in years. This is going to be fun."

One look at Jack told me that Quint was the only one who believed that.

"SO, I'VE BEEN OVER THIS FROM THREE different angles," Quint said an hour later as Jack fed more quarters into the Magic Fingers slot. "No death certificates have ever been issued for that address."

"Is it even an address?" I asked. "I mean ... right now it's just a hovel in the middle of the forest."

"I considered that, but I ran the names individually." Quint was all business now. Apparently the one thing he liked more than flirting and irritating Jack was a mystery. "Death certificates have never been issued for Colin Dempsey, Jessica Dempsey and Emmalynne Dempsey. I found one address for those names and tracked from there. Social Security numbers were issued for all three, but they haven't been used in more than forty years. More than fifty for good old Colin."

"He was a jerk so we're not mourning him," I said.

Quint's eyes flicked to me. I was sandwiched between him and Jack, although Jack was insisting we keep to our half of the bed while Quint spread out on the other half. "How do you know he was a jerk?"

The question caught me off guard. "I ... just have a feeling."

Quint didn't look convinced. "You see mummies, too, don't you?"

I pressed my back into Jack's chest, debating how to answer.

"She's special," Jack countered, pinning his friend with a pointed look. "Don't give her a hard time."

"Fair enough." Quint bobbed his head and went back to staring at his computer screen. "There's no death note in here for Colin and yet you said that was the part of the story everyone accepted."

"It was supposedly a farm accident," I volunteered.

"Well, there's no record of that."

"Records weren't great back then," Jack noted. "Could be an oversight."

"Could be," Quint echoed. "There's no record of the wife or daughter dying either."

"Maybe they moved from this area," I said. "Maybe wherever they moved didn't record their deaths correctly ... when they happened fifty years later because they were old." Something occurred to me. "Maybe Emmalynne isn't dead. She would likely be in her seventies now. She could still be out there."

Quint cocked an eyebrow. "Not using her Social Security number?"

"Maybe she got a new one."

"That's not as easy as it sounds." He switched his gaze to Jack. "She's cute but refuses to see the obvious."

"She has a heart of gold," Jack replied. "She doesn't want to think of others hurting."

"She's standing — er, laying — right here," I argued. "You don't have to talk about her as if she's not here."

"I'm sorry, baby." Jack pressed a kiss to the back of my neck. "Quint is telling you that they're dead."

"So ... what?" Frustration bubbled up and grabbed me by the

throat. "Are you telling me that Hank the cranky bootlegger killed them and buried them in the woods?"

"That's a likely scenario."

"Well, I don't like that."

"I'm sorry." Jack wrapped his arms around me and rested his chin on my shoulder. "Anything else on the family, Quint?"

"Just one thing." Quint shuffled a bit higher on the pillows. "There's a medical note in here — for the whole family — that seems to suggest they had a rough winter in 1972."

"Meaning what?" I prodded when he didn't continue.

"There's not much in here — maybe you can find a local historian who knows more. It says a farmhand died during a blizzard. They had no body to turn over to authorities when spring came because ... well ... they ate him."

My stomach seized and I thought I might throw up. "No way."

"Yes, way."

"Who was involved in that ... incident?" Jack asked.

"The farmhand's name was Alexander Jenkins. The only others listed staying on the property at that time were Hank, Jessica and Emmalynne. So, in theory, Alexander died and they had to deal with the body themselves."

"Ugh." I rolled away from Quint and buried my face in Jack's chest.

"Does that mean anything to you?" Quint asked pointedly.

"Why would it mean something to us?" Jack asked.

"Because you're paranormal hunters. I'm a mummy seer — and, yes, that's real. I read a lot ... and it sounds to me as if you have a wendigo."

All the oxygen rushed out of my lungs. "You know about wendigos?" I asked when I could speak again.

"I know about a lot of things." Quint's gaze was heavy when it locked with Jack's worried stare. "We have a few things to discuss, brother. You've been holding out on me."

Jack looked pained. "Not like you're thinking."

"Yeah, we definitely need to talk."

19

NINETEEN

I liked Quint, but not for the reasons Jack thought. Sure, he was funny and said whatever came to his mind without filtering it — we had that in common — but he was good with Jack. It was as if he knew exactly what to say and do to make my boyfriend laugh. Somehow, despite the back and forth, I fell asleep as they talked things out.

I woke when I felt a soft kiss on my cheek. "Time to wake up, Charlie."

Slowly, I opened my eyes and stretched. My first thought was to look to my right. The spot Quint had occupied was empty.

"He left," Jack said. "He's going to keep digging for us. He said to say goodbye, and if he doesn't see you again, the offer is open."

I wasn't one of those people who could immediately snap to attention when I woke up. It always took me a good ten minutes — and three cups of coffee — to get my brain working. "What offer?"

"He says he has a big house for you. Better than this hotel room. He thinks you would make a cute couple."

I opened my arms and drew Jack to me, sighing as he held me tight and buried his face in my hair. "Yes, but you wouldn't be at the house. That's why this hotel room wins out."

"Good answer." He kissed my neck and breathed me in. "I didn't want to wake you. You look so peaceful when you're sleeping."

"It's probably best you did. I won't be able to fall asleep tonight. How long was I out?"

"Three hours."

"Wow."

"Yeah. I thought it was a bit weird when Quint said you'd fallen asleep. I can't imagine how you managed it with us talking."

"It was the sound of you laughing. You were so happy. It lulled me. I don't ever get to hear that."

He pulled back far enough to eye me. "Are you kidding? You make me laugh all the time."

"I know. It's just ... you were different with him. It was nice to hear you enjoying yourself."

"Is this about you thinking I don't have friends?"

"I know you have friends, but you obviously adore him."

"I didn't realize how much I missed him until I saw him. I don't know if 'adore' is the right word. I adore you with every fiber of my being. He's a very good friend."

"I like him." I flicked my eyes to the window. Jack had drawn the drapes so they were mostly closed, only a smattering of light filtering into the room. "What time is it?"

"Thirty minutes before we have to meet the others for dinner. I went out long enough to see if the others got anything from their documents, then came back to watch you sleep."

"That's not creepy at all."

He pretended he didn't hear me. "The only reason I woke you is because I knew you wouldn't be happy if you missed dinner."

"Definitely not." I rubbed the sleep from my eyes. "Did you and Quint come to any conclusions?"

"He's all for the wendigo theory. Apparently, he's a big believer in the paranormal, something I feel I should've known. I thought he was just messing with me with the mummy thing."

"I still want to hear that mummy story."

He grinned. "I invited him to visit us in Boston. He's going to dig for us, Charlie. I'm not sure what else he has to offer."

I had one more question. "He's suspicious about me, isn't he?" After my minor slip, Quint hadn't come right out and accused me of anything. But he kept watching me, and I knew he was wondering.

"I think he knows you're special, and not just because I said you were. I shut him down when he asked, but he's no idiot."

I rubbed my hand over Jack's cheek, loving the light stubble. He shaved every morning unless we were spending a day in bed, and I had the feeling he could grow a full beard in a few days if he let himself. "If you want to tell him ... ." I didn't finish the offer.

"No." He pressed his lips to my palm. "Quint is smart. He's likely already figured out that you're different. He knows that I love you. He won't push the issue, and I would never volunteer your secret."

"I know." I grinned at him. "I have a way bigger mouth than you do."

"I happen to love your big mouth." He tapped his lips. "Right here."

I leaned in and kissed him, groaning when I pulled back. I would've been happy doing nothing but screwing around with him in bed the rest of the night, but we had a job to do. The sooner we completed it, the sooner we could go home and focus on Sybil.

"I should probably get up and get ready."

"Five more minutes." He was back to holding me tight. "I saw they have ribs on the menu tonight in the dining room. I'm not sure they'll be good, but I know how much you love ribs."

"There's a lot of foods I like. I'm actually pretty easygoing in that department. You don't have to worry about feeding me constantly. I can make do with almost anything. Heck, I have in the past."

"That's why I like spoiling you with food. You're not so jaded that you can't find joy in little things ... like the time you added sprinkles to your hot fudge sundae. That was a big deal for you, and now I always want to add things to your hot fudge sundaes."

"If you recall, I was bouncing off the walls thanks to all the sugar," I reminded him. "You didn't think that was so funny."

"On the contrary. They have hot fudge sundaes tonight at their ice cream bar. I look forward to you bouncing off the walls again later ... when I'm wearing you out because of the nap."

"I see how your mind works."

"Good, because I thought I was being fairly obvious about it."

I PULLED MY HAIR BACK IN A LOOSE BUN and splashed some water to wake myself. Jack and I were the last to arrive at the dinner table.

"How was your day?" Jack asked Chris. I could tell by the way his eyes bounced around the table that he was taking a head count. "Nobody got into any trouble I hope."

"It was a quiet day," Chris replied. He seemed dejected, as if life had kicked him in the teeth and he was still recovering. "Nothing happened. Nothing at all."

I raised my eyebrows as I sat across from him. "I guess I don't have to ask your opinion on nothing happening."

"It sucked." Chris slouched in his chair. He could never play poker because of his terrible body language. "The cameras didn't record anything. There might've been a few shadows on the one, but no matter how we worked to clean up the image, it didn't come together."

"He's a little upset," Hannah offered as she patted his hand. "We did hear those weird screams again. Two of them. I think they belong to an animal, but Chris swears it's a sasquatch."

"I didn't say it was a sasquatch," Chris countered. "I said it could be a sasquatch. There's a difference." It was rare for him to snap at Hannah — he was completely besotted with her — but his temper made a fiery entrance this evening. "Don't talk down to me."

Hannah's eyebrows migrated up her forehead and she stared at him a long time before turning to me. "Did you guys find anything?"

"We might have," Jack replied. He seemed uncomfortable to bear witness to the bickering but he was a professional, so he pushed through. "We managed to track that cabin we found yesterday. The owner's name was Colin Dempsey. He lived there with his wife Jessica and daughter Emmalynne until his death about fifty years ago. In the wake of his death, his brother Henry — now known as Hank the bootlegger — took over the property and lived there with Jessica and Emmalynne."

Chris didn't perk up at the news. "So? Why do we care about the bootlegger? He obviously doesn't have the strength to rip off a teenager's arm."

"I'm not done." Jack shot Chris a quelling look. "You're going to like what I have to tell you by the time I get to the end of the story."

Chris perked up. "Really?"

"Yes. Just ... give me a second." Jack sipped his water and then continued. "Emmalynne and Jessica are missing. Their Social Security numbers haven't been used in forty years. The woman at the bar, Jane, told us that there are two theories about what happened to them. One involves Hank killing them and burying them in the woods. The other involves them taking off and leaving because Hank was a jerk."

"If they left, they would've used their Social Security numbers," Hannah noted.

"True." Jack nodded. "Jane didn't have access to the same information we did. She couldn't know about the Social Security numbers."

"So they're dead," Chris supplied. "That's very sad, but I don't see how that plays into what we're dealing with now."

"Again, I'm not done," Jack stressed. "I contacted an old military buddy of mine. He's a private detective with an office about an hour from here. He helped us run some searches because he has access to local databases we don't."

"Okay." Chris steepled his fingers and waited. He clearly didn't believe Jack was going to deliver on his promise to bestow exciting news.

"One of the stories he managed to uncover was from an old police log," Jack explained. "It involved a terrible winter at the cabin. This was before Jessica and Emmalynne disappeared. They were snowed in for three months with Hank ... and a lone farmhand named Alexander Jenkins."

"You tell a story like Myron's mother," Millie lamented. "Stop dragging things out."

Jack ignored her. "It seems poor Alexander didn't survive the winter. Whether that was by design or accident, the report doesn't say. What it does say is that he died ... but there was no body because the others were forced to consume it."

Casey froze, a buttered roll halfway to his mouth. "Well, I didn't see that coming." He lowered the roll. "Do we really have to have this discussion right before dinner?"

"Sorry." I shot him a rueful smile. "We thought Chris might want to know what we were likely dealing with."

"How does that explain what we're dealing with?" Hannah asked blankly. "Also, cannibalism has been practiced more than you might expect. While it seems ghastly to us, you never know what you would do under certain circumstances to survive."

I couldn't dwell on what she said too long because I knew it would give me nightmares.

"I'm betting Chris has an idea about what I'm getting at," Jack said.

Chris's eyes were so bright they threatened to illuminate the entire room. "Wendigo!"

I grinned at his excitement. It was better than thinking about cannibalism, especially right before I was about to eat spareribs.

"Yup." Jack nodded. "Charlie explained about wendigos this afternoon. I find the stories interesting, but I don't know that a wendigo fits what we're dealing with. We have four bodies. They weren't consumed."

"But we're missing another four." Chris rubbed his hands together excitedly, his earlier petulance forgotten. "A wendigo makes sense."

Jack slid his eyes to me when Chris started babbling to the others. We'd already done our homework on the creature. Now it was his turn to fill in the others.

"Here we go," he said in a low voice. "He'll be insufferable."

"I like when he's excited." I meant it. "Besides, a wendigo makes way more sense than Bigfoot."

"I don't know that we're on the right track," Jack said, "but it seems our footing is better than it was. At least we have something to chase now."

THE WENDIGO WHOOP-DE-DOO

Something to chase was good, but what would we find when the chase was done?

I STOPPED AT THE VENDING MACHINES to study the offerings when Jack was in the bathroom after dinner. Chris was excited to go back to his room and make plans for the following day. That left the rest of us at loose ends for the evening. The town wasn't exactly happening, so I knew Jack and I would return to our room to enjoy the Magic Fingers and bad television. Snacks always helped when there was bad television.

I made my selections and rounded the corner to the lobby.

Jack stood about fifteen feet from the front desk, talking with Mike. Their intensity made my stomach feel as if it was going to drop through my feet. I was convinced things were getting better between them, but here they were arguing behind my back.

I crept a little closer to hear what they were saying without risking them noticing me.

"I know you don't like me," Mike hedged. "I haven't given you a reason to."

"I don't dislike you," Jack countered. "I don't know you well enough to dislike you. I just ... don't need you constantly giving me grief about loving Charlie. It's frustrating, and it makes her unhappy."

"And you don't want her unhappy."

"Of course not." Jack shook his head. "I love her, Mike. I know that's hard to swallow because you missed watching her grow up, but I'm completely in love with her. I always want her happy."

"I know." Mike dragged his hand through his hair. "I get it. I'm cramping your style. She doesn't want a family."

"No, that's not it." Jack fervently shook his head. "She wants you guys so much she can't see straight. But it's hard for her. She can't help falling back on those feelings of abandonment she harbored as a kid. She always wondered why she wasn't good enough to keep."

Mike balked. "That's not why ... ."

"And intellectually, she gets it." Jack was firm. "Childhood emotions are a funny thing. She's working on putting that behind her. You have to give her time. Trust is earned ... especially for someone like Charlie."

"I know you're right." Mike's frustration didn't ebb. "It's hard to love her from afar. It doesn't feel fair."

"Life isn't fair. That's not the only thing wearing on Charlie, though."

"You mean this thing between me and you. It hurts her when we fight."

"It does, but she's stronger than you give her credit for. I was referring to the Rhodes. Charlie loved them beyond reason. She feels guilty for wanting you guys because there's a small part of her that believes she's being disloyal to them."

"But ... everything I've heard about the Rhodes suggests that they would've wanted her to find us," Mike argued.

"They would have. I firmly believe that. Charlie's emotions are a tangled web. She's sorting through them. She needs your patience."

"Which includes me not giving you a hard time," Mike muttered.

"You can give me a hard time." Jack was earnest. "I can take it. But I'm not leaving her. Not for anything. I'm going to love her forever. Fighting with me only hurts her because it doesn't bother me."

"I see it when she looks at you," Mike said. "She loves you with her whole heart."

"She does." Jack smiled. "I love her with my whole heart. We need to work together to keep her safe. You have to meet me halfway."

"I will." Mike nodded, as if convincing himself. "What Millie said today made sense. You're exactly the sort of man I want my daughter to fall in love with. I just wish you weren't going to be around to take her away from me for another five years or so."

Jack chuckled. "I won't take her away from you, mostly because what's best for her is all of us finding a way to coexist. You have to be open to accepting me, just like I'm open to accepting you."

"Because it's best for Charlie."

"I'll always do what's best for Charlie."

Mike nodded again. "That's all I want." Suddenly, he jutted out his hand for Jack. "I love her too. We'll figure this out. All of us."

"Good." Jack shook his hand. "Now, if you'll excuse me, I have to collect my girlfriend. She's already buzzed on hot fudge and sprinkles, and I set her free with a pile of money in front of the vending machine. She'll have her arms filled with candy bars by the time I get there."

This time when Mike laughed, it was genuine. "You guys are a good fit."

"We are. I didn't think so when I first met her. I was attracted to her, of course, but I was afraid our personalities wouldn't mesh. I was never happier to be so wrong."

I slunk back to the vending machine alcove with a smile on my face. Jack and I definitely belonged together. We were working toward a common goal. Now we just had to see it through to the end to get everything we wanted.

That was easier said than done, but it was going to happen. I had faith that we would win the ultimate battle.

Somehow.

20

TWENTY

I didn't initially admit to eavesdropping when walking back to the room with Jack. I was quiet, though, and he questioned me as soon as we were inside.

"Did something happen?"

I nodded as I dropped my snack haul on the ancient dresser.

"Tell me." He looked concerned.

"I fell in love with you even more than before, which I didn't think was possible." I beamed at him as I turned. "I heard you talking to Mike."

"Oh." His lips curved. "Well, I didn't say anything I wouldn't have said in front of you."

"No, but you said all the right things." I leaned back against the dresser and folded my arms across my chest as he kicked off his shoes and avoided eye contact. "When I first met you, I thought you might be emotionally repressed," I admitted. "You were ... standoffish. I'm charming, so I never understand when people don't like me."

That elicited a chuckle. "I didn't dislike you, Charlie. I was just ... feeling things out."

"You didn't want to like me."

"Definitely not. I knew after spending thirty minutes with you that it was a lost cause, though. For some reason — and I cannot explain this, so don't ask me to — I had this feeling when I saw you," he explained as he sat on the end of the bed. "It was as if I could suddenly breathe, like I had been suffocating before you came along and you started filling me with the things I never knew I needed."

"That could be the sweetest thing you've ever said to me."

He grinned as he reached around to the collar of his shirt and tugged it off. "I still fought it. I couldn't help myself. You stirred up all these feelings in me and I was afraid."

I wanted to go to him, run my hands over all that soft skin and firm muscles. I remained where I was, however. "What were you afraid of?"

"That you would change my life." He tossed his shirt on the floor. "I didn't know at the time that I wanted my life to be changed. It felt ... alien. I decided it was best to keep you at arm's length and yet I couldn't follow through on that. My head kept saying, 'She's trouble,' but my heart kept saying, 'You'll regret it if you don't open yourself to her.'"

"Obviously your heart won."

He opened his arms and I stepped between his legs, smiling as he pressed his ear against my heart and wrapped his arms around my waist. "I've come to the conclusion that your heart will always beat your brain and that it's best to embrace it. Otherwise, you end up torturing yourself."

That brought up an interesting question. "Does your brain still tell you I'm trouble?"

He smiled but didn't look up to meet my eyes. "My brain thinks you're smart ... and funny ... and recognizes I can't be without you. It's ceded control to my heart."

"Are you okay with that?"

"I'm okay when I'm with you. That's all that matters." He finally looked up, grinning as I ran my hands through his hair. "I love you, Charlie. I didn't think I could ever feel this way about anyone, but I can't imagine not feeling it now."

"I love you too."

"We're going to figure this Sybil thing out."

"We are."

"Then we're going to start planning for a big future."

"Oh, yeah?" He was feeling playful now. I saw the twinkle in his eyes. "What's that future going to entail?"

"I don't know." He pulled me onto the bed and then started tugging at my shirt. Once it was off, he held me tight against him, relishing the way our skin felt when pressed together. "We have decisions to make."

"What sort of decisions?"

"Well, are you going to want to stay with the Legacy Foundation?"

"Why wouldn't I?"

"It's a lot of travel." He hesitated and then pushed forward. "You're happy when you have a place to call your own. The condo is great, but one day I picture us with a house. You can go all out decorating while I mow the yard and grill on the back patio."

"Don't you want to stay with the Legacy Foundation?" He'd said things before that made me think that wasn't his long-range goal.

"I can work anywhere. My skills will always be in demand. I want you to pick what you want and then we'll go from there."

"And what if I want to stay with the Legacy Foundation?"

"Then we'll stay."

"What if I want to move to another state?"

"Then we'll go." His grin was charming.

"What if you end up resenting me for making all the choices?"

"Baby, that won't happen." He brushed my hair from my eyes. "I can live anywhere. Believe it or not, I can make friends anywhere. I'm a fun guy when an ancient witch isn't trying to kill my girlfriend."

"You're a totally fun guy," I agreed, cocking my head as I considered what he was offering. "I think it's too soon to start talking about any of this," I said. "I'm still happy with the Legacy Foundation. Sybil is definitely a threat. We need to figure out how to handle her before we can look too far into the future."

"I don't disagree." His fingers brushed my cheek. "I don't want you to give up dreaming. If you want to start thinking about the future,

I'm all for that. The thing is, when I do look at our future, the details are vague except for one thing."

I waited.

"I see us with children once we make sure Sybil won't be a threat to them. I'm not sure constant travel with children is conceivable."

I understood what he was saying. "Just for the record, I can't see myself with more than two children. Even one might be best because I'll still want to spend a lot of time with you."

"I'm fine with that. I don't think having a gaggle of children is for us. One is fine. Two is fine. I don't care about those details."

"Okay." I rested my face in the hollow of his neck and breathed deeply. "Now we just have to defeat Sybil. Then we can start dreaming about the future."

"I'm going to dream regardless." He rolled me on top of him and pulled the covers over us. "I'm going to be practical, too. Sybil has to be our primary concern. We need to start making plans for her ... and I think those plans need to involve your crossroads demon friend."

I couldn't contain my surprise as I lifted my head. Harlequin Desdemona Stryker — better call her Harley if you don't want to feel her wrath — had become something of a frequent visitor in our lives. I liked her more than Jack, who found her sassy mouth and constant put-downs annoying. If he wanted to include her, he was really worried. "I'm sure she'll pop up when she has more information."

"I'm sure she will."

"You hate her."

"I don't hate her. I often wish I had a muzzle for her, but I don't hate her." He was serious as he held my gaze. "She can protect you in ways that I can't. I want to keep her close."

"I'm sure she'll love to hear that next time she stops by for a visit."

"I'm not telling her. Her head is already big enough. She'll help regardless because that's who she is."

It was the first time I'd ever heard him be complimentary to Harley. It made me smile. "Well, how about we deal with the wendigo first? Then we'll start brainstorming on Harley when we get back."

"Sounds like a plan." He gave me a soft kiss. "We can't do anything about the wendigo tonight. Chris is researching like a madman even as we speak. We can't help him, but we can help each other."

"Oh, yeah?" He was clearly done with serious discussions for the evening. Playful Jack was my favorite Jack. "What did you have in mind?"

"I think I better show you." He leaned over and popped quarters into the Magic Fingers before moving his hands to my back. "I'm not good at describing things. I'm a shower, not a teller."

I DIDN'T INITIALLY DREAM. WHEN THE DARKNESS of my mind finally gave way to light, however, I was back in Nighthawk. It was the past again — at least what my mind conjured to represent the past — and I blew out a sigh when I saw the people on the street.

"Not again." I wasn't in the mood for some deep dream. I'd been so happy when I curled up at Jack's side. Now, knowing that I would have to learn something new instead of getting the rest I really needed, I was annoyed. "What this time?"

"Oh, that doesn't sound like happiness to see me," a voice drawled from behind me. I didn't have to turn to know who it was.

"Can't you just give me one night without your irritating presence?" I complained.

"Obviously not. This is your head, after all. I'm just along for the ride."

When I turned, I found Sybil sitting on a wooden chair, her feet propped on a split-rail fence. The building behind her appeared to be a post office. "Are you a mailwoman or something?"

Her smile didn't diminish. "Or something." After a beat, she swung her legs to the ground and stood. "Let's take a walk."

I was in no mood to hang around with her. "If you have something to tell me, just spit it out. I don't want to be here."

"You're going to find, *Charlotte*, that you don't always get what you want in life."

I hated being called Charlotte, something she probably knew. If she was even real. I hadn't concluded that she wasn't simply a figment of my overactive imagination. "Thanks for the empty platitude. Can I go now?"

"No." She gestured for me to follow as she crossed the street. She was heading in the direction of the cabin, something I inherently knew, and I spent ten seconds debating what would happen if I didn't follow her.

Ultimately, I gave in. If I wanted restful sleep, I needed to see this through. Whether it was really her or just me trying to rationalize things, I wouldn't be able to rest until I saw.

"I don't know why I'm following you," I groused, shaking my head as I moved behind the brothel with her. "I mean ... you're evil. Nobody should ever willingly follow evil. Jack would not like this."

"Jack is a simpleton."

I slowed my pace. "If you keep insulting him, I won't follow." I was serious. There was no way my imagination was conjuring insults against Jack after our romantic night together. I had only happy thoughts where he was concerned. "I don't have to put up with your crap. This is my head."

"And yet you haven't learned to keep me out yet when you're sleeping," Sybil said with a smile. "That seems like something you should work on. As for me being evil, that's all in the way you look at things."

"Don't you suck people dry to extend your own life?"

"Not necessarily." Her smile never diminished. "Evil is a state of mind. No one person is completely evil. It's simplistic for you to believe so."

"Oh, so now I'm the simpleton." I scuffed my bare feet against the gravel, noticing for the first time that it didn't hurt. There was no pain — real or otherwise — in my dreamscape. I filed that tidbit away to think about another time. "Are you saying you're not evil?"

"I'm saying that I have a specific way of looking at things, as do you. Just because we look at things differently doesn't make me evil or you good."

"Yeah, I'm going to stick with my earlier assessment. You're evil."

She chuckled, unbothered. "You're funny when you want to be."

"Yes, I should be on the comedy circuit," I said, my forehead creasing as we cut through the woods. It took us a few minutes to reach the cabin. It looked in far better shape than it had when we visited the location in the present day.

"Have you researched wendigos as I instructed?" she asked.

"I already knew about wendigos. I didn't need to research." I didn't mention the impromptu research session I'd had after the dream. That was just a refresher course, I told myself. I wasn't doing anything to please her.

"What did you find?" she asked.

"We're researching the family," I replied. There was no reason I shouldn't catch her up. Maybe she could help, even if her only reason for trying to keep me alive was so she could kill me later. "Colin and Jessica Dempsey lived here. Then Colin died in some sort of farming accident and his brother moved in. He took over the farm and apparently performed his brother's husbandly duties."

"You sound as if you disapprove."

"Both men were evil." I knew she wouldn't like my use of the word, but I didn't care. "They tried to control the women, make them do things they didn't want to do. It's entirely possible Hank killed Jessica and Emmalynne."

"Emmalynne is the daughter?"

I nodded. "Her father wanted an arranged marriage. Supposedly she refused, and that caused a lessening of his stature. Emmalynne was considered an old maid at twenty-two. I didn't even know how to fill out rental forms when I was twenty-two."

"And now you know why I've never had a use for men," Sybil offered. "Even though times have changed, and women can elevate themselves in stature, we're still not equal."

"Jack treats me as equal."

Sybil opened her mouth to say something, but I shook my head before she could. "Let's not go to a bad place when we're having such a nice conversation."

She nodded. "Fine. We won't talk about your beloved Jack. That's not important right now anyway." She gestured toward the cabin. "What do you see?"

"My worst nightmare. There's no internet or Starbucks."

"I see a cage," Sybil volunteered. "The men who lived here tried to keep the women locked up. They were essentially slaves who didn't get to make choices for themselves. You know about the bad winter here?"

I nodded. "They ate a farmhand."

"They did ... and that's what set this whole thing in motion."

Now we were finally getting somewhere. "Cannibalism can create wendigos, right?"

"Yes."

"So ... is Jessica or Emmalynne the wendigo?"

She hesitated and then held out her hands. "I can't answer that. There are too many variables. You have to answer that yourself. It's important to keep in mind that multiple people have gone missing from this location. You're fixated on the women, but the men are equally important."

"It's weird hearing you say that. I was under the impression you thought men were somehow lower beings."

"I do believe that, but it's not important for what you're facing." She was serious when she raised her eyes to mine. "There's a taint on this land. It's not a curse, not like what you picture, but sometimes things so horrible they defy human comprehension mark a location."

"Is that what happened here?" I asked. "Did Hank do something to those women that forced this situation?"

"You're still looking at this through rose-colored glasses," Sybil insisted. "People are not all evil or all good. You're painting Emmalynne and Jessica as victims."

"They were."

"But Hank came in and saved them from losing their home."

"Hank is a drunk who hangs out in the woods and warns people away from the darkness," I pointed out. "I hardly think he's a hero."

"Yet if he warned those kids and they'd listened, where would they be now?"

The question made me uncomfortable, and I averted my gaze. "What is it you're trying to show me?"

"That your preconceptions aren't always right." Her tone was firm as she moved to stand in front of me, giving me no choice but to stare into the fathomless depths of her eyes. She was right. They weren't filled with evil. There was no compassion or understanding there either. "Not all families are born good or evil. It's not always one bad apple that ruins things. Stop being so naive when you look at the world."

"Or you could just tell me what you want me to know," I countered. "Why did you bring me to this place? What do you want me to know?"

"Not everything is as it seems, Charlotte. The things you think you know, you don't necessarily know. You believe things are one way but that doesn't make the belief true. You need to open yourself to other possibilities."

"You want me to open myself to you because that will make it easier for you to carry out what you have planned."

"I mean you have to get over yourself. If you can't open your mind, then the doors to the future will always remain closed to you."

She was going in circles at this point. "I don't know what you want me to do."

"Keep digging," she said. "You're close, yet you're still far away. You have to open yourself if you want to see."

"What if I don't?"

"Then your life will become a self-fulfilling prophecy." Her smile turned feral. "Trust me, that's the one thing you don't want."

TWENTY-ONE

Jack was barely awake the next morning when I told him about the dream. He listened while rubbing the sleep from his eyes and frowned when I got to the part about Sybil telling me I needed to better understand the nature of evil if I wanted to get to the bottom of this.

"I need to know if we're dealing with the real thing or your imagination," he said as we climbed into the shower. There was nothing playful about his demeanor this morning. He was deadly serious. "If this is just your mind working things out, then we can break it down. If it's Sybil, then we need to figure out a way to keep her out of your head."

I'd been thinking the same thing. "I might try calling Harley to see what she thinks."

Jack nodded. "Bring her out here. I'd rather have her close if Sybil really is going to make a move when we're distracted with a wendigo."

"She can't just drop everything and come to me," I argued. "I mean ... she has a job too."

"She's dropped everything for you before." Jack insisted. "Call her. I don't care if we have to share our room with her. Just ... see what she says."

I didn't miss the momentary lick of panic as it crossed his features. He shuttered it quickly, but it was obvious that he was worried.

"I'll call her," I promised. "Maybe she can get here this afternoon for a conversation."

"I'll buy her ten meals at Jackal Jane's if she figures out a way to keep Sybil out of your head. I don't think it can possibly be safe for an evil witch to invade your dreams."

"We don't know she's really doing that," I pointed out. "It could be my imagination."

"I want to be sure."

"Then I'll call her." Honestly, there was no harm in placing the call. "You need to settle down. Chris will be gung-ho with plans this morning now that he's had a night to sleep on the new information. The wendigo has to be our priority."

"You're my priority," he countered. "The rest of it, well, it pales. Call Harley. We'll figure out the rest of it as we go."

I did as he instructed. Harley didn't pick up, so I left a voicemail. After that, there was only one thing to do.

"I'm starving. Are you ready for breakfast?"

Despite his earlier intensity, Jack cracked a grin. "I love that I can always count on the fact that you'll drop whatever you're doing to eat. There's comfort in the consistency."

"Right?" I grinned at him and sidled close. "I want pancakes. If we're going to fight a wendigo, I need carbs."

A NEW FACE WAS SITTING at our table when we made our way into the dining room. Jack's hand landed on the small of my back when I stilled. He prodded me forward.

"That's Chad Pace," he said to my unasked question. "He's the local police officer assigned to us. Chris texted and said he would be joining us."

It was rare for us not to interact more with local law enforcement on a case. I'd almost forgotten we had someone at our disposal. "Is he a detective?"

Jack shook his head. "The department here is too small for a designated detective. I'm not sure what Chris hopes to get from this guy, but I guess we'll find out."

I plastered a smile on my face as we approached, moving to the far side of the table to sit. Jack took his spot next to me after shaking hands with Chad. The rest of the group were already engaged in conversation with Chad, and I tried to catch up.

"I pulled the files on the Dempsey house after your call last night," Chad said. He was young, likely in his thirties, and had a friendly smile. There was a wariness to his eyes that set my teeth on edge, however, and I didn't immediately jump on the trust bandwagon. "That was a long time ago."

"Almost fifty years," Chris confirmed.

"My father was assigned the case," Chad said. "He would've been fresh out of the academy and working for my grandfather, who was the chief at that time." It almost sounded like an apology.

"We're talking about the disappearances of Jessica and Emmalynne?" I asked.

Chad sent me a small smile as he nodded. "We are, ma'am."

It was the first time I'd ever been referred to as "ma'am." I wasn't sure I liked it. "I don't think I'm old enough to be a ma'am," I whispered to Jack, who grinned as he rubbed my back.

"Hank didn't report them missing," Chad continued. "In fact, nobody ever reported them missing. One of the locals mentioned to my grandfather that she hadn't seen Jessica in town in more than two months. He assigned my father to go out and check."

"There must be a report on the visit," Jack noted as he smiled at the incoming waitress. She delivered glasses of water and menus. "Thank you."

"There was a report," Chad confirmed once the waitress left again. "Unfortunately, my father passed away from a heart attack two years ago. Truth be told, it's a barebones report. I don't want to make excuses, but it was likely the first one my father ever filled out himself."

"We're not here to cast aspersions on your father," Chris reassured him. "We're trying to unravel a mystery."

"I honestly don't know what fifty-year-old disappearances could have to do with the situation we have now." Chad glanced between faces. "I'm not trying to be difficult; I simply don't understand."

I was mildly curious how Chris would respond. When he did, I was caught between amusement and stunned disbelief.

"We believe that there's some sort of cryptid in the woods," Chris explained, opting for the truth. "Something hunted those kids and killed them. To my knowledge, there's no native animal in this area that could do what was done."

Chad hesitated and then bobbed his head. "I've talked to a bunch of experts in the area. They say a bear couldn't have caused those injuries. A bear will kill, but ripping an arm off that way ... well, there was no other damage to the body."

"What do you think happened to those kids?" I asked.

"I don't know, ma'am. I've done nothing but think about it since the bodies were found." He scratched his cheek and sighed. "Something terrible happened out there. I've tried to wrap my head around a human doing this — it would be easier this way — but I don't know how any one human could've controlled all of them."

He had an orderly mind like Jack. He'd likely been making himself sick trying to figure this out. So far, he'd had no luck, so he should be willing to think outside the box.

"We have a few ideas," Chris offered. He was all business. "Initially, the individual who called our office — I believe that was your chief, Jeremy Winstead — said he thought it was possible that we had some sort of creature, like a sasquatch."

Chad belted out a laugh but sobered quickly. "Yeah, the chief might've mentioned that to a few people. He swears up and down he saw Bigfoot when he was a kid. He's been telling that story for forty years. He was my father's former partner, took over after my father died, so I've been hearing that story my entire life."

"I take it that means you don't believe the story," I prodded.

THE WENDIGO WHOOP-DE-DOO

He worked his jaw, his eyes darting between Chris and me. He was clearly uncomfortable being put on the spot. "Um ... ."

"If you don't believe, it's okay," Jack offered. "I don't believe in Bigfoot either."

Chad looked so relieved I almost felt sorry for him. "It's just ... I've always needed to see something to believe it."

"What about God?" Laura asked, taking me by surprise. She'd been so quiet this trip I almost forgot she was still a member of the team.

"What about him?" Chad asked blankly.

"Do you believe in him?"

"Oh, well ... of course." Chad bobbed his head. "That's different. God is a matter of faith."

"So is Bigfoot for some people," Laura responded. "Chris believes." Her eyes landed on me and I squirmed when I saw the haunted dullness there. "Charlie does. It's okay if you don't believe as long as you're open to possibilities."

Chad studied her for an extended moment and then nodded. "I understand. Bigfoot wouldn't be my first choice as a culprit, though. Half the people in town would believe it was Bigfoot and want to know more. The other half would laugh me out of town."

"We don't believe it's Bigfoot," Chris said.

Chad let loose a relieved sigh. "That's good."

"We believe it might be a wendigo."

Next to me, Jack slapped his hand to his forehead. It took everything I had not to laugh at his expression.

"A wendigo?" Chad's forehead creased.

I opened my mouth to nutshell it for him, but he was talking again before I could.

"You mean that monster-cannibal thing?" he asked.

I was taken aback. "You know what a wendigo is?" I couldn't help being impressed.

"Of course I do." Chad bobbed his head. "This place is thick with legends. We've had legends about wendigo for as long as I can remember. My dad used to tell me stories when I was thirteen or so. At the time, I thought he was trying to scare me from going too deep into the woods. As I got older, I heard even more stories."

"What sort of stories?" Jack asked. He was leaned back in his seat, his fingers light as they traced circles on my back. He may have looked relaxed, but I knew better.

"There're all kinds. Most of them surround Nighthawk." Chad leaned back in the chair when the waitress brought his coffee. Then he waited for everybody to order breakfast before continuing. "It's not just the indigenous folk who believe in the wendigo. Stories have been rampant for years, and nobody who knows the area ever risks being out there after dark."

"I did a little research and know that some hikers have gone missing over the years," Jack said. "Do you believe they were victims of a wendigo?"

"I guess I can believe almost anything. That's a big area and nobody truly knows their way around it. I've lived here my whole life and I'm terrified to be caught out there after dark."

"The report we read on the plane suggested that people camp in that area all the time," Chris noted. "If everybody is afraid of a wendigo, why would they camp there?"

"No locals camp there," Chad clarified. "Anybody familiar with this area would never risk it. Nighthawk is only visited during daylight hours. And if you want to know the truth, the locals don't go there at all these days unless they have no choice. People are afraid of that land. The people who like to hike out there are almost always outsiders."

"Have any of the missing hikers ever been found?" Jack asked.

"Not to my knowledge. We send out search teams of course, but that's a lot of land. If you get lost out there, it's almost impossible to find your way back. Even if you're local and know the area relatively well, you won't risk it."

Jack slid his gaze to me. "I guess that's something to ponder."

"I'd like to go out there with you today," Chad said. "I haven't been out there in years. I went a few times as a teenager. The screams in the woods were enough to turn me off from ever going again."

From her spot three chairs away, Laura looked up. "Screams?"

"We've heard them too," I offered. "They're loud. They're what drew me into the woods that first day to find the campsite."

"Something we're not doing again," Jack said sternly.

I pretended I didn't hear. "They sound kind of human ... and yet kind of not. They could be animals, but I've never heard an animal make a sound like that."

"People have been hearing those screams for decades," Chad said. "That's part of the reason the wendigo legend grew. I want to go with you — as long as you don't mind an extra body."

"That's fine," Chris said. "Laura, are you staying behind again?"

"Um ... yeah." Her face was whiter than I'd ever seen it, and if I didn't know better, I would say that Laura had seen a ghost. I worried she was about to pass out. "He can have my spot in the four-by-four. I'll stay here and continue researching."

"Fair enough." Chris managed a smile, but when his gaze roamed Laura's face, worry momentarily invaded. He blanked it relatively fast. "We'll eat breakfast, hit the bathrooms, and then get going."

"Thanks for including me." Chad was sincere. "I really want to help you folks find answers. Otherwise, we're going to have eight families who spend the rest of their lives mourning without answers ... and nobody wants that."

"Definitely not," Chris agreed. "We're here to find answers — and we're not leaving until we do."

LAURA WAS STILL LOITERING IN THE lobby when I exited the bathroom after breakfast. To my surprise, she headed straight for me.

"Have you really heard screams in the woods?"

I wasn't expecting the question from her. "Yeah. They're weird. In some ways, they almost sound like birds."

"Do the scream for me."

My eyebrows slid up my forehead. "Excuse me?"

"I need to hear the screams." She was insistent.

I glanced around to see if we were alone — I had no idea if I was really entertaining the notion of screaming for her — and then shook my head when I saw two couples at the front desk. "I can't really do that."

"You could." Laura's tone turned accusatory. "You just don't want to because I'm asking."

"That's not true," I protested. "I can't scream in the middle of the lobby." I studied her for a moment. "What's this about?" I wanted to help her. She was so lost. This was the first time I'd seen her show any sort of reaction since we'd left Boston and I wanted to encourage it.

"I've been having these dreams," she muttered, refusing to make eye contact.

"Dreams?" I thought back to my own dreams, Sybil's reoccurring presence. "What sort of dreams?"

"All kinds. I hear screaming. It never sounds human. I thought ... ."

"You thought you might've been dreaming about the wendigo," I finished.

"Which is ridiculous," she groused as she shook her head. "How could I be dreaming about that? It makes no sense. That stupid woman in the dream keeps telling me I have to be careful. She says I need to stay away from Nighthawk. I wish she would just shut up."

My heart skipped. "You've been dreaming about a woman?"

"Yeah. Ever since the asylum. The same woman. She shows up in every dream."

I swallowed hard and forced myself to remain calm. "Does she have a name?"

"I never asked." This time when Laura glared at me, there was a familiar edge to it. She reminded me of the woman I met when I'd first joined the team, the woman who wished Bigfoot would eat me so Jack wasn't so distracted and could focus on her. "Why would I ask her name?"

"I was just curious." Should I tell her I'd been dreaming about Sybil too? That seemed somehow dangerous. I would be exposing myself to Laura's busybody nature. "Well, next time you dream about her, maybe you should ask her."

"What good would that do?"

I held out my hands. "Maybe knowing will be enough to snap you out of the dreams."

"Oh, so now you're a dream expert too?" Laura rolled her eyes. "I'm sorry I even started this conversation." She turned to leave, but I stopped her with a hand on her arm.

"Laura, I know that you're going through something." I chose my words carefully. "Ever since the asylum, you've been having issues."

"I don't want to talk about the asylum," she gritted out.

"Maybe you need to. I know you were locked in there with the ghosts for hours."

"I said I don't want to talk about the asylum!" She practically bellowed it the second time and I felt multiple sets of eyes snap in our direction. If she wanted to make a scene, she'd just gotten her wish.

"Fine. I'm sorry this happened to you." I was resigned. "I think talking to someone might help."

"And I think you minding your own business would help," Laura growled as she spun on her heel. Jack was in her way as she tried to leave. She gave his shoulder a shove. "Keep your girlfriend away from me," she ordered as she passed him. "I don't need her help."

Jack's eyes were on me instead of Laura. "I'll tell her," he said. "Have a nice day, Laura."

"Oh, shut up." Laura was almost to the elevator. "This whole trip is ridiculous. I can't wait to get back home."

Oddly enough, we had that in common. I was ready to go home too, even if it meant facing off with Sybil. But we still had to finish this. We owed it to the kids still missing in the woods.

TWENTY-TWO

Millie didn't care that we had a police officer with us for the ride to Nighthawk. She immediately hopped into the driver's seat of the four-by-four and affixed her goggles.

"Let's get to it," she announced.

Jack glared at her and then pointed Chad toward Chris's vehicle. "You'll want to ride with him."

Chad's brow furrowed in confusion. "Assigned seats?"

Jack shook his head. "Nope. You just don't want to ride with Millie, especially less than an hour after finishing breakfast. She's a menace."

Rather than question Jack further, Chad shot Millie a gently amused look. "She reminds me of my grandmother."

"Is your grandmother nuts too?"

Chad chuckled. "She prefers the word 'eccentric.'"

"Well, Millie is definitely eccentric." Jack directed Bernard toward the passenger seat. "She's your problem today. If she tips us over, I'm going to blame you."

Bernard looked resigned. He had endless love for Millie, but watching her was a full-time job. "I've got it."

Jack and I climbed into the backseat and fastened our seatbelts.

THE WENDIGO WHOOP-DE-DOO

Millie waited until she heard the click before roaring out of the invisible gate she clearly saw in her head. The others were still getting situated in their places when we left them in the dust.

"This is the life," Millie enthused. "I'm getting one of these things for back home."

"Awesome," Bernard droned.

The ride was made in silence. I had to grip the handle on my side to keep my upper body from being thrown about. When we arrived at our destination, I felt sick to my stomach.

"I could circle the town," Millie offered, reluctant to cede her power position. "You know, just to cut down on the walking."

Jack glared at her as he joined me on the other side, his hand going to my back as I tried to keep from losing my breakfast. "You're done."

"Oh, you're such a spoilsport." Millie removed her goggles and tossed them on the driver's seat as she exited. "You need to learn to live a little, Jack."

"I'll keep that in mind."

Chris and the others were several minutes behind, so Jack suggested we start making the rounds.

"I'll check the cameras and you can touch the buildings."

I nodded in agreement. "I bet you never thought you would say anything like that a year ago," I said as we started toward the house of ill repute.

He chuckled. Jack went to the first camera and left me to my business.

I wanted to get as many touches in as possible before Chad and Chris arrived, and I had to be more careful. I was rewarded right away.

You don't seem to understand the truth of your situation.

This time it was a different female voice, and it gave me pause.

You're trying to force a future that's never going to happen, the second female said. *This life you've plotted out in your head can't happen because there's only one person truly invested in your relationship.*

A burst of anger took over and I had to suck in a breath to steady myself. Then I heard Rosalie's familiar voice.

You don't know what you're talking about. This is going to work.

It won't. He already has two feet out of this relationship. He just hasn't told you yet.

And he's told you that's what he has planned?

No. I simply see him better than you do.

Jealousy grabbed me by the throat. It didn't belong to me. It belonged to Rosalie.

Is there something going on between the two of you? Does Pete know? I'm going to tell him.

There's nothing going on between us. I can't believe you would even think that. I just see the truth in his eyes. You refuse to look past that smile of his. You refuse to adjust.

There will be no adjusting. I'm going to get what I want ... one way or the other.

I rested my hands on my knees as the memory faded and sucked in two steadying mouthfuls of oxygen. When I looked up, Jack was watching me.

"Just more of the same," I explained. "I think it was Sadie this time. She was explaining to Rosalie that she didn't have the relationship she thought she did."

Jack nodded in understanding. "How did Rosalie react to that?"

"She accused Sadie of having something going on the side with Paul."

"Do you think that's a possibility?"

I shook my head. I might've been feeling Rosalie's emotions, but I wasn't living her life. My mind was still clear. "No. Sadie told her as much. Rosalie just couldn't see beyond what she wanted. She wasn't a realist."

Jack looked around the town. "You're talking about her in the past tense," he finally noted. "You think she's dead?"

The question jarred me. Up until this point, I'd had hope. Now I wasn't so sure. "I don't know. I can feel her emotions. I still don't understand why she's the one I'm so in tune with. Why am I not seeing flashes from the others?"

"I have ideas."

"You think it's because we're both female."

"That's a simplistic answer, especially the more that we discover through these flashes. Rosalie didn't want to be abandoned. She had an idea how her life was going to go. She couldn't accept things were changing."

It was the word "abandoned" that stuck out the most. "You think I'm projecting my issues onto her."

He shook his head. "You don't have issues. Well, you don't have issues that aren't earned," he corrected. "The Rhodes raised you with love, told you they chose you. You can't help that you always wondered why your biological parents didn't keep you. That's a normal reaction, Charlie."

"I know now," I insisted. "I should be fine with it."

"You'll never be *fine* with it. You'll always wonder what you lost out on. On the flip side, you'll always feel guilt for wondering it, because you think it makes you disloyal to the Rhodes.

"Here's the thing, Charlie," he continued, barely taking a breath. "Nobody is perfect. Nobody reacts exactly how they're supposed to. It's like a person reading a book. They don't understand about mean characters, thinking they shouldn't exist because they don't want them to exist. It's wish fulfillment. They want a perfect world."

"Like Laura would've been written out of our book early if readers had their way," I said.

He nodded, his lips curving. "Exactly. But that's not real life. You can't not feel what you're feeling. Insecurity ... and jealousy ... and whining are normal. People don't want to see it in themselves, but it's reality."

I frowned. "Are you saying I'm a whiner?"

His grin widened. "I'm saying you're perfect for me. The other stuff ... stop beating yourself up over it. You need to feel what you feel. It's okay not to be perfect."

I blew out a sigh. I hated when he was reasonable. "Okay, but I don't want to turn into someone like Rosalie. It's clear she was in love with someone who didn't love her back."

"You don't have that problem. You love me, and I couldn't love you more if you lived in a huge doughnut and swam in a river of sprinkles. Thankfully, there's no trying involved. It just is."

"Ugh. I hate when you're so romantic and we're on the job," I lamented. "I can't jump you because we have an audience."

He winked. "Save that feeling for later."

WE WERE ON OUR THIRD CAMERA WHEN voices wafted through the downtown area. There hadn't been any other flashes despite my determination to touch every building. When I looked up, Chris and Chad were deep in conversation.

"Speaking of people finding each other," I said, smiling. "I think Chris is excited to finally find a police officer who doesn't think he's a nut."

Jack followed my gaze and chuckled. "I like Chad. I don't know that he can help us, but he seems balanced."

"I was surprised he knew the wendigo legend," I admitted.

"Me too. It might be helpful."

I wanted to ask how but went back to watching the video feed. A flash of white on the far-left screen caught my attention and I jabbed my finger. "Go back."

"Hmm?" Jack slid his eyes to me.

"Go back," I insisted. "I saw something."

"You're kind of bossy." He smiled despite the words and did as I asked, this time studying the screen more closely. When he saw the flash, he stopped reversing and leaned closer. When the splotch appeared again, he looked confused. "What is that?"

"What are you looking at?" Chris asked. "Did you find something?"

Jack exchanged a look with me. "Maybe."

Chris was so excited he shoved Jack out of the way to look. Once he and Chad positioned themselves directly in front of the camera monitor, it was hard for me to make out the figure. They rewound and watched the tape ten times before Chris flicked his eyes to me.

"What do you think it is?"

I held out my hands. "I could speculate, but that's not always a good idea."

"Speculate," he instructed.

I licked my lips, darted a look toward Jack, and then went for it. "It seems to be a large figure on two legs. It could be a bear walking upright I guess, but I don't know if there are white bears in this area."

Chris turned to Chad for an answer.

"Some people claim there's an albino bear up here." Chad rubbed the back of his neck. "I've heard stories about that bear since I was a kid."

"How long do bears live?" Jack asked.

"A grizzly bear will live twenty to twenty-five years. A brown bear twenty to thirty."

"Do you think you really have an albino bear?"

Chad looked caught by the question. "I ... don't know. They call them spirit bears up here. They're not technically albinos because they have pigment in their eyes and skin. They have a single mutant gene that makes them white."

I was impressed. "You know a lot about them."

"I was obsessed with seeing a spirit bear when I was a kid." Chad was sheepish. "I heard stories about them on the news one year and told my dad I was going to find a baby in the woods and raise it as my best friend. I was kind of a geeky kid."

I laughed. "I would've loved a spirit bear as a best friend," I offered. "I used to think I would be able to tame a raccoon. My parents thought otherwise and told me to stop staking out the garbage cans because even if I found one, they wouldn't let me keep it."

"Bummer." He shot me a smile. "A pet raccoon would be fun."

"Do you think that's a bear?" Chris was still focused on the footage. "It doesn't look like a bear."

"That's the point," Jack argued. "It doesn't look like anything specific. That's why we have to speculate."

"Well, let's do it scientifically." I decided to take control. "What else could be white up here?"

"A wendigo," Chris answered.

Jack jabbed a warning finger at him. "Let's not get ahead of ourselves. What other animals are up here?"

"Moose," Chad replied. "I think they can be albino. I remember reading about one killed in Canada a year ago. The First Nations were furious because it was considered a spirit animal and a hunter killed it."

"You have moose here?" Jack asked.

"We do." Chad went back to looking at the footage. "But I don't think that's a moose. It's too thin. There's no hind quarters."

"The foliage could be hiding the back end."

"Maybe. It's tall enough to be a moose."

"It's not a moose." Chris was matter-of-fact. "I would lean more toward a bear than a moose, but it seems taller than a bear."

I cocked my head at the footage. "Can you bring the camera to that area?" I had an idea. "Maybe we can do measurements and get a perspective."

Chris beamed at me. "That is an outstanding idea."

"I have one occasionally."

Jack rolled his eyes. "You have them daily. I'll run back to the four-by-four and get a tape measure. Chris, you and Chad move the camera and try to find exactly where the creature was standing. Maybe we can find some prints. Charlie ... ." He trailed off as he looked at me.

"You don't want me wandering into the woods when you're not here to chase me," I surmised.

"Right," he confirmed. "Can you refrain for five minutes?"

"It will be a chore, but somehow I'll persevere."

"Good girl." He gave me a kiss. "I'll be right back."

I fell into step with Chad once Chris had the camera off the stand. I felt the police officer's eyes on me and waited instead of prodding him to ask the question that was obviously plaguing him.

"So, you and Jack?" he said.

I nodded. "Seems so."

"It's nice that you're allowed to have a relationship on the job. I'm guessing you spend a lot of time together."

"It seems like we're always together," I said as we arrived at the location. "It's good I like spending time with him. Otherwise, it would be a big mess."

"Yeah." Chad almost looked wistful. "You're cute together."

It felt like a weird thing for him to say. "Um ... thanks."

"I'm not hitting on you," he said hurriedly. "It's just ... I've always wanted to meet someone who was open to possibilities."

That made me smile. "Possibilities like a wendigo?"

"Yeah. Most of the women here think I'm crazy whenever I bring it up."

I'd felt that way about most of the men I'd met before Jack — and sometimes since getting involved with him, because he absolutely refused to acknowledge I'd seen a Chupacabra. "You'll find someone. It usually happens when you're not expecting it."

"I hope so. What you two have is great."

I started walking up and down the tree line, keeping my gaze on the ground. Chris set up the camera again so he could study it, calling out directions to me so he could gauge landmarks.

"It should be close to where you are now, Charlie," he said as Jack returned, a large measuring tape in his hand. "Like ... right there."

"Okay." I dropped to my knees so I could look closer. At first I didn't see anything. Then, after a few minutes, I found what I was looking for. "Here."

Jack and Chris were arguing math problems as they debated perspective. Jack abandoned the argument and moved toward me when I called out. I pointed to the print I'd found. "That's the same print we found the first day."

"That?" Chad stood behind us, hands on hips, and stared. "How do you know that's not a human print that's become distorted?"

"That's way too big for a human," I pointed out.

"Unless someone slid a little bit," Chad said. "I want it to be a wendigo as much as anybody — so I can have confirmation, not because I want people to die — but that looks like it could be anything."

Sadly, he wasn't wrong. "What about Hank?" I asked. "Why haven't we seen him since the first day?"

"Nobody knows where he lives," Chad replied. "He's thought to have a shack somewhere. He was trying to live in that old cabin but one of those help groups came out to try to take him in. After a lot of arguing — I mean a lot — he led them to where he was really staying. They said there was no running water or heat, but they couldn't justify forcibly removing him. It's not far from here."

I pressed my lips together, debating, and then looked at Jack. "I think we should look for him."

"To what end?" Jack was utterly reasonable as he met my gaze. "What will he be able to tell us?"

"More than we have now. He's out here all the time. If there is a wendigo, he can tell us where to look."

"Everybody thinks he's crazy," Chad pointed out. "Nobody will believe any story we bring back from him."

"He might not be crazy. We don't need to take his word for it. We just need to know what he knows. He might be able to point us toward actual proof."

Chad leveled his eyes on Chris. "Are you okay taking a quick jaunt through the woods? We won't go far because it's not safe without the right equipment, but it might not hurt to look."

"It's a good idea," Chris replied. "It's going to take me a bit to work out the math for the perspective anyway. I'm going to send the problem to Hannah so she can do it for me."

"That's a great idea," Jack said. "Hannah is better at math than all of us. She can stay back with Millie, Bernard and Casey. They can work out the perspective problem. We'll launch the hunt for Hank."

"We'll be in two teams, so we should be safe," Chris said.

"Then let's do it." Jack was grim. "I want answers, even if they prove wendigos are real. I don't want to keep coming out here and getting nowhere."

TWENTY-THREE

Jack took the lead even though that would normally chafe our boss. Chris hadn't yet been to the old homestead, something he bitterly lamented during the walk.

"I still don't understand why you didn't bring me out here."

"We told you about it," Jack pointed out. "If you wanted to see it, all you had to do was ask."

"You went without me."

"We didn't know at the time we were going to find a homestead." Sometimes when Jack talked to Chris, I imagined him as a father. He was patient, although occasionally short because Chris knew how to press every button. I had no doubt that Jack would show infinite patience with a younger child. With a teenager, though, he would likely put his foot down ... at least eventually.

"What are you thinking?" Chad asked from his place next to me. His eyes were keen as he continuously scanned the forest. "Do you think we'll find a wendigo?"

I shrugged. "I don't know. I've never seen one."

"What have you seen?"

"Here we go," Jack muttered from his spot at the front of the line.

I glared at his back. "I think I saw a Chupacabra once." I saw no reason to lie. "Jack believes I'm making it up."

"That's not what I said," Jack countered. "You fell down a flight of stairs. You hit your head and were in the hospital."

"Sounds like a great story." Chad's enthusiasm was on full display. "How did you fall?"

"We were attacked by two people," I replied. "I was trying to survive at the time."

"And she did a marvelous job," Chris said. "I was unconscious for the entire thing. I'm still angry about that."

I smirked. "It's not your fault. They took you by surprise and hit you from behind."

"I need to hear this story from the start," Chad insisted. "I've read about the Chupacabra. It's supposed to be terrifying."

I told him the story, making sure not to drag it out. I explained how we'd been called to Texas, to an abandoned town not unlike Nighthawk. I told him about the body that might've been gnawed on. I explained that it was ultimately a money grab and the two individuals working together latched on to the Chupacabra legend to cover up what they were doing. When I got to the part where I had to use my magic to save Chris and Millie I glossed over the finer details.

"It was kind of a battle there at the end," I explained.

"How did you win?"

I shrugged. "I just ... fought. I don't know that there was any real technique. I knew that Jack wasn't far and that he would come running. I just had to hold on."

"The fight was over when I got there," Jack countered. "Charlie was unconscious at the bottom of these rickety old stairs. I remember thinking as I was trying to carry her out that it would be a real bummer if the stairs gave way and we were both trapped in that basement."

"And the basement is where you saw the Chupacabra?" Chad asked.

I nodded. "Yup. My head hurt. Like ... it felt really heavy. I looked up and there it was."

THE WENDIGO WHOOP-DE-DOO

"Then what happened?"

"I passed out. I woke up in the hospital hours later. Jack was sitting next to my bed. I told him what I saw, but he thought I was a crackpot."

"This is before they were together as a couple," Chris offered helpfully.

"I didn't think you were a crackpot," Jack insisted. "I just ... thought you hit your head. If you remember correctly, I sat by your bed the entire night."

"I know. I had a crush on you after that. I didn't think it would ever be reciprocated, though."

"That shows what you know." Even though he sounded grumpy, he smiled. "I had a crush on you already. That's why I sat next to your bed the entire night. I couldn't bear the thought of you waking alone."

"Oh, that's kind of sweet." Chad beamed at me. "Did you get together after that?"

I thought back to when Jack admitted he had feelings for me. "No. That happened in Michigan ... kind of. And Florida."

"In Michigan." Jack insisted. "I knew then that I couldn't fight my feelings. I guess we didn't technically start dating until Florida."

"I was almost eaten by a Megalodon there," I said, grinning at the memory.

"That is an outright fabrication." Jack was back to complaining. "That incident involved a woman using knitting needles to cover up a murder, for crying out loud."

That was true, but the Megalodon story was better. "I did end up in shark-infested waters and had to swim for my life."

Jack scowled. "Because of Laura. Don't remind me of that. I still have nightmares."

Chad's chuckle was warm. "Sounds like you guys have had a lot of adventures."

"And we'll have even more," Chris confirmed. "We're going to prove the existence of paranormal life if I have to die trying."

"Have you confirmed anything?" Chad asked.

"Well, when we were in Salem two months ago, we saw witches."

Chris's smile never diminished. He could talk about our work nonstop, and he recognized a receptive audience. "Oh, and a couple of weeks ago we were in this haunted asylum and ghosts stole one of our team members."

"For real?" Chad's response told me exactly how badly he wanted to hear the story.

Chris was only too happy to oblige.

I let Chris drone on as we cut through the woods. My eyes were on the ground as I searched for prints. Given the tree roots we had to climb over, brush we had to break through, and uneven ground we had to traverse, finding prints was nearly impossible.

It took us ten minutes to find the homestead because we were coming at it from a different angle. Chris was so excited when he saw it that he quickly wrapped up the ghost story. Then he and Chad started investigating their find.

"Chris has found a kindred spirit," Jack noted as he loitered with me.

"I think Chad loves the idea of traveling with us, searching for ghosts and goblins," I said as I glanced around. The trees had mostly been cleared from the homestead, and the sun poked through. It was a nice break from the claustrophobic feeling of walking through the trees. "I wonder if Chad would be willing to leave this area and join us."

"He'd need a job offer first," Jack said.

"Yeah, but Laura is making noise about leaving." I moved toward the cow barn, hoping to have a few quiet moments with Jack. "She may be serious."

"Good."

"Jack." I was exasperated. "I think she's traumatized. You shouldn't find joy in that."

"I find no joy in her being traumatized, but I won't miss her when she's gone. She offers nothing to our team. Even before the asylum, she wasn't a team player. All she cared about was making sure she was the center of attention."

"She wanted to be the center of *your* attention," I countered. "Like her or not ... ."

"I hate her."

I continued as if I hadn't heard him. "Like her or not, she had feelings for you. She was desperate for you to notice her. When I came along, I turned her whole world into something ... other."

"Other?" He cocked an eyebrow.

"Other than what she wanted," I replied. "She saw her life going a different way. I have no idea if that included marrying you, settling down and having children, but I changed the trajectory of her life."

"She fixated on you to the point of obsession. You didn't do anything to her."

"I'm not saying I did. *She* believes I somehow changed the trajectory of her life. We both know that it was her reaction to me that had things going off the rails. You said it yourself earlier. People feel what they feel, and in her mind, I somehow stole something from her."

Jack sounded exasperated. "You are ... way too sensitive. Laura was horrible. Yes, she's gone through a trauma and part of me feels sorry for her. She's an evil person who has a viable reason to feel sorry for herself now."

It was an interesting take. I brushed my fingers against the barn wall, concentrating.

"Anything?" Jack looked as eager to change the subject as I was.

I shook my head. "Maybe we should go to the back of the building. We weren't out there other than for a quick glance the first time."

"Okay." Jack cast a look over his shoulder to track the progress of the others. He called out to tell them where we were going and got a distracted hand wave for his efforts. "Chris really has found his match."

"I think it's kind of cute," I said with a giggle.

He poked my side. "You're kind of cute."

"Always."

"Now you're even cuter."

I trailed my fingers along the side of the barn. I didn't hear anything until we reached the back corner, and then a new voice joined the fray

This way.

I stopped in my tracks, frowning.

"What is it?" Jack was instantly alert, his eyes going left and right, as if bracing for an attack.

"I ... don't ... know." I looked up at the sky. Clouds that hadn't been there before were rapidly taking over. It looked as if a storm might be coming and yet I'd watched Jack check the weather reports at breakfast and knew it was supposed to be a sunny day.

"What did you hear?" Jack demanded.

"This way."

He waited. "What way?"

"No, that's what I heard." I shook my head. "Somebody said, 'This way.'"

"Rosalie?"

It was the obvious guess, but I didn't know if it was correct. "It didn't sound like her. It was a whisper. I ... don't know who it was."

"Sadie?"

I made a face. "Didn't I just say that I don't know who it was?"

"Okay, crabby." Jack made a sound like an angry cat and smiled. "I was just asking. You know I get antsy when stuff like this happens."

I couldn't blame him. "I just don't know."

"Okay, well ... let's see what's out back." His hand was on the holster of his gun when we turned the final corner. He saw whatever was there to be found before I did, and I didn't miss his sharp intake of breath. He extended a hand to keep me behind him, but I stepped around it as my gaze fell on Hank.

The older man sat on a ravaged chair, the fabric faded and mildewed. I was guessing small animals and bugs had made it a home. Hank didn't look bothered by any of that as he sat and drank from a metal tankard.

"I told you to go," he said when his eyes landed on us. He didn't look alarmed by our appearance. "I warned you about the Darkness, just like I warned the others. You're going to meet the same trouble because you refuse to stay away."

Jack darted a look in my direction, as if debating, and then he relaxed his stance and dropped his hand away from his gun. Right now at least, Hank didn't look to be a threat. This could be our best opportunity to get information from him.

"Do you live here?" I asked before Jack could form a question.

"Sometimes." Hank shrugged. "Sometimes other places." He sipped from his tankard. "I'd offer you something to drink but you look far too sensitive to handle it."

"Is that gin?" Jack asked, finding his voice. "She'll go blind if she tries to drink that stuff."

"This is the real deal." Hank tipped the tankard toward us. "I've been perfecting my recipe for years. Or is it decades now?" He scratched the white whiskers on his chin. "Doesn't matter. I know what I'm doing. Doesn't mean I want to share with the likes of you."

"Why not?" I gave him a wide berth as I circled to my left. It gave me a clear view of what was behind the chair, which turned out to be nothing.

"I guess I'm set in my ways." He took another sip, his gaze completely for me. He either didn't mark Jack as a threat or didn't care enough to be afraid. "You remind me of someone." He looked lost in his memories.

I decided to go for it and ask the obvious question. "Emmalynne?"

He shifted in his chair, surprise evident. "How do you know about Emmalynne?"

"I know a lot of things." I didn't even attempt a smile. "I know that you took over your brother's life after he died. I am kind of curious if you're the reason he's dead. Whenever that particular detail comes up, I have questions."

Hank snorted. "What is it you think you know?"

"I know that this was your brother Colin's house. I know that he lived here with his wife and daughter. I know that he had big plans to marry Emmalynne off to the son of a mine owner, but she didn't want to be married."

Hank made a disgusted sound deep in this throat. "That girl. She was headstrong when she should've been subservient. Colin thought he could beat it out of her, but it never took."

My stomach clenched at the word "beat." "Did your brother abuse his daughter?"

"Abuse? Why is discipline considered abuse?"

"I think that's your answer right there, Charlie," Jack said in a low voice. "He'll never be able to rationalize the things that you hate about this situation. He'll never be able to explain it in a way that's comfortable for you."

I knew it was true, so I simply nodded. "Did you kill your brother?"

"Why would you ask that?" Hank's face was blank. "He was my brother."

It wasn't a denial. Did he realize that? It was hard to tell what he did and didn't grasp. He was in the throes of severe alcoholism. The tint of his skin — it was an unhealthy pale yellow — indicated his liver was likely shot. It was now or never if we wanted answers.

"You killed him?"

"No." Hank was solemn as he shook his head. "Emmalynne killed him."

I stilled, dumbfounded. "But ... ."

"Oh, I see how it is." Hank wagged his finger. He almost seemed amused. "You think that girl was a victim. You think the world mistreated her and she was unfairly punished. I know how it is in the world today. We're living in the end times and nobody knows it."

"Nobody but you?" Jack challenged.

Hank shrugged, seemingly unbothered by Jack's accusatory tone. "I don't know what you want me to say. Things were better in this world when kids understood discipline. It's not just girls like Emmalynne who refuse to follow the rules. Girls like this one." He inclined his head toward me. "They refuse to follow the rules."

"Don't talk about her," Jack growled.

Hank continued as if he hadn't heard the admonishment. "The world has gone to hell. That's why I choose to stay out here. Things are simpler out here. I don't have to try to fit in and adjust my way of thinking – the right way of thinking."

I didn't care how he thought, what he believed, or how he had come to the conclusion that this was the end times. All I cared about were answers, and I was going to get them, even if I had to start shaking him.

"What happened to Emmalynne and Jessica?" It was time to get to the heart of matters. "I know you told the police officer who came out here to do a welfare check that they'd left, but that's not true. Did you kill them?"

"I killed Emmalynne." He said it so calmly it stole my breath. "I warned her what would happen if she didn't stay away from that boy. She wouldn't listen, kept sneaking out even though he was married to another woman, so I killed her when she wouldn't follow the rules. It was punishment, not murder. Keep it straight."

My mouth dropped open. "And you think that's okay?"

"No. I think that was the beginning of the end. I didn't know then what I know now."

"And what's that?" Jack demanded.

"That some things, even if they're done for the right reasons, can never be forgotten ... or forgiven. That's why I'm here now. Somebody has to keep control. If I don't ... well ... it will all be over, and not in a good way like it should be."

"Because of the wendigo?" I asked. "How does that come to play in this? Did Emmalynne turn into a wendigo?"

"Not Emmalynne. It was her mother. She haunts this land. She will inherit it when I die. She tortures me ... and enjoys doing it."

And just like that, what I thought I believed turned out to be another false tale. Nothing was as it seemed.

TWENTY-FOUR

"I don't understand." I was practically breathless. "Jessica is the wendigo."

"Started after the bad winter." Hank grimaced, as if the memory disturbed him. It should. He'd set all of this in motion.

"Farmer's Almanac said the winter was going to be bad, but I didn't think it would be as bad as it was," Hank explained. "The year before was terrible, but we survived. That winter, the bad winter, things were worse."

"You had a farmhand," Jack noted. "Alexander Jenkins."

Confusion washed over Hank's features. "How did you know that?"

"We've done research. There was a report on Alexander. He died during the winter."

"He did."

"And you ate him," I added.

Hank's eyes clouded with an emotion I couldn't identify. "We survived," he countered. "Don't look at me that way. You're not the one who was starving. I had two other mouths to feed, and when Alexander killed himself ... well ... it seemed like it was the answer to our prayers."

My stomach twisted. "He killed himself?"

Hank bobbed his head. "Cabin fever."

"Like in *The Shining*?"

Confusion etched across Hank's face. "Am I supposed to know what that is?"

"It's kind of like *The Shining*," a new voice offered from the other side of the barn. When I jerked my eyes in that direction, I found Chad and Chris emerging.

Hank didn't look surprised by the appearance of others. "You're David Pace's son," he said after studying Chad. "Recognize you anywhere. For a second there, I thought I'd fallen through time again. Happens when I brew a bad batch."

Fallen through time? I wanted to know more about that, but Jack offered me a small, almost imperceptible, headshake. "Alcohol psychosis."

Hank let out a rough laugh at his own folly. "That's what it felt like. Couldn't keep my timelines straight. Kept seeing Jessica ... as she'd been before. Then I saw the after and was reminded. The before was much better."

"Because she's a wendigo?"

He shrugged. "Don't know the word for it. Like to think of her as a grief monster. She survived so much, Colin's drunkenness and wandering ways. She survived the disappointment of Emmalynne ruining the family name. That bad winter was the start of her downfall. She was never the same after that."

"Because of the cannibalism," I said.

"She didn't like it, refused to do it. I had to wait until she was weak enough that she had no choice."

I thought I might wretch. "You forced her to eat Alexander."

"I made sure she survived," Hank snapped. "She would've gone to bed and never woken up if she'd had her way. I'm not sorry. Alexander wasn't doing anything for anyone. We'd gone through all the horses and cows. We still had a month of winter left. I did what I had to do."

That's when the unthinkable occurred to me. "Alexander didn't kill himself. You killed him."

"That's not how I remember it." Hank averted his gaze and stared at the empty field. "Things had to be done, so if that's how it happened, I'm not sorry for that either."

I licked my lips, debating how to proceed. That's when Jack decided to take control of the conversation.

"So you killed Alexander – something you lie to yourself about now so you're not the villain – and forced Jessica to eat him. Then what?" Jack demanded. "You said that was the start of the end for her."

"She was delirious at first," Hank explained. "She was so weak I didn't know if she would survive. Emmalynne was acting sickly too, but she didn't put up a fight when I told her how things had to be. In some ways she had more strength than her mother.

"We made it through that month living off what was left of Alexander," he continued. "I was ready to put it behind us when the weather broke. I just wanted to forget, but Jessica couldn't. She'd taken on another sickness. She was ... different. Her eyes were red and she was pale. Her hair had started growing faster. She looked like a witch I once read about in a book."

"The wendigo," I said, more to myself than anybody else. "The transformation was already taking root."

"I guess." Hank gave a haphazard shrug. "When spring hit, I started going out more. I was going to ignore what happened with Alexander, but the cops showed up asking questions. That was before your daddy's time," he said to Chad. "I thought about lying but figured that would come back to bite me. Besides, Emmalynne blurted out the truth before I could think of a lie to protect us."

"So, Emmalynne put you at risk," I said. "I'm guessing she couldn't shoulder the guilt any longer."

"There you go making that girl a victim again," Hank muttered. "She wasn't a victim. She was a devil. Jessica couldn't see it either. I always could. I told Colin she would be trouble, but he insisted he had things under control. Then what did she do? She turned around and ruined that engagement. And that ruined the family. Colin might've died in an accident, but I knew it was coming once Emmalynne said she didn't want to marry that boy."

"Did Colin really die in an accident?" I demanded. "Did you kill Colin, like you killed Alexander?" That made more sense.

Hank's eyes were narrow strips of hate. "Does it matter? It was a long time ago, another lifetime."

"You should pay for what you've done," I insisted.

"Oh, I've paid." Hank let loose a disgusted sound. "I've paid and then some. There's nothing the law could do to me that hasn't already been done."

"You're still alive," Chad noted. "If the truth of what you've done had been made public ...."

"This isn't much of a life, boy. If you want to take it, go nuts. I won't stop you. In fact, it will be a relief."

"Tell us the rest," Jack insisted. "Tell us what happened with Emmalynne. We know you killed your brother and took over his life ... and wife. We know you killed Alexander Jenkins and consumed him to survive the winter."

"We also know that Jessica had begun transforming into a wendigo," I added. "She couldn't deal with what you forced her to do, and that anger turned her into something else."

"It started to," Hank clarified. "I still thought I could turn things around. Then I made a mistake. I caught Emmalynne sneaking out one night. She'd kept up relations with that O'Neill boy even though she'd been forbidden from seeing him. He'd gotten married when she was promised to someone else. She didn't care. She claimed she loved him."

"Maybe she did," Jack argued. "Maybe he loved her. Maybe some people are meant to be."

"Hogwash." Hank hawked and spit. "Love may be real, but responsibility is more important. Emmalynne had responsibilities. She refused to meet them. She was pregnant. That's what she told me. She was pregnant and she and that boy were going to run away together.

He was going to leave his wife and they were going to start a new life far away from here."

"You stopped her," Jack pressed.

"She wouldn't shut her mouth. She kept saying hateful things. I told her she couldn't do what she was planning and to turn around and go back into the house. She wouldn't ... and I just lost it. She said I wasn't her father, never would be her father, and even though he was a terrible man, she wished I'd died instead of Colin.

"After all I'd done for her," he continued on a growl. "I made it so she didn't starve to death. I made it so the farm wasn't lost. I did all of that and she didn't show me an ounce of gratitude. She blamed me for all her problems."

"So you killed her," Jack said.

Hank nodded. "I shut her mouth once and for all. It felt good in the moment. Watching the life drain out of those eyes, those eyes always judging me. I shut her up."

"And then what happened?" Chris asked, entranced by the story.

"And then Jessica found out I killed Emmalynne." Hank's voice cracked. "I told her why I did it. I told her that it had to be done. Emmalynne was going to just keep dragging us down. We could've had a good life if she'd just come around to my way of thinking."

"She finished the transformation," I said, briefly shutting my eyes. "She became a wendigo."

"I don't know what that is." Hank was morose. "She became darkness itself. She grew taller in that very moment. She started screaming. At first I could make out her words. Then I couldn't understand. She took off, leaving me behind. She wouldn't let me explain."

"That wasn't the end of it." Jack's tone was grave.

"She kept coming back," Hank confirmed. "I'd see her, walking the property line. She looked different each time. She wasn't human any longer. She had those red eyes.

"I thought she was going to kill me as payback," he continued. "It would've been better if she had. I think she realized that's what I wanted. Instead, she dug up Emmalynne from where I put her, took her away. She still comes back, at least once a week. I see her through the trees. She leaves those twig things she makes to let me know she's still around. I hate them. It's as if she's waiting for something to happen."

I had a feeling I knew what that something was. "She knew that killing you would be easier than letting you suffer," I said. "She wanted you to be tortured, like she was. You took everything from her, so she made sure you could never have anything."

His lower lip quivered as he nodded. "She made sure I could never leave. I tried a few times, but she always stopped me. When I finally managed to get a truck, she destroyed it. Ripped the wheels clean off. She followed me at night, too, always screaming. She never stops screaming. I wish I knew what she was trying to tell me."

"She's trying to tell you that you're a murderous ass," Chad snapped. He looked shell shocked by the story. "You killed her husband. You killed her daughter. You forced her to eat another human being. You made her life hell."

"And she's made his life hell in return," I said. "That's what she's living for. What I don't understand is why she went after the kids. I mean ... they hadn't done anything to her."

Jack's eyes were sad when they landed on me. "Charlie, there's more to the story. He hasn't touched on it because he doesn't want to be complicit. Those kids weren't the first ones she killed. Those missing hikers? Jessica ended them. I'm betting there are missing hunters too."

I was baffled. "But why?"

"The answer was in the story," Chris provided. "She might be a paranormal creature ... but she still has to eat."

A shudder ran through me and I had to turn away, briefly shutting my eyes as the reality of what they were saying washed over me. I understood now why Jack occasionally referred to me as naive. The story had made me feel for Jessica, want to help her.

"She has no choice," Hank said. "She has to survive somehow. People have the right to survive."

"She's no longer a person." Chad's statement was accusatory. "She's a monster. You created that monster, and in her zeal to punish you she's killing others. There were eight kids in these woods a week ago. They didn't want anything but to have a good time. She killed them."

I turned back to Hank, my stomach quivering. "Did you hear those kids die?"

"I told them to go." He said it as if it was somehow something to be proud of. "I warned them that the Darkness would come."

"Did you tell them it would come in the form of a monster that would rip off their arms and gouge out their eyes?" Jack demanded. "Did you tell them they would be served up as dinner?"

"I told them to go." Hank insisted. "They should've listened. That's on them."

"No, it's on you." Chad removed the cuffs from his back belt loop. "You're coming with me, Hank. Stand up."

Rather than acquiesce, Hank sipped his homemade gin and regarded the other man with laughing eyes. "Where is it you think you're taking me?"

"I *know* I'm taking you to jail. You might've escaped punishment for decades, but that's over. You're coming with me to face trial."

Hank let loose a hollow laugh. "You really think she's going to allow that?"

Fear reared up and tickled my heart. When I lifted my eyes again, I found the sun had been completely obliterated by the clouds. Shadows stretched from the trees, and the wind picked up, whipping my hair with each burst. Apparently, I was the only one who noticed.

"She doesn't get a say," Chad argued. "You set all of this in motion. You're going to pay. You're coming with me."

"I don't think that's a good idea," I said in a low voice.

"You don't get a say either," Chad challenged. "I like you, Charlie, but this is a matter for law enforcement."

He truly didn't understand. "She won't let you take him. She's torturing him. If you take him out of her reach her whole reason for being will be gone. She won't sit back and let it happen."

"She has no choice." Chad reached for Hank's arm. The older man didn't resist. The second the first cuff landed on his wrist a terrifying scream echoed through the air.

"She's here," Hank said, reverence illuminating his face.

"What was that?" Chad's face had drained of color.

"Do you even have to ask?" Jack drew his gun with his right hand and reached for me with his left. His eyes were on the tree line. "Charlie, come to me."

I shook my head. "Put your gun away, Jack," I said. "Don't let her see you as a threat." As if to prove my point, I shoved his shoulder. "Get away from Hank."

"But ... ."

I grabbed Chris's hand as we passed. I couldn't control Chad, but I could do my best to protect the others. "The gun won't hurt her. It will only tick her off."

"Charlie, what's happening?" Chris's face twisted in concentration.

I didn't know exactly what was going to happen. I only had an inkling ... and it wasn't good. "She won't let us take him." I cast one final glance over my shoulder, my eyes pleading with Chad. "I know you have a job to do, but if you try to take him, you're going to die."

Chad looked caught, uncertainty flashing in his eyes. For a moment, I thought he was going to listen. I really believed he would join us, but his duty wouldn't allow that.

"You don't have a say," he said. "He's making it up. This whole wendigo story is a cover. I wanted to believe too, but he's the murderer."

"He's a murderer," I agreed, "but he's not making it up."

Chad reached for Hank's other hand.

I prepared myself for one more verbal stand. I would beg him if I had to, but it was already too late.

The first rain droplet was followed closely by another scream. Hank's hands were in cuffs. He was going willingly.

Jessica came from the barn, blowing through doors that had long ago fallen into disarray. She was on Chad in an instant, claws slashing as the police officer's eyes went wide. In his last moment he saw his mistake.

Blood flew from his throat as Jessica slashed with claws the likes of which I'd only seen in horror movies. Chad was dead before his body hit the ground, and then Jessica lifted her head to the sky ... and screamed again.

"Run," I ordered, shoving Chris and Jack with everything I had.

TWENTY-FIVE

I bolted to the right and Chris bolted to the left. Jack, sticking with me, viciously swore under his breath. He kept behind me, as if serving as a wall between the wendigo and me.

We ran for several minutes before I climbed between a clump of four trees that had grown together in such a way that we could hide between the trunks.

"Look at me." Jack's voice was a raspy whisper.

When I did, I found his eyes were fierce. "What?"

"You're okay?"

"Are you okay?"

"I asked you first."

"Well, since we were together for the entire run, I guess it's fair to say I'm feeling exactly what you're feeling."

He gave me a dark look but pulled me in for a hug. I could practically hear the gears of his mind working. He was coming up with an escape plan, but there was one problem.

"Where did Chris run?" I asked as I pulled away.

Jack looked back in the direction from which we'd run. "I just ... don't know."

"Maybe we should go back and find him."

The look he shot me was all "Are you kidding me" instead of "What a good idea." I held firm and continued to stare back.

"We can't go back," Jack argued. "That ... *thing* ... is back there."

"I'm well aware." I looked to his hand to reassure myself that he hadn't drawn his gun. "You can't shoot at her."

"If I can kill her, then all of this will be over with."

"A gun won't work on her."

"You don't know that."

I hesitated and then shook my head. "I don't," I conceded. "It's a feeling. I just ... think she still has some rational thought."

"Rational thought?" Jack's anger was palpable. "Did you see what she did to Chad?"

"I also understand the reason she did it. She doesn't want Hank to escape. Chad was going to take him away. That's why she did what she did."

"Then tell me why she killed those kids."

I had no answer. "Maybe they were going to give Hank a ride out."

"You're just grasping at straws."

He was right. "We have a problem." I decided to be the rational one for a change.

"Oh, do you think?"

I didn't appreciate the sarcasm. I understood why he was defaulting to it. He was torn by duty and love. As the head of security, it was his job to go back for Chris. He would never leave me, though, and there's no way he would drag me into danger.

"There's a murderous wendigo out there that might have some capacity for thought," I said. "Our boss is somewhere out here ... and he has no way to protect himself."

"You're saying we don't have a way to protect ourselves," Jack shot back. "You're saying *Predator* rules apply, that I can't use my gun. We're basically screwed."

My brow furrowed. "*Predator* rules?"

"The movie," he said. "In the movie, the predator only marked people who were carrying guns. That's how the woman survived."

I'd seen the movie, and recently. Jack turned it on when we were

THE WENDIGO WHOOP-DE-DOO

packing several days before. I'd only watched it with one eye — honestly, I found it ridiculous because there were too many plot holes to ignore — but I understood why he would glom onto it. He was ex-military. He needed things to make sense. Even if he had to use movie logic, he would fight until it made sense. "Okay, well, let's say we are in *Predator*. What would you do to get us out of that situation?"

"I would ease through the woods until we got to the four-by-fours and run."

"You wouldn't leave Chris."

"Fine. I would put you in a four-by-four and tell you to run. Then I'd go back for Chris."

"Well, that's not happening." He was crazy if he thought I would flee. "We have four people at Nighthawk. Have you forgotten them?"

He shook his head. "No, I haven't. I just ... cannot let anything happen to you."

"Well, I can't let anything happen to you. We have to work together." It was utterly reasonable for me to suggest that and yet he was fervently shaking his head.

"Baby, I feel paralyzed." It had to be hard for him to admit. "Above all else, I need to keep you safe. I can't even think about going back for Chris until I know you'll be okay."

I rested my hand on his chest and sucked in a calming breath. Part of me wanted to soothe him. The other part wanted to yell at him. I refused to make things worse for a change. "You're forgetting something," I said in a gentle voice. "I have magic. We're not completely weaponless."

He blinked several times in rapid succession, telling me his fear had glossed over that fact. "So, what do you want to do?"

"We need to go back to Nighthawk."

"And get the others? Go back for Chris as a strong unit?"

I shook my head. "No. They're sitting ducks out there. We need to get them in the four-by-fours so they can escape ... and maybe get help back in town. Once they're gone, we need to go back for Chris."

Jack protested. "No. I'll continuously panic if you're in danger."

"Well ... I'm sorry about that." Now was not the time to coddle him.

"You need to suck it up. We have to get Chris, but first we have to get the others out."

Jack pressed his lips together, as if debating. "Fine. I don't like this, but I know you won't back down. Let's get the others out of here. Then we'll figure out the rest."

IT TOOK US TWICE AS LONG TO find our way back to Nighthawk as it should have. Jack insisted we take regular breaks so he could listen to the sounds of the forest. He explained, in hushed tones, that as long as we heard birds and other small animals rustling we were likely okay.

When we finally emerged in Nighthawk, none of our group members were immediately visible.

"Maybe the wendigo got them," I said as my heart constricted. "Maybe she came straight here and never followed any of us."

"Or maybe they're screwing around by the house of ill repute." Jack leaned to his right and pointed, relief washing over his features.

When I leaned with him, I saw our group. They sat on a blanket under the overcast sky, munching on snacks, oblivious. "Come on." I ran to them, Jack on my heels.

Millie was the first to catch sight of us and she enthusiastically waved. "We have Doritos."

"You have to go right now," I insisted, slapping away the chips she offered. "Don't pack up. Don't grab the cameras. Just ... go."

Casey's eyes filled with alarm. "What happened?"

"We ... uncovered a few things." I looked to Jack for help. "We have a better understanding of what's going on here."

"We do," Jack agreed. He was fully in charge now. His voice was even but there was a forceful nature to his tone. "Charlie's right. You need to get to the four-by-fours and take one of them back to the vehicles. Make sure you leave the key in the other one for us."

"What are you saying?" Millie demanded. "What happened?" It was only then that she realized we were down two team members. "Where's Chris?"

THE WENDIGO WHOOP-DE-DOO

Jack's expression must've said it all because Hannah's face drained of color.

"Please tell me he's all right," she said in a low voice. "Where is he?"

"We got separated." Jack might've been panicking in the woods directly following the event, but he'd pulled it together. "We're going back. We need you guys to get out of here. Go back to town and get help."

"Help for what?" Millie demanded. She wasn't the type of person to run, especially when someone she loved was in danger. "You tell me where Chris is right now," she ordered.

We didn't have time, so I kept it short. "We have the full story. Jessica Dempsey is the wendigo. She's been torturing Hank for decades because he killed her daughter ... and turned her into a cannibal. I really wish I could smack him around." I babbled when nervous.

Jack placed his hand on my back to steady me and took over. "We were at the homestead. Hank told us the story. Chad decided he was going to take Hank in for murder even though Charlie told him not to. When he put cuffs on Hank, that's when it happened."

"That's when what happened?" Hannah, always steadfast in her devotion to Chris and love of science, was near tears. It was heartbreaking.

"The wendigo came and killed Chad." Jack was matter-of-fact. "The rest of us bolted into the woods. Charlie and I got separated from Chris. We have to go back for him."

"Of course we have to go back for him." Millie was all business. "Let's do this."

"No." Jack vehemently shook his head. "You can't be part of the team."

"Why?"

"We need help out here." Once Jack committed to a plan of action, he usually stuck to it. We'd decided what needed to be done. He wasn't going to back down. "You need to get us that help. On top of that, the bigger the team we take into those woods, the more likely the wendigo is to track us."

Millie glared at him. "He's my nephew."

"You'll slow us down." Jack was brutal with his response. It was what we needed now. Millie had to see reason. "You can't run through those woods, Millie. You move slower. If we get separated, we won't be able to focus on Chris."

"But ... ." Millie looked to me. "He's my nephew." She was imploring me to step in. I couldn't.

"Jack's right. We have a better shot of finding Chris on our own."

"We have a better shot of evading that wendigo, too," Jack added.

Millie's gaze was dark as she searched my face. She understood. If I ran into the wendigo again and those not in the know weren't with us, I could use my magic. Jack was former military and had his own set of skills. We were Chris's best hope.

"I think you should take me with you," Casey said. "I can help."

He didn't want to be separated from me. He didn't want to return to the hotel to tell Melina and Mike that I was in the woods hunting a wendigo while he was safe.

There was nothing I could do for him — or them, for that matter. "You need to make sure they get back."

"Call the police when you get there," Jack insisted. "Tell them some sort of animal attacked Chad Pace. Tell them to get a team out here — an armed team — and fast."

Casey looked conflicted. "I can't just leave you."

"You have to," I insisted. "There's only one way we're going to get a happy ending here."

Casey pressed his lips together and held my gaze. Ultimately, he nodded. "Okay, we'll head back to town and get help."

"I can't leave Chris," Hannah insisted. "He's out there and he needs me."

My heart broke for her but there was no time for coddling. "Chris would want you to go back. He'd want you safe. You can't help us."

"I don't understand how *you* can help," Hannah shot back. "Doesn't it make more sense for you to escape with us and Casey to go with Jack? They're more physically fit than the rest of us."

Thankfully she didn't come out and say that they had better survival skills because they were men. That would've pushed me over the edge. "Casey is going with you. I'm going with Jack. We're going to find Chris. It *has* to be this way."

Millie and Casey were the only two who could fully understand why it was necessary that I go with Jack. In an effort to help, Millie slid her arm around Hannah's shoulders. "Charlie and Jack have got this," she insisted. "We have to trust in them. The best way for us to help is to get more people here."

"Make sure they know that we're out here," Jack said. "If they come with guns, make sure they understand that we're not dressed in orange and that they call out before they shoot."

Millie nodded in understanding. "No mistaking you for deer. Got it."

"One more thing." I dug in the pocket of my jeans and returned with my cell phone. There was no service in the woods. That's why we couldn't call for help from Nighthawk and then hunker down and wait. "You need to do something for me." I pressed the phone into Casey's hand.

"What?" His face was blank.

"As soon as you have cell service, go through my contact list. Find the number for Harley. Call her and tell her what's going on. If she doesn't answer, keep calling."

"Harley?" Casey had met her, understood that she was magical. Still, he stared at the phone as if I was asking him to make contact with an alien. "Can she help?"

"She's the only option we have right now."

"Okay." He shoved my phone in his pocket and then grabbed Millie's arm. "We're going. It'll take at least two hours for a rescue team to get out here. Can you guys survive that long?"

"Of course we can." I managed a smile. "Jack has special training."

"What do you have?" Hannah demanded. She was still fighting the idea of fleeing rather than joining the team that would hunt for her boyfriend.

"You have to trust us, Hannah," Jack argued. "You have no choice. This is the way it has to be."

"But ... ."

"Honey, they're right." Millie grabbed Hannah's shirt and started tugging. "We're wasting time. Jack and Charlie should already be out there looking for Chris. Come with me."

"I can't." Hannah was anguished. "I ... love him."

"I know you love him," I reassured her. "We'll remind him of that when we find him."

"And we *will* find him, Hannah," Jack interjected. "You have to trust us. We can't hang around here any longer. We have to go back in."

"Just find him." Tears coursed down Hannah's cheeks. "I can't live without him."

Jack's eyes landed on me. "I understand. We'll find him. We won't stop until we do."

With that, Jack and I headed back to where we'd lost sight of Chris, trusting the others to make it out of Nighthawk on their own.

It was time to face off with a wendigo.

TWENTY-SIX

Once we were away from the others, Jack fixed me with a "What next?" look.

"It's time for magic," I explained as I flexed my fingers. "I'm going to try to cast a spell that will lead us to Chris."

He nodded, as if I'd just said the most normal thing in the world.

"Bay can do it," I said, referring to the Michigan witch who had taken me under her wing. "So can Zoe." Oh, how I wished for the magical mage. She wouldn't fear a wendigo. In fact, she would be making jokes as she casually taunted our enemy and looked forward to a big dinner.

"I get it," Jack said, "but I can't help you. You take the lead."

I knew how hard that was for him. "Thank you." I closed my eyes, tugging on the magic that was always inside. I wasn't as good at this spell as the others I'd come into contact with, but I had no choice. "Here we go."

Requiro. I didn't say it out loud. The word reverberated through my mind. The magic flared almost instantly, and Jack's sharp intake of breath told me it had worked. When I opened my eyes, there was a dull purple line on the ground. It glittered as it bobbed and weaved through the trees in the direction of the cabin.

"Let's go," I said, starting forward.

Jack grabbed my hand before I could take more than two steps. "No matter what happens, we have to stick together," he said.

"Of course."

"I mean it. The only reason we should separate is if ... well ... there's no chance for me. If that happens, I don't want you feeling guilty about leaving me behind."

He had to be joking. "I'm not leaving you under any circumstances."

"I want you to if you can get away and I can't."

I couldn't believe he was actually suggesting it. "You wouldn't leave me."

"That's different."

"Because you have a penis?"

His lips curved down. "Because ... I cannot live without you. And it's my job to make sure this team is safe. You're the most important member of my team."

"Well, Jack, you're the most important member of my team. I'm not leaving you under any circumstances."

"You might have to."

I jabbed a finger at him when he opened his mouth to argue. "It is not going to happen, Jack. We're in this together ... until the end. I would rather die with you than live without you."

"Well, I don't like that."

The way he said it had a ghost of a smile playing around the corners of my lips. "Neither do I, so let's make sure it doesn't happen."

He growled as he fell into step with me, his fingers linking with mine. "Let's get this over with."

THE LINE LED BACK TO THE HOMESTEAD. We released our grip on one another and started looking around. When we reached the spot behind the barn, we found Hank still sitting in his chair. He'd refilled his tankard in our absence, the cuffs still attached to one wrist.

Chad's body lay on the ground, ignored by Hank.

THE WENDIGO WHOOP-DE-DOO

"Having fun?" I asked angrily.

"As much fun as I can manage," he replied blandly. "I'm surprised you're still alive. I guess that means Jessica went after the other one."

My stomach did a little flip. "Did you see which direction Chris went?"

"That way." Hank waved haphazardly. "He's already dead. You should run while you can. The Darkness won't miss twice."

"Neither will I," Jack growled. "When we come back, we'll be taking you with us."

"If you say so."

The magical line stretched from the back of the barn into the woods. I treaded carefully as we re-entered the forest.

"I'm really starting to hate that guy," Jack muttered.

"I've hated him pretty much from the start."

The rain that had started during the wendigo attack had dissipated when we were heading back to Nighthawk. It now returned, this time in the form of a torrential downpour. But I barely paid any attention. My entire focus was on the ground.

We walked for what felt like a really long time. Jack kept his ears on the animals, stopping our progress when it was too quiet for his liking and only restarting when the bird sounds resumed. When we reached the end of the glowing line, it seemed to run directly into a small rock outcropping.

"I don't understand," Jack said as we looked around. "Why would the line lead us here?"

That was a good question. When I turned to the left and brushed my hands over the foliage, I found what we'd initially missed. "A cave."

Jack peered over my shoulder, a muscle working in his jaw. "Well, that's just great. I was just thinking that what we needed to really enhance this situation was a dark hole in the ground."

I fought back a laugh.

"I don't suppose you brought a flashlight?" Jack asked.

"We don't need a flashlight," I reassured him, squeezing my hand once and then holding it palm up as a ball of fire appeared. "I'm more than just a pretty face," I said to his look of wonder.

"You're everything," he agreed, pressing a kiss to my forehead. "You're ... absolutely everything."

The naked emotion on his face, in the words, had my heart stuttering. "I love you, Jack. This is going to be okay."

He nodded. "I love you more than anything, and this *is* going to be okay." He was firm. "Just ... don't be a hero."

"I can't help it. I fell in love with a hero and I want to be just like him."

"Don't say things like that." His expression was pained. "Let's just do this."

"I'll go first."

Jack looked as if he wanted to argue, but because I had the magical fire he acquiesced. I waited until I'd ducked inside the cave to scatter the flames. The ball floated upward and broke into a million pieces, reminding me of twinkle lights as we started moving forward.

"Is this where she lives?" Jack asked, his voice echoing despite how quietly he'd spoken.

"It makes sense. It's not far from the homestead and ... well ... movies have taught me that monsters often live in caves."

"Well, if it's in the movies it must be true."

"Totally."

He smirked as he looked around. "Kind of close quarters."

"I don't think we're going to have to go far."

"Here's hoping."

The trip through the cave seemed endless despite my words. We were careful as we traversed the space, watching the ground as much as the area in front of us. I was about to comment on how far in we'd gone when the walls opened up and we found ourselves in a decent-sized cavern.

We were not alone.

"Chris?" I headed toward the first body on the ground. It belonged to a male and I was almost certain he was wearing the same blue shirt Chris had been when we scattered at the homestead. I was careful as I rolled him, my breath clogging in my throat when he was on his back. His eyes were closed and he was unnaturally still.

"Let me look, baby," Jack said, dropping to his knees. His fingers went to Chris's neck and checked for a pulse. "He's alive."

That was good, but we still weren't out of this. "I ... ." I didn't finish because something caught my attention in the far corner of the cave. My inner danger alarm wasn't dinging, so I knew it wasn't the wendigo.

I lowered myself to the ground next to the other body, my hand shaking as I reached out to touch a slim shoulder. The girl jolted at my touch and whimpered.

"Don't hurt me," she pleaded, cringing away from me.

"I won't," I promised as I tugged on her shoulder, relieved at the sight of her filthy face. "Rosalie."

"Do I know you?"

I shook my head. "I feel as if I know you. You're Rosalie Partridge."

"I think I'm dead," she muttered. "I think I'm dead and this is obviously Hell."

"You're not dead," I reassured her, fighting the sympathy that threatened to overwhelm me. I wanted to wrap my arms around her, make her believe that she was safe and everything was going to be okay. But I couldn't promise that. We might've found our missing team member and a terrified girl, but we weren't in the clear. "How long have you been in here?"

"What year is it?" she asked dully.

"It's about four days after you were due to return home from your camping trip."

"Only four days?" Rosalie's eyes were flat and she seemed frail. When I glanced around, I didn't see any water or food. She was probably weak from lack of both.

"We're going to get you out of here," I promised, looking to Jack. He was still close to Chris, but his attention had been diverted to the cave. "Do you have any water?"

Jack jerked his eyes in my direction and nodded. "Not much."

"She needs it." I leaned Rosalie against me and gave her some water. "Small sips," I said as she greedily sucked from the bottle. "You'll make yourself sick."

"I'm dying."

"You're not dying. We're going to get you home. I just ... are there any more of you? Did any of your friends survive?"

"They left me," Rosalie gasped. "Paulie left me. He got away. I think that was his plan."

"Some members of your group tried to get away," I conceded. Now was not the time to tell her about Paulie's death. "Some of them didn't escape. Do you know what happened to Sadie?"

Rosalie lifted a shaky hand and pointed toward the corner, where numerous twig creatures – obviously Jessica's doing – were strewn about. "She was dinner two nights ago. Last night it was Vincent. Tonight it's my turn."

I thought I might be sick. "Rosalie ... ." Before I had a chance to say any more there was a terrific crack, followed almost immediately by a bright flash from the narrow tunnel we'd used to find the cavern.

"What was that?" Jack demanded, pressing his body on top of Chris's prone form to protect him. "What the hell was that?"

"Oh, you bring me to the nicest places," a female voice drawled as a silhouette became visible. "First it was New Orleans. Then it was Charleston. Now it's a hole in the ground. I love what you've done with the place."

My heart leapt into my throat at the voice, and when the figure grew close enough to make out, I saw Harley studying me with unreadable eyes.

"You just can't go a full week without finding trouble can you, Charlie?"

I had to blink back tears. "You came."

"I'm not supposed to be here." Harley started forward, pulling up short when Rosalie started whimpering and shaking. "What is going on here? Why are you in a cave?"

I didn't have time to explain. "Wendigo."

Harley's eyebrows hiked up her forehead. "Enough said. That explains the smell." She glanced around. "That's your boss?" She pointed to Chris.

THE WENDIGO WHOOP-DE-DOO

"Yeah. That's him. This girl went missing with her friends several days ago."

"Paulie left me," Rosalie said dully. "He just ran away."

"Well, Paulie sounds like a douche," Harley said. "You're better off without him."

"He's already safe at home," Rosalie said to herself. "I bet he's packing to move away to college right now. He doesn't even miss me."

Harley hunkered down directly across from the girl and felt Rosalie's forehead. Briefly, she shut her eyes. When she opened them again, she looked concerned. "Rosalie, you have internal injuries. You have two broken ribs, which means you can't walk. If one of those pieces breaks off and punctures your lung, it's game over."

I scowled at her. "That's a great bedside manner you've got going."

"I try." She looked to me. "What's the plan here, Charlie?"

"We have to get them out. We have a four-by-four on the other side of Nighthawk. If we get them there, we can transport them back to town."

"Okay." Harley pressed her lips together and glanced around the cave. "Are those bones?" She inclined her chin toward the corner.

"They are," Jack replied. "I think those are the remains of the other kids who were with Rosalie."

"Paulie." Harley made a face.

I shook my head. "Paulie is dead, but he's not in here. Four other bodies have been recovered."

"Well, that's lovely."

"I told them they shouldn't have shot at the bear," Rosalie said dimly. "They heard it. They saw it. I told them we should leave. They wanted to kill it."

"The bear?" I brushed her hair from her eyes. I was desperate to do something to ease her fear.

"The wendigo," Jack said. "They saw it when they were camping and decided to go after it."

"I didn't know they had guns," Rosalie explained. "Chase had them hidden in the tent. When they pulled them out, I said it was a bad idea. They didn't listen. Paulie never listens."

Rosalie hadn't wrapped her mind around the fact that Paulie was gone, but this was not the time to break that news to her.

"We have to get them out," I insisted to Harley. "Can you do that popping thing you do?"

She shook her head. "Papa Legba can track me that way. If he knows I'm here ... ." She trailed off. "He thinks I'm spending too much time on you. He assumed I was trying to get you to make a deal — and approved — but he's not as amused now. He said I should've closed the deal given the amount of time I've spent on you."

"So you can't help us?"

"Oh, I'm going to help." She flashed a smile that didn't touch her eyes. "I just can't do it the way I'd like to. We need to make a stretcher for them."

"And then what?" Jack demanded. "They're too heavy for Charlie and me to carry out."

"As much as I'd like to watch you flex, Mr. Muscles, that's not my plan." Harley was good at getting under Jack's skin. "Once they're on the stretchers, Charlie can use her magic to kind of motor them out. Then we just need to make it to the four-by-fours."

She made it sound so easy. "And then what?"

"And then you run."

"We can't ignore the fact that there's a wendigo," I argued. "It will keep killing. I thought Casey would've explained when he called."

Harley's expression twisted into one of confusion. "Casey didn't call me."

"Then how did you know we were here?"

"I didn't. I went looking for you when Sybil tripped the protection spell I've had chasing you. Once she gets close, the spell alerts. I came to warn you that she's coming."

My heart sank. "She's coming now?"

"Well, that's just great," Jack growled. "And I thought things couldn't get any worse."

"Things can always get worse." Harley fixed me with a serious look. "We need to make the stretcher and get the hell out of here. Leave the wendigo for somebody else to deal with."

It wouldn't have been my first choice, but I didn't see that we had many options. "Where do we get the supplies for a stretcher?"

The question was barely out of my mouth before Harley snapped her fingers and caused an old tree to appear in the cave tunnel. "Let's do this," she said as she headed toward it.

Jack followed her, tension rolling off him in waves. "We have the branches to make it work. We need rope."

Harley nodded. "Leave that to me. Start breaking apart the branches."

If she was worried, I knew I should be too. But I couldn't embrace the fear. My mind was too close to overloading.

Was this it? Would I meet my fate at the hands of Sybil after all?

TWENTY-SEVEN

Jack's military experience was helpful in building the stretcher. Harley's way of getting rope was to conjure it from a store, muttering the whole time that it was unlikely Papa Legba would track the slight magic she employed.

"So you stole it?" I asked as she uncoiled the rope and pitched in to help Jack.

"Don't look at me that way," Harley groused. Her hands were lightning quick as she used her magic to cut through the rope, doling out lengths to Jack. "They won't even notice it's missing."

"I know but ... what if an employee gets fired because the inventory is off?"

Harley pinned me with a glare. "Charlie, don't make me come over there and paddle your good girl behind. Just shut up and let us work."

I ran my tongue over my teeth, debating, and turned back to Rosalie when Jack didn't look in my direction. The girl had finished the water and was now resting with her eyes closed.

"Are we almost finished?" I asked after a few more minutes.

"Almost." Harley put her hands on the stretcher and pulsed it with magic. "It should hold. We need to get both of them on here." She went toward Chris first. "Jack, help me."

THE WENDIGO WHOOP-DE-DOO

I'd never seen her move this fast. Usually, she was all about the quips and mental torture. Jack wordlessly moved to Chris's shoulders and nodded as Harley lifted his feet. Within seconds they moved Chris onto the stretcher.

"She's more delicate," Harley said to Jack. "You need to lift her but try to keep her straight."

"I've got it." Jack grunted as he slid his arms under Rosalie, who whimpered as he lifted her. Once he had her on the stretcher with Chris, he took his time to situate them. "This should work."

"It's our only option, so it has to work." Harley turned to me. "Do your thing."

"I ... don't know what to do."

"Levitate the stretcher and tether it to us for the walk."

She made it sound like something I should know how to do. "I've never done that."

"There's a first time for everything." She grabbed my arm and dragged me to one end of the stretcher. "Normally I would buy you some wine before feeling you up like this, but we don't have time." She plastered herself to my back and linked her fingers with mine, as if cuddling me. "Concentrate, Charlie. This isn't the sort of magic I possess."

Her urgency was terrifying. "Okay ... I ... okay." I closed my eyes, feeling the magic pulse through me. Harley let me build it and then helped me direct it.

"There you go." She was trying to be encouraging, but I couldn't miss the hint of impatience. "Just tether it to us now."

After a few seconds of my concentrating, the stretcher lifted from the ground. There was a low hum, almost as if it was happening through some sort of industrial design.

"Nice job." Harley slapped my back. "Let's get out of here."

She moved to the front of the stretcher.

"Are you claustrophobic?" Jack asked as we followed her. He looked as concerned as I felt.

"I'm not a fan of caves, if that's what you're asking, but I'm fine," she reassured him. "Let's just ... get out of this freaking hole."

The trek back seemed to take longer than the initial trip. When we finally made it through the trees and brush, I sucked in a breath of fresh air. I hadn't realized how stagnant it was inside the cave until this moment.

"Which way?" Harley asked, pulling her phone from her pocket.

"There's no service out here," I said. "You can't play Pokémon."

She slid her eyes to me. "And here I thought they would make the wendigo cave into a gym," she drawled. "I'm so disappointed."

I held her gaze. "Harley, you're starting to freak me out."

"Fear is a healthy emotion. Let's go with it." Her annoyance was evident when it landed on Jack. "We need to get out of here."

Jack's eyes roamed her face, as if looking for an answer that he should know but was incapable of sussing out. "How close is she?" he asked.

"Close enough that I feel her dampening field. She's trying to cover her approach. She doesn't want Charlie to sense her. We have to go right now."

I hurried closer to Jack. I was about to tell him to go ahead of us and get the four-by-four ready when he turned and shook his head.

"Whatever you're about to say, don't," he growled. "We agreed to do this together."

"Oh, we're all stuck together," Harley agreed, lifting her head and darting her eyes to the right. "I don't think we're alone any longer."

I realized the forest sounds Jack was always telling me to pay attention to were no longer present. It was as if we'd been tossed into a snow globe and the only sound I could make out was that of our ragged breath.

"Sybil?" Jack asked Harley, his eyes terrified. His hand was automatically going to the weapon on his hip.

"Not Sybil." Harley growled as she swiveled, her hands immediately going up at the same moment a bone-rattling scream filled the air. As if in slow motion, the wendigo — which had apparently been hiding on the ledge over the cave — jumped toward us, claws extended.

I raised my hands to protect us, magic instinctively flaring to life, but the wendigo bounced off the shield Harley had raised and flew back into the rock wall with enough force that it echoed. I watched, dumbfounded, as the creature that had once been Jessica Dempsey shook its head. When it opened its eyes, the red glowed hot.

"This is not an appropriate time," Harley snapped at the wendigo. Her eyes briefly landed on me. "Keep those hands ready, rock star. I have a feeling we're going to need them."

The wendigo shrieked in rage. When she hurled herself at us again, she got the same result. She bounced against the shield and was thrown back into the wall.

"You don't learn very fast, do you?" Harley clucked her tongue. "We don't have time for you ... Jessica." It was as if Harley had picked the name out of thin air. She wrinkled her nose as she regarded the creature with fresh eyes. "Interesting. You're ... you're not a true wendigo."

The words caught me off guard. "Can she be saved?"

The look Harley shot me was pitying. "Not everybody can be saved, Charlie. That ... thing ... certainly can't. She's been lost a long time. She barely remembers being human. Well, except for one face."

"Let me guess," Jack said, glaring at the hulking creature. The wendigo was tall — eight feet of solid horror — but it was thin to the point of malnutrition. What used to be hands had elongated into claws, and the skin had turned to a rubbery gray texture. "Do you see a drunk old dude with white hair drinking homemade gin in a rotting chair?"

Harley nodded. "How did you guess?"

"That's Hank." Jack murmured. "He's Jessica's brother-in-law. He killed her husband and daughter and ... is the catalyst for all of this." Jack gestured to the wendigo.

"Don't forget the part where he killed the farmhand and made her eat him," I added.

"Oh, that's just gross." Harley's hands landed on her hips. "Don't people know that cannibalism never leads to anything good. I mean ... look at Jeffrey Dahmer. That guy was a freak. He was the sort of freak the neighbors pointed at and said, 'It's only a matter of time.' If people haven't realized by now that cannibalism is not the way to go, I don't even know what to say."

"This was like fifty years ago," I said, shaking my head. "It's not like they did it last winter."

"Fifty years is nothing in the grand scheme of things." Harley sighed. "Listen, Jessica, I'm sorry this happened to you." She sounded reasonable, even though she was facing off with a creature that should only be making cameos in nightmares. "I could give you a long speech about how this is Hank's fault, but the truth is that you're to blame.

"Losing your humanity is never easy," she continued. "It sucks. It's harder for you too. I've seen people willingly give their souls away in exchange for a new truck. I've seen others gladly hand theirs over to get revenge on an old friend. You, however, made none of those choices. They were all forced on you.

"Here's the thing, though," she said. "You made the choice to kill those kids. You might've done it out of hunger, but these woods are teeming with game. You decided that they were yummier."

I stared at her, dumbfounded. I couldn't believe she was actually having this conversation with the wendigo.

"There's no salvation for you," Harley said. "There's no going back. Your daughter is dead. Your husband is dead. Why are you hanging on? You should let go of this life. That's the only way you'll find peace."

Now I was legitimately confused. "Can she leave this life?"

"Of course she can." Harley said. "She can let go. That's what most wendigos do. They live fast and die quickly. Very few of them last more than a few months. You've been out here for fifty years, lady monster. There must be a reason."

There was: Hank. "The reason is sitting behind the barn at your old house," I called out. "He's getting drunk and blaming everybody else for the problems he created."

"Hank?" Harley asked.

I nodded. "She's been keeping him here all this time, torturing him. Hank's nutty but still alive."

Harley looked at the ground, a hint of a smile on her face. "I admire your dedication. There are few people in this world I'd commit to torturing as thoroughly as you've tortured Hank. I commend you." She mocked clapped.

"Now it's time to let go," she continued, barely taking a breath. "You can't win this game. You need peace and he needs to die. If you want this to be over, track his horrible ass down and kill him. There's no need for the rest of us to be caught up in this. It's between you and Hank."

The wendigo's head cocked, as if it had been listening. When it raised its chin, its eyes drifted to a spot in the distance.

"We can't give you anything," Harley said. "All we can do is kill you. I would really rather not waste time getting into a battle when you're low on our list of worries."

"She's not that low," Jack muttered.

Harley ignored him. "Kill Hank. He has it coming. You must know that by torturing him you've tortured yourself. It's time to end this. There's no reason to drag it out. Enough people have died."

"Paulie," Rosalie whispered, her eyes closed. She was in her own head space. It was best she stay there until this was over.

The wendigo raised its head again and wailed, the sound long and thin. Then, as if somehow coming to some magical epiphany, the creature bounded around the magical dome Harley had erected to protect us and raced in the direction of the homestead.

"Did you just send the wendigo off to kill a man?" I asked.

Harley shrugged as she dropped the dome. "He deserves it. She'll end herself when her reason for living is gone. It's easier for us if she puts an end to this nightmare."

It sounded reasonable enough and yet I still felt unsettled. "All those kids died for nothing."

"Didn't Rosalie tell you that they pulled a gun and decided they were going hunting for a bear?" Harley challenged. We were moving again, back toward Nighthawk ... and freedom. "If they'd left the gun in the tent, they'd probably still be alive."

"Just because they made a mistake doesn't mean they deserved to die," I insisted.

"Very few people do," Harley said as we crossed the final hill that led to the homestead. "But we can't go back and erase their stupidity."

"Harley is right, Charlie," Jack said. "You saved Rosalie. I would've bet money she was gone. You made something out of nothing again. Take that as a win."

"Listen to Tall, Dark and Whiny," Harley said. "Occasionally he's not an idiot."

"I hate when you visit," Jack groused.

"Yeah, well, you love me today and you know it. In fact ... ." Harley trailed off, her eyes going to the barn in the distance. "Is that Hank?"

I followed her gaze, cringing when the wendigo raged in front of his chair. The creature let out a terrible scream, and I held my breath as one hand was raised high in the air.

I wasn't close enough to see Hank's face when the wendigo slashed its claws at his throat. Was he frightened; grateful it was finally over? All I could see was the wendigo's wrath.

Hank didn't cry out in pain, and when the deed was finished, the wendigo stopped screaming. For one breathless moment the creature stood over its nemesis, chest heaving, and I thought Harley had been wrong. I believed the wendigo wouldn't be fulfilled until it had killed us too.

A plume of red smoke — it was magic, but my mind didn't immediately register that — billowed from the barn and grabbed the wendigo by the waist. It was like a huge magical hand, kind of like the one in the old *The Stand* miniseries ... but with better special effects.

The red magic lifted the wendigo into the air, as if somehow freeing the soul inside ... although I had no way of knowing if Jessica's soul had somehow remained, even fragmented, during her decades of torture.

"Is this her release?" I asked, hoping it would be over quickly.

Harley didn't respond, jolting when the wendigo started to fight the magic, which appeared to be squeezing the creature. After a few seconds of struggle, the wendigo screamed once more before being slammed to the ground.

Even from where we stood, the sickening sound of crunching bone told me the wendigo was dead. Nothing could've survived that blow. I thought it would be somehow more peaceful. And then I looked at Harley's face. She was so white she was almost transparent.

"That wasn't her release, was it?" I asked.

"Not at all." Harley looked as if she was about to pitch forward. "This is something else entirely."

"What?" Jack demanded.

"We're too late." For the first time ever, I thought Harley might cry. "There's nowhere to go now. She's here, and we're in a crap-ton of trouble."

Sybil had finally found me.

28

TWENTY-EIGHT

"**Y**ou have to run." Jack shoved me back toward the woods, the terror on his face threatening to break me. "Run right now."

I couldn't. The headshake I gave him was soft and pitying. "I can't run from this."

"She can't," Harley agreed. She was grim. "She has to survive this." She licked her lips, as if debating, and then stepped to her right. She was creating distance between herself and the floating stretcher ... and she looked ready for battle.

"What are you doing?" I demanded, fear coursing through me. Was she trying to make herself a target? "This is my fight."

"That's where you're wrong, Charlie. You're never alone. You need to realize that." Calm, which was something I could rarely say about Harley, she pasted a wide smile on her face and unleashed a goofy wave. "How's it going?"

Sybil, dressed all in black, merely stared.

"You really were in my dreams," I called out. We were still a decent distance from the barn, but we were in the open, vulnerable to attack. There was no running. I had to figure out a way to keep us all safe.

"Did you think I wasn't?" When Sybil spoke, her voice was soft, almost mellifluous. "You really need to learn to protect yourself in dreams, Charlie. That's when you're most vulnerable."

"Thanks for the tip." I attempted a smile ... and failed miserably. "Do you need something specific?"

"I came for you."

"You're not taking her," Jack growled. His hand kept moving to the gun on his hip, but he didn't draw it.

"Let's not do that, Wild Bill," Harley drawled. "It won't help, and it could very well make things worse. Let's try a diplomatic approach." She held out her hands as she regarded Sybil with what could only be described as a deranged expression. "So ... the Pokémon sucks here, huh? I think a haunted town should have a few stops. I plan to message Niantic and explain that dead zones are not okay."

Sybil's perfectly arched eyebrows drew together. She was slowly drifting toward us, carefully, as if trying not to spook a feral cat. "What are you?" She seemed confused as she cocked her head. "You're not a witch."

"I'm not," Harley agreed. "If you're thinking of trying something funny, you should know it won't work on me. You don't have the power to end me."

Sybil's laugh was loud and raucous. "You wouldn't believe how many times I've heard that. It has never once been true."

"Try me."

Sybil lifted her hands, causing my heart to stutter, and aimed her magic at Harley. The wall of magic she built was black and I opened my mouth to tell Harley to run. The magic hit the crossroads demon square in the chest before I could get out a single word.

Harley's smile was malevolent. "I wasn't joking. You don't have the power."

"That's ... interesting." Sybil looked more annoyed than amused. "What are you?"

"Someone you don't want to mess with." Harley's tone was no-nonsense. "You should turn around, Sybil. You won't get what you want today."

"No?" Sybil glanced back at the spot where the wendigo had fallen. "I think otherwise. I took out your enemy. That at least deserves a conversation."

Harley flicked her eyes to me, as if debating, and then nodded. "Sure. Let's talk. Stop right there."

Sybil was only thirty feet away at this point. "Are you going to stop me?"

"If I have to."

"Well, let's see about that." Sybil took another step. That forced Harley to whip out her hand in a horizontal arc, and as she did magic erupted from her fingertips. The barrier that appeared was almost transparent. Because it was still raining, however, the water caused the barrier to glitter. She'd built a magical wall ... and it was like throwing down a gauntlet.

"What is this?" Sybil reached out her hand to touch the barrier, making a face when her magic collided with Harley's and drawing her fingers back quickly at a sizzling. Her fingertips looked black. "White magic?"

Harley shook her head. "Nope. Just the sort of magic you can't overcome."

"You're a demon." It wasn't a question. Sybil looked on Harley with fresh eyes. "Why would a demon insert herself in this situation?"

"Well, you'd have to ask my mother — Satan rest her sorry soul — but she always told me I was built for evil. I always tried to upend expectations. So, whenever I can, I go against what she believed to be my true nature. You know, just to keep the game going."

Sybil didn't look impressed. She also didn't look fearful. "You may have the power to protect yourself, but you obviously don't have the magic to take me out. Perhaps you should remove yourself from this situation. It has nothing to do with you."

Harley shook her head. "I'm good."

"And we want her here," Jack added. "You're the one we want to leave."

Sybil's eyes were dark when they landed on him. "I don't really care what you want. You're a peasant in a sea of goddesses."

THE WENDIGO WHOOP-DE-DOO

"Oh, I've always wanted to be in a sea of goddesses," Harley said. "Can I be queen? I think I should be the queen."

"You're nothing," Sybil hissed. "You're a busybody demon, and when I figure out your place in this, you'll wish you'd never been born."

"You remind me so much of my mother." Harley pressed a mocking hand to her chest. "I can't wait to disappoint you too."

This conversation was going nowhere. I knew Harley well enough to recognize she wouldn't turn down the snark. She would continue hurling insults until Sybil reacted.

"What do you want, Sybil?" I asked, doing my best to keep my voice level. I'd hoped I would have more time before this happened. "We're on a clock. We need to get these people back to town."

"Let your friends take them back," Sybil said. "I'll not do a thing to stop them — as long as you remain so we can chat."

It was an interesting offer — and I honestly considered it — but I knew better. Even if she let them escape, there was no stopping her from killing them later. And Jack would melt down if I tried to separate from him. He would never allow it and would likely be hurt in the process. I had to keep him close.

"Just tell me what you want," I insisted. "That's the only way we'll be able to work this out."

Sybil's smile was back. "I want us to join forces, Charlie."

"Oh, well, what a fun offer," Harley drawled. "Charlie is flattered that you would think of her, but she has other plans for her day. You can leave now."

"Shut up, *demon*," Sybil hissed. Harley was getting under her skin, likely her goal. "Nobody is talking to you. I'm here for Charlie."

"What is it you want?" I asked.

"Only what I was promised."

"You want to absorb my powers and use them for yourself," I said.

"No, that's not quite it." Sybil let out a low laugh. "I'm sure you've been told many stories. The truth is, I don't want to hurt you, Charlie. That holds no appeal for me. I simply want us to ... get to know one another."

"And then what?" I was confused. "Do you see this turning into a *Thelma and Louise* thing? Are we going to go on murderous adventures together? Are we going to conquer the world?"

"I have no interest in conquering the world." Sybil was matter-of-fact. "I don't even want to rule a small portion of it. I simply need what was promised to me."

"You mean me. Why do you need me so badly? It can't possibly be that you just want to hang out."

"Why can't it be that?" Sybil demanded. "I know you've been told things by the people who managed to hide you for so many years — and kudos to them on how they did it, because I never thought they would go that route. But that doesn't mean they told you the truth."

"So you want to hang out?" I didn't believe her for a second. "Are we going to drink tea and lament the state of the world today?"

Sybil's lips twitched. "Something like that. I don't want to hurt you. I didn't spend years searching for you because I want to destroy you. I was close once. Did you know that? You were in a foster home and I managed to track you. Unfortunately, I was just a little too late. You'd already been moved, and your foster parents didn't know where to find you.

"They had a rug rat of their own," she continued. "A little snot-nosed monster. She carried your bear. I sensed you all over the creature ... so I took it. I planned to deliver it to you in person. They wouldn't tell me where you were, though, no matter how ... convincingly ... I questioned them."

"I don't understand."

"They didn't know where you'd been taken, and after that, whenever I looked for you, I ran into a wall of magic. I never understood it ... until now." Her eyes narrowed on Harley. "You've been hiding her all this time."

My mouth dropped open as I turned to Harley. "Is that true?"

Harley shook her head. "I didn't meet you until New Orleans. You intrigued me from the start. I'm not the one."

"Someone did," Sybil insisted.

"Someone certainly did," Harley agreed. "I've run into the same wall of magic when researching Charlie's background, but I'm not responsible. I'm not sure who is, but it's a powerful individual."

"I don't understand." I felt lost.

"There are things you need to know, Charlie," Harley explained. "I've been searching for weeks. This is bigger than all of us. You have to understand that. I don't know who protected you as a child, but once you were moved from that temporary foster home — those people were killed in a home invasion less than forty-eight hours after you were moved — you were essentially hidden from the magical world until you were eighteen."

I was horrified. "Home invasion?"

"What are the odds of that?" Sybil asked with faux innocence.

"Excellent," Harley shot back. "You did end up with her bear."

I felt sick to my stomach. "You killed them because they wouldn't tell you where I was."

"It was a simple request." Sybil made a big show of staring at her fingernails. "They had one job to do and they failed."

"You were put under a magical veil, Charlie," Harley explained. "I don't know who did it, but I'd like to find out. What's important is that whoever carried it off protected you for a reason."

"Nonsense," Sybil said. "There was no reason to protect her from me. I'm family. We're bonded by blood."

"Which is why she wants you so very badly," Harley said, her eyes on me. "She needs your blood, Charlie. Not to enhance her powers, but because she's dying."

Sybil's eyes flashed dark and dangerous. "She doesn't know what she's talking about. She's talking out of her posterior."

"I do that often," Harley readily agreed. "But not this time. Charlie, look at me."

I did as she instructed.

"I've been digging. I don't know who protected you. But I do know why she wants you. Her whole goal is to live forever, but not as a wraith. She knows she'll lose her sense of self and purpose if she goes that route. She's been using magic to extend her life for a long time, but she's stretched thin now. She's reached the limit of what magic can do for her. If she wants to be reborn, to continue living as she has, she needs a new body from her family line to be born into."

That's when the reality of what I was facing smacked me square in the face. "She wants to take me over."

Harley nodded. "She wants to rip out your soul and install hers in your body. A male heir won't work for her because the magic won't be strong enough. Your family's entire line has been building to you because you're the only one strong enough."

"She's making that up," Sybil stormed. "None of that is true."

Harley jabbed a silencing finger at Sybil. "Don't listen to her. Never trust her. No matter what she says to you, it's a lie."

I'd already figured that out. "So ... what do we do?"

Apology etched across Harley's face. "You can't do anything. You're not ready."

I didn't understand.

"I can do something, though." Harley was grim as she glanced back at Sybil. "In fact, there's only one thing I know to do. It won't be easy but ... I have to. For you."

She sounded as if whatever she had planned would be terrible ... and deadly. "You can't sacrifice yourself." I was breathless. "I won't allow it."

Her chuckle was low and humorless. "I'm not a martyr. I'm not sacrificing myself."

"Then what are you going to do?" Jack demanded.

"The only thing I can." She turned to me. "Remember what I told you. I can't intervene ... and yet I will. You might not see me for a bit. I will have other things to deal with."

I wanted to ask what that meant. Papa Legba would punish her for getting involved. Would it hurt? Could he kill her? Would it be something worse than death? "Harley ... ."

"It's fine," she reassured me. "This is the only way." Now she turned to Jack. "I'm sorry that you're going to be left with the aftermath. You're a big, strong dude, though." She slapped his shoulder hard

THE WENDIGO WHOOP-DE-DOO

enough to rock him. "Chase the information I haven't been able to find. Someone protected her as a child. We need to know who."

"I ... ." Jack broke off, bewildered. "I'll do what I can." He grabbed her arm before she could walk away. "I don't know what you're about to do but thank you."

Her sunny smile was back. "I'm doing what needs to be done. It will give you a bit of breathing room, but not much. Once it's done, you'll be safe to get Rosalie and Chris back to town. Don't dawdle. Get out of this place. You're done here."

Jack nodded. "I promise not to give you grief when I see you again."

"Oh, don't go changing your personality on my account. I like when you're a big crab." Harley planted her eyes on me one last time. "Don't fall apart. I'm not dying. Neither is Sybil. I don't have that power. Just ... try to be okay with this. Remember, this is how it has to be."

With those words, she turned her full focus on Sybil, who had been listening. The ancient witch didn't look worried — perhaps she'd lived so long that she no longer felt fear — but there was a hint of doubt creeping over her face.

"Ready to play a game?" Harley asked, moving toward the barrier. "It's a game I saw in a movie once. It was called *Saw*."

My eyes went wide. "*Saw*? What the hell, Harley?"

Harley didn't respond. She walked right up to the barrier, let loose a devastating grin, and then walked through the wall. It was of her own making, so apparently the rules she'd put into place for Sybil didn't extend to her.

Sybil gasped. She immediately raised her hands and unleashed a torrent of magic on Harley.

The blond crossroads demon shrugged off the magic before unleashing her own. Harley's purple magic wrapped around Sybil like a giant fist, almost identical to the scene we'd watched play out between Sybil and the wendigo.

"*Louvri*," Harley intoned in a language I didn't recognize.

Sybil's eyes went wide. "Crossroads demon," she eked out.

The magical fist raised Sybil above the ground. Harley moved to the spot directly beneath the fist and turned, her eyes seeking — and finding — me.

"Remember what I said," she intoned as the ground opened beneath her. It looked as if she was about to fall into a fire pit. For a moment, she hovered above it, Sybil flailing against the magic that held her in its iron grip. "This is only the beginning."

And just like that, the magic slammed Sybil toward the ground. Instead of hitting earth and rock, the magic punched through and into the hole. Harley was dragged with it.

I screamed her name and raced forward. The magical barrier that had been protecting us disappeared when Harley did. By the time I got to the spot where she'd been dragged under, she was gone. The ground closed tight again, as if nothing had happened, but I heard the echo of a laugh.

"She's gone," I said to Jack when he reached my side, tears streaming down my cheeks. "She's ... just ... gone."

Jack slipped his arm around my waist and pulled me to him. "You heard her. She'll be back."

"What if she just said that to make me feel better?"

"That's not Harley. If she said she'll be back, she will."

"But ... ."

He shook his head. "She'll be back. We have to get out of here now. She told us what to do."

I couldn't shake the horror coursing through me. "She sacrificed herself."

"Only a little." Jack said. "You heard her. She's not a martyr. She *will* be back."

I had to believe that so as not to fall apart. I looked to the bodies behind the barn. The dead wendigo was still there, crushed and sightless. Hank was dead on the ground, about ten feet from Chad Pace. "We need to get Chris and Rosalie to the hospital." It was all I could think to say.

"We will. They'll be fine." He glanced at the woods and shook his head. "Then we'll get out of this godforsaken place and go home. That's what Harley wants for us."

Given what she'd done, Harley deserved to get what she wanted today. "Okay." I was still shaky but we had a job to finish. "Let's get out of here."

TWENTY-NINE

Chris remained unconscious during the trip back to the four-by-four. Jack loaded him in the passenger seat of the vehicle and then helped me get comfortable with Rosalie in the backseat. I was alert for the ride. I didn't even settle when we reached the Tahoe, when we had to move Chris and Rosalie again. We did it silently. We were both too wrecked to speak, which is why, when we were on the road, Jack speaking almost jolted me out of my skin.

"Baby, can you look up where the hospital is?"

I reached for my phone, frowning when I realized I didn't have it. "I need your phone. Casey has mine."

"Oh, right." Jack handed his to me. I used one hand to stroke Rosalie's hair — she was asleep and didn't stir — and the other to search.

"They don't have a hospital," I said. "There is an urgent care."

"Direct me. They'll arrange for transport."

I did as he instructed, making sure to text Millie between barking out directions so she could meet us there.

Hannah, Millie, Casey and Bernard were in the lot when we pulled in. Hannah wept as she rushed to Chris. It was only when she started talking to him, brushing his hair from his face, that Chris stirred.

"He might have a concussion," Jack said as Hannah and Bernard helped Chris out of the Tahoe. "Be careful with him. Casey, can you help me?"

Casey went to the back door of the Tahoe, his eyes going wide when he caught sight of Rosalie. "You found her."

"Yeah." Jack was grim. "We found her. She has internal injuries. We need to be really careful getting her out."

Casey and Jack were gentle as they grappled with Rosalie, who whimpered as they moved her. I scurried over and opened the door, watching as first Chris and then Rosalie were transported inside.

The medical workers hopped to it when they saw who we were bringing in. Jack gave them a brief rundown, said we'd found Rosalie in a cave, and then dragged his hand through his hair as the girl was taken into the inner sanctum of the facility.

"We've called the police," the nurse behind the desk offered. "They said that one of their officers was with you."

"He didn't make it," Jack replied solemnly. "We can direct them to the body ... along with two others."

The nurse's eyes went wide. "Oh, my ... ."

"Just send them to me when they get here," Jack instructed. He grabbed my hand and pulled me to him, resting his cheek against my forehead. There'd been little time for consoling until this moment. It was necessary and yet I couldn't give in to what I felt. I was still too raw.

"This way." Casey led us to the small waiting room. "Hannah, Millie and Bernard are with Chris. You need to tell me what happened so we can come up with a story. We don't have much time."

"We're going to tell the truth," Jack replied dully. "At least as much of the truth as we can. The wendigo attacked behind the barn. It killed Chad Pace. We found you guys, sent you back here for help, and went looking for Chris. We found him in a cave. Rosalie was there. We took them out, and when walking by the barn again we saw the wendigo attack Hank and kill him."

Casey swallowed hard. "So the wendigo is still out there?"

"No." Jack leveled a serious stare on Casey as he released me. "Sybil showed up and killed the wendigo. I have no idea how we explain that."

"Sybil?" Casey looked as if he was going to fall over. "You can't be serious. Where is she?"

"We have no idea." Jack related the tale as if he was reading recipe directions. He was quick, because he had no other choice, and when he finished, he pinned Casey with a pointed look. "We can't mention Sybil. We're just going to say we took off when the wendigo was attacking Hank. They'll have to come to their own conclusion as to what happened to the wendigo."

Casey nodded in agreement. "What about Harley?"

I had to bite back a sob. All I could see when I closed my eyes was her face when she took Sybil into the fiery pit.

"Harley says she'll be back," Jack replied, stroking my hair. "I have to believe she knows what she's talking about."

Casey didn't look convinced. "Does that mean Sybil will be back?"

"Definitely." Jack looked out the glass doors of the clinic. "The police are here. Let me do most of the talking, Charlie. If they ask you a direct question, answer it. No mention of Harley or Sybil."

"Okay." My voice was barely a whisper.

"I'll tell them you're in shock," Jack added.

"That's not far from the truth," Casey said. He handed me back my phone. "I'm going outside to call Mom and Dad. They'll want to know about this."

"Good idea," Jack said. "We're going to be here for hours. Rosalie is going to be transported to a hospital. Chris might too."

"What do we do after this?" Casey asked. "I mean ... are we heading right back to Boston?"

"Not tonight." Jack understood the workings of a police investigation, so he laid it out. "They're going to question us here and again tomorrow. We have to be open to them if we don't want suspicion to fall on us. Once they cut us loose, we're going back to the hotel. Charlie needs sleep."

I didn't know what I needed but sleep sounded good.

"We'll play the rest by ear," Jack added.

"Okay." Casey's eyes were searching as they roamed my face. "I'm sure Harley is okay, Charlie. I ... don't know what to say about the rest of it."

"There is nothing to say," I offered. "It happened. Now we have to deal with it."

"We'll deal with it together," Jack insisted. "You need some sleep. You'll feel better in the morning."

I was fairly certain that wasn't true.

THE POLICE DIDN'T BELIEVE OUR STORY at first. They were beside themselves thinking that one of their own had fallen in the line of duty. It was still early enough in the day for them to send paramedics and searchers to the old homestead. They found things exactly as we'd described. So, after Jack related the story three times without a single detail changing, they allowed us to return to the hotel.

Chris had been transported to a neighboring town with a hospital. He was being kept overnight for observation. Millie, Hannah and Bernard went with him. Rosalie was also transported to that hospital. The doctors reassured us she would likely be okay, but it would take a long time for her to fully recover.

I said goodbye to Rosalie, who was barely conscious. She waved when I left, and I doubted I would ever see her again. That was okay. To her, I would always be a reminder of her ordeal. For me, I couldn't look at her and not see Harley. It was best to say our goodbyes ... and mean them.

Mike and Melina were in the lot outside our hotel room. They both hurried in my direction when I exited the Tahoe. I allowed them to hug me before Jack gently pulled me from them.

"She needs a shower and sleep," he said quietly. His gaze was pointed when it landed on Mike. "She just needs sleep."

"Casey told us what happened," Melina said. "Shouldn't we be running? Sybil knows we're here."

"Harley said Sybil would be otherwise engaged for a bit," Jack replied. "We can't leave anyway. The police don't want us to. They'll be questioning us again tomorrow."

"Screw the police." Mike was vehement. "We need to go into hiding."

That was the first thing I'd heard in more than an hour that had me wanting to respond. "We're not going into hiding."

"We have to." Mike insisted. "Sybil will come after you again."

"Yes, and when she does, we'll be more prepared." I was adamant. "Harley put herself at great risk to protect us. She said we had to find whoever hid me as a kid, that it was important. She also said I needed to practice so I would be strong enough to face Sybil next time. We're going to do that."

"But ... ." Mike turned his helpless stare to Jack. "You can't be okay with this. She's not safe."

Jack slid his eyes to me. There was no doubt, only ferocity. "Charlie is the boss here," he said. "She makes the decisions. Harley had no reason to lie to us. If Harley believes that's what we need to do, then that's what we're going to do."

"But ... ." Mike looked frustrated. "She could die."

"She's not going to die," Jack growled. "And she's not going to give up the things she loves most and go into hiding. You need to get with the program. Charlie is in charge."

"We understand Charlie is in charge," Melina said hurriedly. "We just think it might be smart to go into hiding until she's ready for a fight."

"That will mean giving up our jobs, and possibly our freedom if we run from the police now," I said. "We're not doing that. We're going to do what normal people would do and wait for the police to come to us tomorrow."

"They'll have questions about the wendigo," Jack said. "Chris should be up to answering some of them. We'll be going back to Boston with our group, as expected."

"But ... what if Sybil comes back?" Mike demanded. "What if she tries again?"

THE WENDIGO WHOOP-DE-DOO

"She will try again," I replied. "We know what she wants now, to take me over. That's how she's going to extend her life. We know what we have to research and how to prepare, so that's what we're going to do."

"Charlie." Melina sounded exasperated. "You're not safe."

"And I won't be until we deal with Sybil. I'm not going into hiding to prolong the agony. We're going to start working on the problem. I guarantee that Sybil isn't coming back tonight ... or tomorrow ... or maybe for a week. Harley said she would find a way back. We have a little time."

"Why should we believe Harley?" Mike challenged.

I pinned him with the darkest glare in my repertoire. "Because she's part of the team. She risked herself for Jack and me today. We might never see her again because of her sacrifice. You're either going to believe Harley or get off my team."

Mike was taken aback. "Sweetheart ... ."

Jack's hand moved up and down my back. "Harley proved her merit today. I don't always like her, but I trust her. She has Charlie's best interests at heart. You need to accept that."

Melina grabbed Mike's hand and gave it a good squeeze to keep him quiet. "So what do we do?"

"For tonight, we go to bed. Tomorrow, we're probably going to have to jump through some hoops. Once we get back to Boston, we start researching and preparing. That's all we can do."

"Okay." Melina made an attempt at a smile. "Is there anything we can do for you?"

"We're going to bed," Jack replied. "Tomorrow, once we get some food in Charlie, we'll start planning. For tonight, we're done."

"Okay."

I managed a half-hearted smile. "We made it through the first battle. That's the most important thing. We still have a war to win. We need to start preparing because I'm not going to lose. Harley bought us time. We're going to use it wisely. That's all there is to it."

With that, I strode into the room and flopped on the bed. Jack followed me, locking the door before joining me. I heard the coins slide into the Magic Fingers slot and closed my eyes as the bed began to vibrate.

This was nowhere near done, but Jack was right. I needed rest and time to think. After that, it was anybody's guess what would come.

Made in the USA
Monee, IL
04 January 2022